THE SPREAD

THE SPREAD

THE SPREAD

JACQUELINE DRUGA

PRESS

Published by Vulpine Press in the United Kingdom in 2022

ISBN: 978-1-83919-485-6

Cover by Jacqueline Druga

www.vulpine-press.com

ALSO BY JACQUELINE DRUGA:

ONE

To No Purpose

TX-36 S
Two miles outside of Rosenberg, Texas

Run.

The only thing that James Conrad could think of at that moment was to run.

Run.

His mind scrambled, trying desperately to remember the instructions on what to do, how to handle it, all those things the authorities said to do. At that moment though, he couldn't think of a single one. His mind was a blank. Just…run. As fast as he could as far as he could.

Would it make a difference?

He had seen a bar right on the side of the road when he drove by, probably only a half mile beforehand. He even thought about stopping by for some normalcy, a beer and shot, perhaps. He slowed down to take a peek. Motorcycles were out front, neon signs glowed, country music played. Although it was odd at the present time, the bar was busy, hopping and normal.

1

How were they doing that? With all that was going on. Maybe they didn't know. Maybe they didn't care what was happening or weren't afraid.

James was.

Like many, James was heading anywhere that wasn't a big city.

Safer in small towns, rural areas.

Escape from Houston as if he were in some sort of movie.

He packed what he could, what he needed and wanted, and took off.

No longer could he hide or avoid it. When the phenomenon hit his area, he knew he had to go. Being a single man, with no wife or kids to slow him down, gave him the freedom to hit the highway right away; he could even run for the hills if need be. His job as an insurance man wasn't exactly needed anymore.

From his perspective, the world was going down.

He worried when he left. Lots of calamity, chaos and riots. The power had gone out the day before and with the temperatures rising, it was almost unbearable.

No police directed the congested outbound traffic.

Impatient and aggressive drivers slammed into slow moving cars, pushing them out of the way, causing even more of a bottle neck on the road.

James left his house in the middle of the afternoon.

Now it was nightfall, but he made it out.

He was glad to see the glow of the Houston fires in his rear-view mirror.

James was hungry. He had a bunch of those peanut butter and jelly sandwiches that were round and without crust.

He ate two in the car as he sat in traffic and another as soon as he got out of Houston.

His stomach was in a knot. It probably had more to do with him rationing water. He didn't want to drink all that he had in case he couldn't find a place to stay.

Online hotel reservations were impossible, and the cell phones were out.

Most of the towers in Houston were down.

He kept his phone close, in the front pocket of his t-shirt, just in case he needed it, not that there was anyone waiting for his call.

He watched the signal, regardless.

There was a small flow of traffic on the road. It moved at a steady pace, but much slower than the speed limit would normally allow. It was impossible for anyone to drive fast on this road even if it had been empty. It was like a maze or video game. There were a lot of abandoned cars just left on the road, not to mention all the dead animals.

Animals dead from… *it.*

The phenomenon. They weren't roadkill, James could tell.

Considering the highway circumstances, he was cruising pretty well when he saw the man on the side of the road. He was an older man, wearing a baseball cap and waving out for a ride, trying to flag someone down. It was nearly midnight. He stood behind an old beat-up car, a big one, a duffel bag at his feet.

The man was probably someone's grandfather. He could have been James' grandfather.

As everyone else drove by, James slowed down, put on his turn signal, lifted his hand to alert the gentleman he was stopping, and finally pulled to the berm of the road. It possibly wasn't the best idea. Authorities were warning people not to stop because of marauders and such. But this was an old man, and he certainly wasn't safe.

James pulled in front of the disabled car and placed on his blinkers. They were the only lights going and they reflected off of the vintage Oldsmobile. He looked in his side mirror and could see the old man. James watched as he bent down for his bag.

Hearing a long honk of a horn, James looked ahead. It was probably one of those aggressive drivers again.

"What the heck, dude," James said. "Chill out."

Shaking his head, he realized the old man should have been at his car.

What was taking him so long? James thought and looked again at his sideview mirror.

The man was gone.

James reached over, opening the side door, figuring he was coming up that side of the car.

Smart. Walking on a dark highway wasn't a good idea.

He pushed the door open wide enough for the old man to get in. But he never came.

There was silence.

Looking again in his mirror, James saw nothing. He double checked to make sure he could open his door, that no cars were coming, then stepped out of the car.

"Hello?" he called out, walking toward the beat-up Oldsmobile. He saw the duffle bag on the side of the road.

No old man.

Pulling his phone from his pocket, he turned on the built-in flashlight.

All kinds of things ran through his mind. Did the man fall, have a heart attack? There had been some reports of people doing bad things, he hoped some trap wasn't set for him on the road.

Just as he reached the end of the Oldsmobile, where the bag was, he heard the slam of a car door, followed quickly by the screech of tires.

James spun around and stumbled back in shock as he watched someone speed off in his car.

"No!" James screamed. He started to chase it, but what use was there?

The old man must have set him up. Played on his good Samaritan nature than stole his car. Authorities warned people about that.

Did James listen?

No.

Angry about it and at himself, James, furious, kicked out and slammed his foot into the Oldsmobile.

That hurt.

The pain from his foot ricochet up his leg causing him to drop his phone as he reached down.

Surely, he broke a toe or something.

He cursed out, loudly and rapidly, every bad word he could think of as he hopped about waiting for the pain to wane.

When it did, he was glad his phone wasn't broken. At least he didn't think it was. He could see the beam of light from the flashlight shooting up at him.

He bent down and grabbed it. When he lifted it, he saw it.

The blood on the duffle bag.

Slowly, light outward, James walked to the back of the car. The light from his phone reflected off of the pile of a red mushy substance.

In the dark, it was hard to tell but it looked like remains. Human remains that had to belong to the old man because his hat was just to the right of the pile.

Had some animal annihilated him that quickly?

Light still aiming at the pile, James started to call 911.

Three numbers.

But before he could press 'call', he saw something move in the remains. At first, he thought it was an optical illusion, a trick of his cellphone light, but then he looked again.

There *was* something moving in there.

It was hard to see in the dark, even with the flashlight, but James knew, or at least thought he knew, exactly what it was.

The same thing that was happening in Houston and in a lot of major cities.

With that realization, James sprung back, keeping a distance from the remains and came up with an idea.

Run.

It was the only thing he could do. Get away as fast as possible. He ran back in the direction from which he came.

The bar with the motorcycles, neon sign, and country music was his goal.

It wasn't far.

James could make it as long as he ran as fast as he could, and didn't look back.

TWO WEEKS EARLIER

TWO

DEITY

The Talbot – Super Yacht
Galveston Bay

One more night, Martie Morgan thought as she chopped the green onions with precision. *One more night and I'll be home in my own bed.*

Not much left to do. Finish and serve the main course and dessert. Prepare snacks for the guests that wandered into the galley for food late on Mainstays Loveseat Sleeper Sofa night, then prep for breakfast.

She would be home in Houston in time to take her kids for a mid-afternoon lunch.

They were at her ex-husband's house. Her oldest son, at seventeen, didn't need a babysitter and truly argued the case to stay home alone. It wasn't that Martie didn't trust him, it was that Martie's youngest son was nine and a handful.

Their stepmother, Carrie was in the midst of a very difficult pregnancy with twins and Martie didn't want to add that to her plate. Especially since the cruise was a week long.

Martie liked Carrie, they all got along well. She didn't want to put her through any unnecessary burdens.

Almost over.

The cruise from hell was winding down.

For the most part, being a chef for a celebrity on a yacht wasn't a bad gig. It paid well, *very* well when she was given the hours. Which was quite a bit in the spring and summer when Skyna Lord, her husband, his friends and business acquaintances used the ship.

Skyna Lord loaned the yacht and staff out a lot. That was the one positive thing about Skyna, she kept her staff paid so they didn't go elsewhere. She even would bring Martie to her house to cook, just so Martie wouldn't go elsewhere either.

Probably because the staff knew her secretes.

Martie was hired to be chef on the Talbot. Unless there were more than sixteen guests. Martie didn't need an assistant cook. She did it herself, relying on the help of a small top side staff. Two servers, a food runner and dining room attendant. It was enough. If she did need help, there was always the lower galley chef who did the meals for the crew.

Martie was Skyna's.

She had been working at a hotel when she was chosen to compete on one of those cooking shows. Skyna was a judge.

The rest was history. They hit it off, Skyna praised her cooking and hired her for the yacht and the plane. Though Martie only prepared food for the plane, she was never onboard like the yacht.

They got along at first, then Skyna treated Martie like everyone else.

Horribly most of the time, as if she were beneath her.

All smiles, Skyna seemed generous to her guests, inviting them on cruises. Those were tough, big shot Skyna acting like a queen. Martie liked it when people borrowed the Talbot, they were so much better and nicer.

Martie never knew exactly who was boarding until they did, she was only told how long they'd sail and any food allergies they might have. Except, of course, when Skyna was taking the yacht, then everything had to be perfect. It never was, despite how hard Martie and the crew tried. The fashion model, turned actress, turned billionaire's rich wife, then reality show star was as difficult as they came.

She was always right even when she was wrong. When Skyna drank and fought she was intolerable, and she drank and fought often.

Skyna's friends dealt with it because they didn't want to lose Skyna as a friend.

Behind her back they were like, "She was horrendous, horrid." But to her face, they proclaimed, "You go, you were so right to do that."

Except Brick Dogman. Probably not his real name. Martie only new him as Brick.

Dashing, chiseled-face actor with a beaming smile. His teeth weren't Hollywood perfect straight, his far left front incisor had a sight turn to it, making him look real. His processed blonde hair was always styled perfectly like a box office superhero. Even though in every movie he played the arrogant bad guy, in person he was kind and down to earth.

Brick was from Missouri and hung out with the kitchen crew a lot. Claiming he hated the stuffy and fake parties and only came for the food.

He always followed that statement with a wink.

Usually when Skyna would start her alcohol infused rants, Brick would argue with her, put her in her place, tell her to stop.

Martie never witnessed it firsthand, but the security crew shared video footage from the CC cameras. Skyna's husband seemed to enjoy the chastising of his wife.

Except on this cruise, Skyna had enough and kicked Brick off the ship. Right there in the middle of appetizers, miles from shore, she threw a fit until Brick gathered his things and they loaded him into a boat that was store in the lower level of the yacht.

Martie got to witness the Brick and Skyna fight. Appetizers were served on the deck. Martie was inspecting the buffet table and the dining room when it all happened.

Of course, dinner was delayed.

And it was everyone else's fault.

"An hour late?" Skyna blasted in the kitchen. "You couldn't keep working and cooking during all this."

"Your husband told me—"

"My husband doesn't sign your paychecks!" she cut off Martie.

Thinking, *'technically neither do you'*, Martie just nodded. "My apologies. Perhaps the guests will be really hungry and enjoy the meal more."

"Or maybe they'll vomit and drop dead from your cooking." She gobbled down that glass of wine and stormed to the galley door. Then she stopped and like a light switch, changed from angry to pleasant. "Oh, by the way, everything smells divine."

Another smile, another nod from Martie.

As Skyna pushed open the galley door, she was knocked some off her feet, when the yacht jolted hard. So much so that Martie caught the tray of vegetables before it flew off the counter. She did a quick visual check of her kitchen.

"I'm okay, thank you for asking!" Skyna spoke loudly and sarcastically. "Not like the food can suffer a traumatic brain injury or anything."

"Um, I'm sorry," Martie stammered. "Do you think something hit us."

Loudly, Skyna replied. "Do I look like I know?!"

She huffed and stormed out about the same time Kelly, one of the servers stepped in.

Kelly whistled. "Oh, she's in rare form. Maybe not. I thought we were anchored."

"We are," Martie replied.

"What the heck was that?"

"I have no idea what that was. I'm sure the Captain will tell us."

"Is the soup ready?"

Martie looked at the clock. "Six minutes. Are the two tables ready?"

"Two tables set for eight."

Martie cringed. "Yikes. Remove a setting. Brick got kicked off and Skyna will have a fit if she sees it."

"Oh, shit. That's right. I'll go do that. I'll be back for the soup."

Kelly hurried from the galley and Martie returned to the mini potato puffs. Delicate little things that would go amazingly with the lamb chops.

The six-minute timer went off and Martie turned off the burner and removed the pot from the heat. She transferred the soup into the ceramic tureen and placed it on the edge of the counter for Kelly to retrieve.

She didn't come back.

Seven minutes.

Ten minutes.

Finally, Martie worried. She didn't hear fighting, but that didn't mean anything. The galley was contained, firewalls kept it a quiet area. More than likely there was drama. Knowing the soup was now late and Skyna would have a fit, along with the fact that she was curious as to what was going on, Martie lifted the tureen and carried it from the galley.

She moved down the small corridor which led to the server area right outside the doorway to the main dining room.

No servers were there. The coffee carafe was open, and the recently brewed pot was next to it. Almost as if whoever was prepping it, stopped in the middle.

But there was no noise. It was eerily quiet, in fact. At that point she was no longer surrounded by a protective wall, Martie should have been able to hear something. *Anything.*

After setting the tureen on the back beverage counter, Martie lifted her phone from the front pocket of her chef's jacket. It was hard to get a signal, but the Wi-Fi was working, and she had Wi-Fi calling enabled. She double checked that and placed the phone on the counter. She thought about that 'thud' the jolt of the ship. What if someone came aboard, hijackers or as farfetched as it seemed, pirates?

The soup was scalding hot, and Martie lifted the tureen, if needs be she would throw it. She thought ahead, made a quick mental plan in her mind of how she would run, where she would hide.

It was too quiet for there not to be something wrong.

Taking a deep breath, she pushed on the swinging door. It made it three inches and stopped.

Thinking, 'what the hell', Martie nudged harder. Immediately her imagination went into overdrive.

Something happened.

Someone was blocking the door.

But if it were hijackers or pirates, would they keep it blocked?

Again, she tried and that was when she saw the foot. White socks, black pants, slip proof shoes.

Martie backed up.

It was one of her servers.

Setting the tureen down on the counter, she lifted the phone. Her heart thumped out of control, and she could feel the nerves vibrating through her body.

Giving it all she had, she pushed on the door. It moved the leg enough that Martie could slip through into the main dining room.

There she froze in horror, her phone toppled from her hand and landed without a sound. It never hit the floor because it landed on Kelly's body.

What Martie saw in that room caused her to scream and run as fast as she could.

THREE

AUTHORITIES

Galveston, TX

Eight days.

Eight days was all Chief of Police, Richard 'Rocky' Therman had left until he retired. Eight glorious days. He wasn't sure how he'd spend his days after he was done working; the gym, the beach, with the grandkids, or running security at Sunrise Hills Retirement Home. He was offered that position and it came with free meals. That was a nice bonus.

Rocky was at the point in his long stretch where he was now training his replacement. She seemed nice enough, a little wet behind the ears. He didn't know why someone outside of the department got the promotion, but he was sure city council had their reasons.

Rocky liked his replacement and was positive she would have no problem earning the respect of those in the department, just as he had done. Dawn Bates went to West Point, graduating top in her class, she served her country for ten years, then worked her way up through the Philadelphia PD to detective and finally captain.

On her off time, she volunteered as an EMT. Quite an impressive resume.

"So why Galveston?" Rocky had asked the council, curious to know if she had some sort of sordid secret that brought her so far away from her home. To go from high crime to Galveston was a complete switch.

The answer was easy, they had asked her the same.

Dawn grew up in Galveston. She lived there until she went to West Point. She had been away since, making Pennsylvania her home, but she wanted to come back for her ailing mother. With her two kids in college, and her husband a freelance artist, Dawn saw the opening at the Galveston Police and applied.

Getting the position brought her back to her mother, who ironically was at Sunrise Hills.

Dawn was on her third day of training when Rocky suggested they do a late shift together. She was fine with that. After all, she had to learn it all.

Rocky liked her. He thought she was a genuine person and smart. Not to mention beautiful. The misogynist in him worried when he first met her that she didn't like to get her hands dirty, then after a few minutes, he realized Dawn was as real as they came.

That was reiterated when she dove into her Sloppy Pete's double decker burger. The stack of napkins weren't enough.

They did rounds. It was quiet for the most part, then again, it was early. Not that Dawn would be doing rounds as the chief, but she needed to see what her crew would be doing.

They grabbed a burger for Stew who was dispatch at the station and stopped by to drop it off, check in and head back out.

"Oh, wow, Sloppy Pete's," Stew sniffed the bag. "I love Sloppy Pete's."

"We all do," said Rocky.

"Chief, I was about to call you," said Stew. "We got a weird call from Houston Emergency network."

"Really?" Rocky asked. "What made it weird."

"They got a call from a seventeen year old kid. His mother sent him a Facebook message telling him to get help. Apparently, she's a chef on a yacht in the bay and everyone is dead on the boat."

"Wait. What?" Dawn stepped forward. "Did you talk to the kid?"

"No, we never got to talk to him. He got frustrated and hung up on Houston. They sent the transcript." He handed the paper to Dawn. "Just came in a second ago, I haven't had a chance to read it."

Rocky watched Dawn take the paper and look down to it.

"He called over an hour ago," she said. "We *just* got this?"

"Yes, Ma'am."

"Why was there such a delay?" Dawn said. "Take a look." She handed it to Rocky. "He was pretty specific. The operator dismissed him."

"The Talbot," said Rocky. "Anchored. Yeah, you're right, he was pretty specific. I wonder why the officer was so dismissive. What have we done?" he asked Stew.

"Nothing yet," Stew replied. "That just came in."

"Okay." Rocky rolled it up, placed the paper in his back pocket and looked at Dawn.

"Marine response?" Dawn asked.

"Yep." Rocky turned to Stew. "Get a hold of GMR on duty tonight, tell them we'll meet them at the docks, we're gonna look for this Talbot."

"Yes, sir."

The Galveston Marine response was a multi organization department that took care of emergency search and rescue on the bay.

The docks were located far from the station and Rocky and Dawn headed there, lights on to make good time.

They parked the patrol car near the docks and walked toward the police boat.

"The kid stated his mother said it looked like they all dropped dead," Dawn stated as they walked briskly.

"I know. Weird." As they moved toward the end of the dock, Rocky spotted the captain of the police boat and another officer talking to a civilian. Then as he moved closer, he recognized him. 'Is that the movie star?"

"Brick something or other, yeah," said Dawn. "Doesn't look quite as dashing wet."

Rocky chuckled. "Hey, Willie, what's going on." He handed him the transcript sheet. "Here's the call we go. We ready to roll?"

"Absolutely, Chief," Willie replied. "This fellow just rolled up. Just dealing with him."

"You don't say." Rocky glanced at Brick. "Why are you on the police dock. Do you need help?"

"No, sir, not now," Brick replied. "Thank God for the fisherman with a speedboat. Kind of weird huh? Or else I would have been stranded on some little dingy in the middle of the bay."

Dawn asked. "Why were you on a dingy in the middle of the bay?"

"Not on purpose," replied Brick. "Was on vacation on a beautiful yacht, the Talbot. But I got kicked off. Literally for arguing with the host. Like put me on a boat and said go."

Dawn looked at Rocky then back to Brick. "You were on the Talbot? When was this?"

"Two hours ago. The fisherman got me right away." It didn't take long for Brick to noticed that Dawn, Rocky and Willie exchanged glances. His eyes shifted from each of them. "What's going on?"

Rocky shook his head. "Nothing. Just stay put with this officer. Don't go anywhere."

"Okay." Brick said. "Why?"

"Just stay put," Rocky ordered, then looked at the officer. "Keep him here until you hear from us."

"Yes sir," the officer replied, then escorted Brick down the peer.

"We're ready." Willie handed the paper back to Rocky. "Not that I can see very well in this light, but this looks like the woman said everyone just dropped dead."

"That's what it says," replied Rocky.

"Then maybe, because of the circumstances we should alert TDCW?" Willie suggested.

"That's a good call." Rocky looked at Dawn. "What do you think?"

Dawn exhaled. "I don't know. That's a new one to me," she said. "What is TDCW?"

Houston, TX

It was new. Brand new but a bright shining star in the area of public health.

Not department but division. Nor was it public, but rather community. Health was changed to welfare. Texas, well that stayed the same. TDCW. Texas Division of Community Welfare. A state department created after a series of public health concerns left the public weary and leery of so-called experts in the field of public health and scientific warning.

Par for the course.

Where many in the medical and virology field labeled Mark Reigns a genius, and gave him the nickname 'Answer Man'; his mother just said he was psychic. Not that he wasn't smart, he had to be to become a doctor, but to earn the reputation of always and only being one percent wrong, that didn't take brains as much as it took intuition.

Of course, Mark argued he had to have a backlog of knowledge to be able to do what he did.

Since he was in high school, before he even went to medical school, he could look at a rash, mark or hear about an ailment and guess what it was. Ninety-ninety out of a hundred times he was right.

They invented a category in the Guinness book of world records just for him. Although admittedly, he was the rash king. He could look at any skin anomaly and get it right all the time. It was the viruses and sickness that threw off his percentage.

It was that keen ability that made him want to be a doctor. Not the fifteen minutes of fame he got when he was a resident and did the talk show circuit.

Harvard Medical even put him under a rapid fire of testing. Multitudes of scholars watched.

He took that test and emerged victoriously, arms in the air, dancing like Rocky Balboa.

Then he went and got drunk with his brother.

He wanted to use that insightfulness where it would do the most good, and because he liked helping kids, he chose the field of pediatrics.

When he was approached about the position for Director of the TDCW that was about to be launched. He laughed saying he was a pediatrician. What did he know about public health.

Then they told him the perks and salary.

With the normal work hours, Mark was all in.

He did his job well and as director of the TDCW people trusted him. They liked him, listened and in the three years since the division launched, they were highly regarded and trusted.

If Mark said be concerned, people were. If he said it wasn't a worry, no one gave it a second thought.

Texas was miles ahead in the field of public health alerts, and the rest of the country was still waiting to catch up.

There were times when authorities and politicians tried to sway him, but Mark had his reputation. He chose his doctors and virologists personally, a team of five, and they all had the same integrity as him. If they went out into the field to investigate an outbreak or an unknown medical situation, Mark trusted what they had to say.

Did Mark's special talents come into play? Absolutely. Ninety-nine percent of the time he could peg what the health emergency was. Only once in the three years was he wrong. Just once. He stated an outbreak infecting twenty-two people at a restaurant was salmonella when it was intentional poisoning. A mistake he wouldn't make again.

"Okay, okay, okay," Mark said rushed into the phone as he walked into the headquarters. "I get it. Give me a minute. Or three. Thank you." He put his phone in his pocket, grabbed his lab coat and walked from reception into the back room which they called 'front lab'. It was there they handled incoming calls and reports and the virologist or doctor on duty would field them or investigate.

There was one person in the room and Mark spoke directly to him upon entering, "Doctor Wolfenstein, go home." He said to the young man sitting before a computer counter with his feet up.

"You sure?" the young doctor asked.

26

"Yes. Jason, I'm sorry, I'm late. I changed your reservations to nine, called your wife and apologized, sent forty through the cash app for the sitter and…" He reached into his pocket, pulled out his wallet, opened it and handed Jason a credit card. "Dinner is on me."

"Are you sure? You're only a half hour late."

"I'm positive. I promised I'd fill in so you could have a nice anniversary and my brother held me up."

"Is he in town?"

"No, he still held me up. Now go."

The young doctor stood. "Thanks."

"Anything?"

Wolfenstein shook his head. "Nope. Nothing on alerts, from the health department or police. It should be a quiet night. Call me if it isn't.

"I'm sure it won't be. I'm going to transfer all calls to my office."

"Alert system as well."

"Yep. Got it. Go." Mark nodded. He waited for Jason to leave. He then transferred everything so that even the smallest alert would go directly to his computer and phones.

After that, he secured the front lab door and went to his office.

It was a great office, spacious and the lighting was warm. He loved it there.

Mark powered up the computer at his desk and the one on the counter behind him. The one behind him would get the alerts. That was more the official computer. After double

27

checking the phones, he pulled out his cell, laid it on the desk and sat down in his thick leather chair.

His desk computer was booted and after a few clicks of the keyboard he placed on a microphone headset as the screen changed. Just as Mark sat back, in the top left-hand corner of the screen a small video screen appeared.

In that square was another man wearing a headset.

"I see you," that man said. "About time."

"Some of us have to work, brother," Mark said as he opened his bottom drawer and grabbed s bottle and small glass. When he said the word brother, he meant it. The man in the square video was his brother, Cal.

"Some of us delegate authority so we can have time off, brother. We paused this long enough."

"You're right."

"I will say you made record time leaving my house," Cal said.

"I got pulled over but I showed my TDCW card," Mark said. "They let me go."

"Man, that wouldn't work with my guys,"

"Yes, it would."

"You're right." Cal lifted a bear bottle and took a drink. "Ready. Wait. Are you drinking. Is that a drink I see." Cal leaned into the camera and squinted.

"Just one." Mark held up the glass. "So are you."

"But unlike me you actually are on duty."

"Cal, please." Mark lifted a game controller. "It's one drink. And nothing is going to happen tonight. Trust me," he said. "Let's get back to the game."

Six minutes exactly they were playing. Rapid gunfire, hands moving with controls, brother bantering, and the phone rang.

"What the hell?" Mark said.

"What? What is it?" asked Cal.

"The phone is ringing. The…phone."

"Answer it.'

"Hold on." Mark put the game on pause, took off his headset and lifted the incoming line. "TDCW Director Reigns speaking. Yes, this is the actual director. The director, yes, what is it?" Mark listened. "Has anyone been in there? So, we don't know anything. Sickness, murder. Keep me posted and I can be there in fifteen. Thanks." Mark hung up. After staring at the phone for a second, he put his headset back on.

"Mark, what is it?" Cal asked.

Mark shook his head. "Nothing. I'm sure it's nothing." He looked back at the game. "Now where were we?"

FOUR

ALL ABOARD

The Talbot – Super Yacht
Galveston Bay

It wasn't for Martie to be a hero, nor did she act like one in the after moments of discovering the Skyna, the guests and the crew all motionless in the dining room. She could have checked to see if they were alive or bleeding, but she didn't.

There was a thump, something hit the boat, so something caused their deaths, no doubt. Because of that, she backed up quietly, turned off all the burners, along with warmers, grabbed the biggest knife she could find and locked herself in the galley pantry. It wasn't big, it was a squeeze, but she was safe. There she had enough signal to send a message to her son.

He was always on social media; he would get it for sure.

After that, the signal went out.

While waiting in the pantry Martie had a lot of time to think. Scared out of her wits, she rewound what she saw in her mind, Because of what she witnessed, she believed the boat had been hijacked and someone used gas to attack them. Everyone was head down on the table, faces smashed in the empty soup bowls, glasses tipped over. No one moved. Then again, Martie didn't stay to look long., She took off.

Was the captain okay? The maids, the other crew. Martie didn't know. She hoped they were. She had to worry about herself, for the sake of her kids.

The galley was safe, walls and doors made to contain a fire should there be one.

It felt like hours had gone by, three or four, when in actuality it was less than two. It didn't matter to Martie. She'd stay in that pantry until someone in authority or help came for her

The rescue boat pulled alongside the Talbot. Willie called out over the loudspeaker alerting the ship that they were going to board. Rocky stood with Dawn, listening to the buzz of the drone while trying to hear her conversation on the phone.

The stern of the yacht contained a garage style dock. Probably where they stored small boats, like the one the actor, Brick, used when he was removed from the yacht. The gates were still open, and Willie had the rescue boat pull around to the stern. It would be easier to enter that way than all of them climbing up the side.

Dawn ended her call.

"What did he say?" Rocky asked.

"He said there were fifteen other guests beside him," Dawn replied. "And a dozen crew. Give or take."

"We're looking at close to thirty." Rocky shook his head. "The ship is quiet. Surely, we'd have heard something."

Willie approached. "We've tried by radio as well. But…Take a look." He handed him the tablet with the screen footage from the drone. "Our dining room."

"Jesus," Rocky gasped out, then share the video image with Dawn.

Two long dining room tables, one empty chair, the others filled, and everyone was face down.

"We can see the floor," said Willie. "So, we don't know if anyone is there. We should wear the masks in case this was chemical."

"I agree," replied Rocky.

"Wait," Dawn called out. "Can you tell the drone to hold position."

"This is video footage," Willie said. "Why?"

"I see movement. The fingers," she pointed. "Eye lids. See. There again."

"Shit. They're not all dead," Willie said with shock. "Let's prepare for a rescue, I'll alert the coast Guard that we're going in."

"Medical ship ASAP," Dawn said.

"I'll call TDCW and have them ready," added Rocky, lifting his phone. "We have that Director working tonight."

Willie paused and looked back. "That 'Answer man' genius." Willie whistled. "Thank God, at least we'll have an answer. He's never wrong."

<><><><>

Beep.

"Eighty-nine point three," said Dawn, pulling back the thermal reader. "Pulse steady and slow, breath shallow." She crouched down to the crew member they found laying just inside the ship when they entered through the stern. She was certain there were more and the rescue workers that went ahead of her and Rocky, probably found them. For the moment, she tried to learn what she could from that one man on the floor.

She turned him over to examine him., "Slight bleeding in the eyes and mouth." She glanced up to Rocky. "Chemical maybe. I've not seen a virus that doesn't have a fever."

Rocky nodded. "I don't know. Our Whiz guesser Doctor Reigns will know." He looked at Willie. "ETA on the coast guard."

"Eight minutes."

Willie's radio sounded off.

"Cap, we're in the dining room," the radio voice said.

"Any alive?" asked Willie.

"Looks like they all are, one way or another," replied the man on the radio.

"On our way."

Rocky asked. "What does one way or another mean?"

Willie shrugged. "Beats me." He lowered his radio and directed a fireman to stay with the fallen crew member.

33

When they arrived at the dining room, the four emergency workers from the marine rescue were already moving the guests from the face down positions, sitting them upright or laying them on the floor. Trying to get them comfortable while waiting on the Coast Guard.

Some whimpered a little in pain, not much. They fluttered their eyelids as their fingers were mildly triggering. The tiniest of bloody tears were in each of their mouths. Their coloring all slightly off, but not drastically gray.

Dawn felt a bit overwhelmed, the medic in her wanted to provide help, but the cop in her didn't want to compromise the scene. She opened the mouth of a woman, moving her gloved finger around the inside of her lips. The woman only blinked. "Has anyone gotten any kind of verbal response?" Dawn asked.

"No," answered another worker. "I'm not even sure they can voluntarily move."

Dawn looked at her fingertip and rolled the thick blood around. "It's coagulating so the bleed happened immediately and stopped." She gazed up to Willie.

"Nerve toxin?" Willie guessed.

Dawn glanced at the woman then to the table. "Or poison."

"Well, Doctor Reigns will know," said Willie.

Rocky looked around. "Has anyone located the chef? The person that called for help."

"My guess," Willie said. "The galley. Let's go check."

"Captain," the male voice, muffled from the mask called out. "I think you should see this. We found three more on the bridge."

"Are they alive?" Willie asked.

"No, sir, they are dead."

"Are you sure."

"There's no way they're alive," he replied. "And they aren't like this."

"You said three?" asked Willie.

"We think it's three."

Dawn was curious, as she figured Rocky was as well. The three of them hurriedly followed the crew member up to the bridge.

In all the years of being a cop, a detective and medic. From injuries on foreign soil to the street of Philadelphia, Dawn had never seen anything like it. In fact, it was the first time she could recall her stomach turning.

The bridge was a high-tech area for the Captain and his navigation team. A large private area.

One of the windows contained a baseball size hole and the bodies were on the floor.

As far as Dawn could tell there were three because the remains were separate and spaced apart.

They were without a doubt dead. There was nothing left to be alive. The only thing recognizable in each of them were bits and pieces of internal organs. No faces, limbs, not even clothing. They were piles of fresh, pink innards pudding.

Instinct caused Rocky to bring his hand to his mouth, but it hit against his gasmask. "My God. What would do this?"

Dawn shook her head. "I don't know. But I bet that doctor, that answer man, will know what this is." She sighed, looking at the bodies again. "Hopefully."

<><><><>

When Mark and his small team arrived at the dock and met Lawrence Zulinsky from the health department, it was already clear there was some sort of medical anomaly aboard the Talbot.

What it was remained to be seen and they all waited on Mark for a good guess.

To his face and behind his back, Mark called Lawrence a dick. He was just arrogant, but knew his stuff.

The four of them were dressed in Biohazard suits, except for the hoods. They'd put those on just before boarding.

"One survivor," Lawrence said. "They found her in the closet in the galley."

"The chef?" Mark asked.

"Yes. She is in shock right now. Not talking. She called it in but shows no signs of whatever it was that infected the guests and workers. Well, with the exception of what mutilated the three crew."

"You know my first through was poison," Mark said. "Because the chef was quick to call and say everyone was dead when they weren't."

"That's not your guess?"

"Not really. Nothing viral I know can mutilate those bodies. Has to be a weapon."

"So *that's* your guess," said Lawrence.

"No. Not until I see everything up close. Then I'll give my best guess."

"We look forward to it."

The problem was, to really get a good guess or answer, Mark had to see the victims up close and examine them. Unfortunately, but the time they arrived, suited up and boarded, the Coast Guard was already removing the last of the victims to take them for medical tests and treatment.

Lawrence wanted to assess the situation with Mark before they decided where to quarantine everyone - a hospital wing, military installation or if need be, on a quarantine ship.

Just as he entered the dining room, Mark paused as two medics pulled a gurney. He stopped them to look at the man lying there.

"Have you checked the vitals?" Mark asked, giving a quick visual exam.

"Major Franklin, physician on duty did when he came in. Said they were low but not dangerous. No responses yet, verbal or otherwise, muscular either."

Lawrence lifted the man's hand and tapped his wrist. "No reflex. He looks in shock."

"We'll both know better once a complete battery of tests are run." Mark walked into the dining room.

Lawrence followed. "No guesses?"

"Not yet."

"Damn it."

Mark chuckled then slowly walked around the first dining room table. "So, they're saying that upon first assessment they looked like they just dropped."

"Face first into the place settings."

Mark slowly paced around the table and stopped. "Did they all have mouth bleeds do we know?"

"Yes. Minor."

Mark swirled his finger. "Some plates have blood. Some don't. Let's collect these and test them." He stared at the plate at the head of the table, a small quarter size smear of blood was on the golden design of the china.

"They haven't removed the mutilated bodies," said Lawrence. "Shall we."

"Yes." Mark took a step, stopped and returned to the plate again.

"What is it?"

"Holy shit." Mark reached to his utility belt and pulled what looked like a pair of tick goggles. He placed them over his hood, and made an adjustment on the side. The goggles made a whirling sound. "Jesus, the blood. There's something moving in the blood."

"Can you get a good look without a microscope?"

"I have a decent look. You can see it without the goggles." He lifted them from his hood.

"What is it?" Lawrence asked.

Mark returned to staring at the small smear of blood. "It's like nothing I have ever seen. And to be honest, this is the one percent" he said shaking his head. "I have no idea what it is."

FIVE

THE LAW OF BROTHERS

Needville, TX

Irritated and slightly loud, Cal Reigns blasted an, "Oh, come on!" into his gaming headset as his hands move ferociously, up and down, thumbs clicking away. "You could have had him. You missed." He grunted. He was probably angrier that Mark left in the middle of the game, Sons of Apocalypse. Granted Cal could have waited until Mark logged back in, but he didn't want to. He wanted to get to the next level.

Brothers. A year apart, so much alike, yet totally opposite. Mark was academic, Cal better at the physical sports. One brother helped people medically, the other through the law.

Cal was a police officer. Actually, the chief of Police. A job he inherited three years earlier when the previous chief died, and no one wanted the position.

It wasn't exciting. Nothing ever happened in Needville. They closed the police station at eleven and forwarded all calls to the county police.

Even then, it was an oddity for there to be calls overnight. Occasionally a drunk driver would pass through coming from Ma and Joe's bar on 36.

That was it.

The last time there was trouble in the middle of the night, Cal made the arrest. Of course, he was at Ma and Joe's open mic night. When leaving, he saw a man pummel another guy, get in his car and take off.

He went south.

Cal followed until he was in his jurisdiction, put on the lights and pulled him over.

That was the extent of the excitement.

Like he did on this night, if Cal wasn't playing his guitar at some open mic, he was playing video games. He took the evening off, made sure everything was covered because Mark was coming over to grill.

They had steaks, hung out, played some games and Mark left. He had to fill in for someone at the lab and promised to log back in.

He did, but only for twenty minutes.

Cal regretted his decision to get a fill in for Mark.

He grunted again. "Another miss, are you kidding me? I gave you the log in because you said you could play. No wait, you assured me you could play. Mom, what the heck? Did you lie?"

"No," his mother answered through the headset. "I can play. Just not this one. I like the ones where things race in little cars."

"Oh my God. Things race in little cars? This is the apocalypse, Mom. You have to defend and fight not drive little cars. Why did you say you could play."

"Cal, you sounded so sad that you couldn't play. I just couldn't let you feel badly," his mother said.

"Mom, this is serious stuff."

"It's a video game, Cal."

"And your point."

"No wonder everyone says you're the douchebag brother."

Cal saw it.

He shrieked.

Golden_Doc_Boy has left the game.

"She stopped!" Another angry grunt and Cal dropped the controller and swiped up his beer bottle.

Empty.

"Shit." Grabbing his phone he sent a text to Mark, 'Mom hung up on me. Not sure what's up with her.' He wrote then hit send and watched. It was delivered and for a minute it went unread.

Mark had seemed more annoyed about having to go on site, maybe it was more serious than he originally thought.

Wanting another beer, Cal walked to the kitchen of his single story, four room house and realized as he reached for the fridge, he didn't have any.

He deliberately didn't buy any because he knew Mark would lay into him about how many beers he had in his fridge. Not that Mark didn't drink, he did, but he liked to judge Cal a lot.

42

That's what big brothers did.

Looking at the time, Cal saw it was still early. It was trivia night at Ma and Joe's, and though it got a bit insane there and competitive, he figured he'd get in on the third game. If not, he'd yell out answers to piss off people.

He grabbed his jacket and keys and headed out.

Ma and Joe's was only a few miles up the road.

The typical eight vehicles were parked out front along with a half dozen motorcycles.

It looked normal but something was off.

Where was the yelling, the fighting? Trivia night was cut-throat at Ma and Joe's. Many a fight had broken out there over bad answers.

But it wasn't loud.

It was quiet.

Cal walked in. One person sat at the bar and everyone else was across the room gathered around and blocking the big screen TV.

Thinking the trivia host was probably showing one of those 'find the clues' videos, Cal approached the bar. Even Glen the bartender was engrossed in watching whatever it was.

Of course, Glen was the main culprit in getting annoyed at people who guessed wrong answers. He found enjoyment rousing people up.

Glen was a good guy as well as a phenomenal musician and showman. Cal had known Glen since grade school. Played in many bands with him. Glen had dreams. He even took a job as a truck driver to take his music on the road. He bragged that he was not only going to be the best-selling black country artist of all time, but the highest grossing and bestselling country artist ever. That didn't come to fruition. Something happened and Glen was back in Needville. He did sell a few songs to some really famous artists though. Now he and Cal were local players. They were typically the only ones that played at open mic night. Needville wasn't a place folks drove all the way to for music.

That's why the stranger caught his attention.

The only person who wasn't engrossed in watching was the man at the bar. Cal didn't know him, and Cal knew everyone. He didn't seem like the typical tourist making his way through town.

Average built, the man sitting there wore all black. His hair was shoulder length, brown and wavey like some sort of rock star. He rested both his hands on a glass of brown liquid, probably bourbon. His hands and fingers covered with tattoos, and he had silver rings on every single finger.

Cal made it a point to stand next to him and then called for the bartender.

"Glen, can I get a beer?"

It took Glen a second to give Cal his attention. "Oh, yeah, sure, sorry, Cal, didn't see you."

Cal looked at the man, he brought the drink to his lips slowly, sipped it and brought it back down.

"So, uh, you passing through?" Cal asked.

"Not sure," he answered staring forward. He took another sip of his drink and then finally glanced at Cal. "Maybe."

44

There was something mysterious about his features. Especially his eyes, they were really green. His age was hard to tell.

"Maybe?" Cal asked, pulling out his wallet. "Not much around these parts to stick around for," Cal said with a chuckle. "What brings you here?"

"I'm a scout."

"Like a talent scout? Cool." Cal pulled out money. "I play guitar. I'm Cal." He extended his hand.

"Jude." The man didn't shake it.

"And I'm the better musician." Glen set down the bottle. "Don't harass my customers, Cal," he said then looked to Jude. "Ignore him. He's the law around here and does that. Leave him alone." Glen wagged a finger. "Should I start a tab?"

"Um…you know what? Yeah." Cal took a swig of his beer. "Hey, Glen, what is everyone watching. They're engrossed."

"News," Glen replied. "And you know it's interesting when it puts trivia on pause."

"It's not time for the news," Cal said.

"Breaking news. You weren't watching?"

"No." Cal shook his head, then took his beer and made his way to the masses to see what they were watching. "What's going on?" he asked a woman standing there.

"Oh, Skyna Lord. Terrorist seized her yacht. All kinds of celebrities on board. They think they hit it with some sort of biological or chemical weapon."

"Serious? Who would do that?" Cal looked at the screen. The words at the bottom clearly stated that a biological attack was suspected. It showed a large yacht, a Coast Guard ship and a bunch of smaller boats around the yacht.

The view zoomed in to one of the boats showing the men on it wearing part of their biohazard gear.

Cal's eyes clocked in, he took a drink of his beer and swallowed hard.

"Hey, Cal," Glen called his name. "Think you can find out more? I mean you are chief of police around here."

"I can do you one better." Cal set down his beer and pulled out his phone. "See that guy on the right, on the boat. Dark hair and glasses? That's my brother." He proceeded to dial. Unlike the text message, Cal wasn't letting any calls go unanswered. Like everyone else in the bar, Cal wanted to know what was going on.

SIX

STILL CONFUSED

The authorities made Martie wait in the galley after they discovered her. She hid, scared to death to step out of the panty, and after being found she still didn't have the reassurance she so desperately needed.

An older police officer discovered her and told her it wouldn't be long.

That didn't make her feel less anxious nor did she have any answers to her questions.

She asked a lot.

What happened? Was she the only one alive on the ship?

No one told her anything. They made her sit in a chair while they bagged her culinary creations as if evidence. Each lamb chop, vegetable, potato, placed in a bag as leftover examinations.

Then finally they took her from the Talbot, nut not until she had walked through the yacht, now empty and void of the bodies. After they took her in a smaller boat to an isolated facility she didn't recognize. It wasn't far from Galveston and was close to the water. The plain white, concrete building looked like a military installation. Surrounded by a fence and armed guards

Inside it was very clinical, white and clean.

Once there, she was barraged with questions. How did she feel? How long was she in the dining room? Did she notice or smell anything suspicious beforehand.

They had all those questions, yet when she told them about the thud and jolt, they dismissed her.

She just wanted to go home. Home to her children, hold them, sit with them, bury what she had witnessed underneath glass after glass of wine.

That wasn't happening, at least on this night.

Martie comforted herself by remembering she wasn't supposed to be home for another twelve hours, that the officials that held her weren't really keeping her from her family.

The experience was not like being home or even on the ship.

They took her as if she were a criminal. Men and women in white suits that covered their bodies, making them look like space aliens. She undressed, they took skin samples, she showered.

After being given new clothes, they took at least six tubes of blood to test.

Her room was nice, very hospital looking with a plastic wall that faced a nurses station or observation station. She had her own bathroom and there was a curtain she could draw over the plastic for privacy.

The nurse that brought her in assured her the plastic was for her comfort, that they didn't want to hook her up to monitors and would visual monitor her in case she had a delayed reaction.

It took a while for anyone to come back to the room. She picked at the turkey sandwich they gave her, and she paced. Finally, someone named Lawrence from the Health Department came it. He gave her another set of clothes, an iPad because there was no television, and her phone in a plastic bag.

"Just be responsible with what you tell people," he said. "You can call whoever you want, just know it's responsible to be discreet until we know anything."

"Thank you, I will," Martie replied.

"We apologize for the wait, the inconvenience and anything that you are doing for us to help figure out what happened to those on the ship." He pulled up a chair. He wore a mask and sat down a couple feet from her.

"How are they now?" she asked.

"Stable, not responding yet, but not dying," he answered.

"I would think the CDC would be here, are they?"

Lawrence shook his head. "No. Texas has its own sort of CDC."

"Oh, yeah, I heard about that. The head guy is supposed to be a know all doctor and can guess exactly what things are."

"That's correct. I'm sure he'll be in to see you."

"What does he think this is?" Martie asked.

"He doesn't know.'

"What?"

Lawrence scoffed a chuckle. "I know right. He doesn't know. So that tells me this is completely new."

"Like a weapon?"

"Possibly. We don't know."

"Thank you for your honesty and transparency," Martie said.

"What reason would I have not to be. I just don't have any answers. That's why we're watching you, testing you. If it's a virus, then we need to see if you have it, immune or a carrier. That's why you are quarantined."

"For how long?"

"We don't know. If it is a virus, we need to isolate it and watch you for it."

"It it's a weapon or sorts," Martie said. "Could those firewalls of the galley protect me?"

"It's possible."

Nodding, Martie stood up and paced to the plastic. "Am I the only one under quarantine."

"No, actually, Ish Goldman is also quarantined."

"Who?" asked Martie. "Maybe he was a new crew member."

"No, he was a guest." Lawrence snapped his finger once. "I'm sorry, you probably know him as Brick Dogman."

"Brick Dogman's real name is Ish Goldman."

Lawrence nodded. "It is."

"He was kicked off the boat an hour before it all happened."

"Yes, but he could have been exposed. He's right there." He pointed to a curtain on the right side of the room. "Plastic separates you, but you should be able to talk to him."

Martie walked over. She parted the curtain just a bit then quickly shut it and spun around. "He's naked."

"Then he needs to learn to close his privacy curtain."

Martie partially smiled. "He wasn't there when it happened. I really believe we were attacked."

"Why do you say that?"

"The thud and jolt."

"I'm sorry, the thud and jolt?"

"I've told everyone. They kind of dismissed me. Ten minutes before I found everyone there was a thud and the boat jolted."

"That's a big ship to jolt."

"I know. We had been anchored for an hour."

"And you say ten minutes later you found them?" Lawrence asked.

'I'm positive because I was timing the soup and my server never came back," Martie stated.

"Thank you for that information, that can be helpful." Lawrence sighed out. "Martie. Can I call you Martie?"

"Please."

"We don't know what happened yet, but I can promise you, we will keep you posted and for what it's worth, I think you and Ish are going to be just fine."

"Thank you."

"I'll let you call your family."

Martie gave an appreciative nod and waited for him to leave. He seemed nice enough and honest. She glanced to the curtain that separated her and the actor. Briefly, she wondered why he was just standing there naked, then figured it was something those Hollywood people do.

She was glad she had her phone and removed it from the plastic. A charger was in there as well and she would find an outlet. She was happy to have her phone. Not only to call her family, but it was a means to finding out what really was being said and was happening outside the quarantine walls.

Did anyone even know? If they did know, did they even care?

<><><><>

"I'll tell ya, Cal," Mark spoke hushed in his private office in the corner of the treatment room. "It's looks like a damn plague ward in here from the turn of the century."

"Which century?" Cal asked.

"Not this one."

"Take a picture. I wanna see."

"Promise not to post or share?"

"I don't post anything, Mark, come on. Take a picture."

"Hold on." Mark stepped from behind the curtain and aimed the camera of the phone to get the entire room in the shot. Three rows of eight beds. Every patient laid freakishly the same, on their back, white covers to their chest. IV units and monitors hooked to every one of them. He snapped it and sent it.

"Got it," Cal said. "Dude, seriously. Are they alright?"

"Physically, they're getting there, yeah. They just aren't waking."

"Maybe whatever it is affected the brain," suggested Cal.

"That's where I'm going. Has to be. And you say there's like a lot of attention on this."

"Mark, it's all over the news. I mean you have a boat load, excuse the pun, of celebrities all hit with something. And the media is saying it was a terror attack, a weapon. So, you know people are scared and glued to the set. Hell, trivia night was put on pause."

"I wonder why the media would think that."

"People talk," Cal said. "Someone that was on the site said something. Called it in. So is it a weapon."

"I don't know, I think it is. Unlike anything I've ever seen."

"And you're sure it isn't some new virus?" Cal asked.

"I told you what I saw."

"That thing in the blood."

"It's in the blood, it's on the blood. Nothing under the microscope," Mark answered. "Almost completely visible to the human eye."

"What did it look like?"

Mark paused and thought. "Okay, remember when mom was on the gluten free kick and didn't need to me."

"Yeah."

"She was eating those Asian rice noodles almost daily. The super thin ones that when uncooked they were translucent and looked like plastic or fiber."

"Yeah, yeah. It looked like that?" Cal asked.

"It did. But no immediate other samples showed it.'

"Maybe, just hear me out. Maybe it was a noodle. It was a dinner table."

"No," Mark replied. "It was one of those fancy dinners with perfectly cooked lamb chops."

"Yeah, they wouldn't go with lambchops."

"They could."

"Nah," Cal said. "They wouldn't."

"Anyhow," Mark added. "it moved."

"It moved?"

"Yeah," Mark said. "And when I tried to get it. It was gone, like absorbed or something."

"Work on that."

"If I can find another." Mark lifted his head and noticed through his small window one of the nurses waved for him. "Hey, I have to go. I have to call you back. Keep an eye on mom."

"I will. Mark?"

"Yes."

"Be careful."

He gave his brother his assurance that he would, then hung up the phone.

He wasn't sure what the nurse wanted. It didn't seem like an emergency, until he drew closer and saw the woman patient shift her eyes to him.

The first one to wake up and Mark was excited. He picked up his pace.

He paused at the foot of her bed, "Well, hello," he said. The moment it came from his mouth he cringed at how corny it sounded. He flashed a smile walked to the other side and did a quick peek at her monitor. "Jess," he spoke to the nurse. "Everything looks pretty normal."

"Everything but her temp. It's still low."

"Like how low?" Mark asked.

"Eight-eight."

"Yeah, that's low but her pulse is normal. Well, if she's up the others will be too. I hope." He gave his attention to the patient. "How are you feeling?"

"Tired. Drained perhaps. I can't really judge," she replied. "I'm laying down and haven't tried to stand."

"Doctor Reigns," Jess said. "This is Skyna Lord, the Talbot is her boat."

"How bad was this?" Skyna asked. "I see all my guests and crew. But did anyone..." her words trailed off.

"We lost three, I'm sorry," Mark replied. "Miss Lord, we really don't know what happened and anything you can remember will help us tremendously."

"I think I remember it all."

"You do?"

Skyna nodded and sat up in bed some and spoke in a very calm even tone. "We were hungry because we had to remove an unruly guest after the appetizers were served on deck. No, wait, that isn't true. He and I got into a fight. I was unkind and my decision to remove him was hasty. But, in light of everything, lucky for him."

"So, you were all hungry and gathered in the dining room."

Skyna nodded. "We had cocktails and sat at the table to wait for the first course. Which was going to be a wonderful vegetable bouillabaisse. Martie, our chef, that is her specialty. It smelled divine in the kitchen."

"But you didn't smell anything off?"

Skyna shook her head. "No, we all sat, were laughing. Kelly had poured me another glass of wine, and I suddenly felt dizzy, like extremely dizzy. There was a burning in my mouth, and I reached up when I felt it. My noise was bleeding. But I wasn't the only one. Everyone was doing the exact same thing. There were some hysterics around the table for only a few seconds. I looked at the blood on my finger and I passed out. I remember my head falling, I don't remember hitting the table."

"Was there any point you came to?" Mark questioned.

"It wasn't long. I can't speak for the others, but I heard our chef scream. I can only figure she saw us. But Doctor, I couldn't move. I couldn't call for help. I was completely paralyzed. It was so frighting."

"I can imagine."

"I was like that for the longest time." Skyna said.

"Miss Lord, by chance did you have noodles?" Mark asked.

"Excuse me?"

Mark held his fingers close together. "Little rice noodles. Tiny, thin, wiry Asian noodles. Kind of look like plastic. Did you have them?"

"When?"

"For dinner, an appetizer?"

"We were having lamb. They wouldn't go with lamb."

"They might—"

"No," she cut him off abruptly. "No, they wouldn't."

Mark turned his head to the nurse when he heard her cough and tried to cover a laugh. "What?" he asked.

"That was just really an out-there question," Jess said.

"Not really, if you knew all the facts." Mark heard a clearing of a throat and turned around. Lawrence stood with a folder all the way at the other end of the hall. He summoned Mark with a wave.

"Will you excuse me?" he said to Jess and Skyna and made his way to Lawrence.

Before Mark could say anything, Lawrence huffed. "Where is your PPE?"

"I don't need any."

"Yes, you do," Lawrence insisted.

"No, I don't. It's not viral."

"We don't know that."

"I'm about as certain it isn't viral as I am Asian rice noodles don't go with lamb," Mark replied.

"Oh, I don't know, they might."

"Thank you." Mark lifted his hand. "So, what's up?"

"Blood results are in."

"Awfully thin folder."

"It's just one."

"Why one?" Mark asked.

"Because," Lawrence dropped his voice. "Mark, every single reading is the same. The lab ran them three times."

"What do you mean the same?" Mark asked.

"RBC, WBC, platelets, the levels and numbers are the same in every single male patient and female patient. No percentage variation."

"That can't be."

"It's like whatever hit them made their levels optimal, except…" he opened the folder and showed Mark. "Look at the red blood cell count."

"Nine point two million?" Mark stated in disbelief. "That can't be right. Way too high. What is the hematocrit?"

"Seventy-four percent."

"In all of them?" Mark questioned and received a nod. "Every single one of them can't have a condition that causes extreme erythrocytosis."

"True," Lawrence said. "But you do know Carbon Monoxide poisoning can cause this."

"Not this high."

"Yes, this high."

Mark shook his head. "No. Nope. No. It's not carbon monoxide. Carbon Monoxide doesn't decimate a body like it did to the three on the bridge. It's not Carbon Monoxide. That's an easy answer to appease but not the right one."

"Then what is it?"

"I don't know, but I will find out."

And Mark was. He was determined. He was certain he knew what it wasn't, he just had to figure out what exactly it was that caused everyone to drop on the Talbot. Once he figured out what it was, he needed to figure out if the threat was over. Something inside of him screamed that it wasn't.

SEVEN

DEEP SEEDED

HTD – Hospital for Tropical Diseases
London, UK

She always had been an odd one, but that was one of the reasons Farina Ainsworth's husband, Brett, adored her so. He told her that many times. Her quirky ways, no matter how many years passed made her more enduring and youthful.

Farina didn't feel youthful after a twenty-hour shift.

They had met as children in India when Brett's father was doing work there.

Nine years old.

Almost forty-years had gone by.

They clicked; they stayed in contact.

He came back many times, visiting her when she was in medical school. Shortly after her internship, they married, and she secured a position in London where Brett worked as an inspector.

They lived busy lives, darting a kiss as they passed each other on opposite shifts.

Things eased up when she got the job seven years earlier at HTD. More meals together, movies and down time. And three days earlier was the first time in all those years their careers had crossed paths.

She stared at his photograph on her desk, which set next to her computer. Farina wanted to call him, get his advice but she knew he was sleeping and would be getting up soon enough. The last time she spoke to him, she told him she would be leaving work and he said he had a plate in the fridge for her.

That was eight hours earlier and the only thing Farina had to eat were crisps from the hospital cafeteria.

It wasn't as if Farina wasn't busy. She was. Her evening into the early morning hours wasn't spent watching a pathogen, it was spent watching the American news.

The story of the super yacht owned by celebrity Skyna Lord. How Skyna and other famous people boarded the Talbot for a five-day pleasure cruise of pampering, fun and luxury.

One day remaining, twelve hours before they were set to dock, the cruise came to an end.

Health agency ships along with the Coast Guard surrounded the ship, removing the twenty some ill passengers and three dead crew.

As of the last repost, one crew member, a look out, was unaccounted for and the media was labeling the twenty-two year old college man a suspect.

Speculation and conspiracy were abound.

It went from super flu outbreak, intentional poisoning to a terrorist attack.

Everyone had a reason for what happened.

Farina didn't. She was dealing with her own crisis that occurred three days before the American's. One that didn't make the news, it wasn't a yacht, it involved a dozen unknown partiers remaining from a rave, Yet, the circumstances, so eerily similar it made her skin crawl.

She wondered if the ill celebrities also made a sudden recovery.

The slight tap to the door, caused Farina to jolt. She turned in her chair. "Susan," she spoke to her brilliant lab assistant. "You look tired, you need to go home."

"So do you." Susan stepped in. "We both need to rest."

"Yes, yes, we do."

"Have you reached out to the Americans yet?"

Farina shook her head. "Not yet."

"Can I ask why?"

"I'm afraid. I'm fearful that we are dealing with the exact same thing."

"There's only one way to find out. You have to ask about the three deaths."

Farina nodded as she lifted a pencil and nervously tapped it. "And the missing person."

"And the missing person, yes."

"Susan, what do you think?"

"I think it's related, how, I don't know. But…Doctor Mark Reigns is on it."

"He is so intimidating," Farina said.

"But if anyone knows what this is, he does."

"Under normal circumstances, yes," Farina folded her hands in a prayer fashion, resting the tips of her fingers under her chin as she turned her chair again and faced the computer. She glanced at the news story she had paused on the screen. The yacht, the headline of 'Hollywood Terror Attack'. She inhaled deeply, closed her eyes for a second then exhaled. "I don't think even the brilliant Doctor Reigns can figure this one out. Something tells me, it's beyond what we know."

EIGHT

STRANGER IN A FRIENDLY TOWN

Needville, TX

Cal wasn't used to working Friday morning. It was the day he slept in and prepared for the not so crazy Friday nights in Needville. But having arranged schedules to spend time with his brother the night before, Cal was now working a double on a Friday.

Not that he had to be at the station that early. County Police had the calls until seven. And Mary, dear sweet Mary who should have retired ten years earlier was on dispatch. She'd let him know if anything happened.

Until he hit the station, Cal went along with his normal morning routine he had whenever he did work the day shifts.

That meant stopping at his mother's. He checked on her every day. Even though Cal was certain his mother could handle just about anything, Mark was insistent. If she was going to live alone, they needed to check up on her. Mark feared if they didn't their mother would lie dead for days before someone found her.

"She's not that old, dude," Cal told him.

"Still, you never know."

"Fine."

Cal did go to her house. Every day because he was closest distance wise to her. A few blocks from his own home. Once a month he'd hint to her to move in with Mark.

She didn't bite.

Doing the same as he did every morning that he went to his mother's, Cal parked in front of the driveway and walked around to the back.

It was routine.

He'd go around to the back yard, smell the cigarette smoke before he got there and see his mother sitting on the back patio having her coffee, a smoke and reading the newspaper on her tablet just as he said, "morning mom."

On this day he didn't smell the smoke.

Not thinking twice about it, Cal called out his typical, "Morning, Mom." As he rounded the bend and then he stopped cold.

Nothing.

She wasn't there.

He looked down to his watch to make sure he wasn't exceptionally early or late.

Nope. Eight fifty-three on the dot.

Suddenly, all that neuroticism of Mark plowed through Cal's mind, and he feared for his mother.

She was dead. She had to be. She was a creature of habit. Just as his brother feared, Cal was certain his mother was laying on the floor somewhere.

Heart racing, and just in case foul play was involved her pulled out his pistol and reached for the sliding patio door.

It was unlocked.

"Damn it, mom," he cursed because she left herself vulnerable. Was she going to be one of those unsolved mysteries?

He opened the door and walked into the dining room that was when he heard the noise.

A gurgling.

It wasn't until he stepped into the kitchen that he realized it was the coffee maker. His mother stood by it looking impatient as she waited the forty some seconds for that coffee pod machine to fast brew her coffee.

"Mom?"

His mother jumped and screamed. "Oh my God, Cal." She grabbed her chest. "You scared me."

"Are you okay?"

"Yes."

"You're usually out on the patio by now."

"And you're usually not here on a Friday," she said

"Does that make a difference?"

"Yes, Cal. It's my sleep-in day and why is your gun pulled?"

"Oh, sorry." Cal put the gun away. "You have a sleep-in day?"

"Um, yeah, I do. Fridays. You don't work Fridays. Hold on." She lifted a finger, grabbed her cup from under the brewer and took a sip. "Ah, yes, that's better. Did you want a cup?"

"Yes. Thank you."

His mother pulled out a coffee pod and cup and proceeded to make him a cup. 'Why are you here on a Friday so early?"

"Checking in and, well, breakfast."

'Breakfast?" she asked.

"You make me breakfast every day," Cal said.

"Not on Fridays."

"Ah, seriously? Does this mean I have to go fast food."

"No, Cal, I'll make you breakfast. Although you are a grown ass man who could make his own."

"Yeah, but it wouldn't taste as good."

"Can I have a smoke first?" She handed him his coffee.

"Sure. I can wait."

"Gee, thanks." She sipped her coffee.

"Were you up late?"

"Until four." She grabbed her pack of cigarettes from the table and walked outside, immediately lighting one.

"Why were you up so late?"

"Watching the news. Shame about those celebrities being targeted by terrorists."

"Was bound to happen." Cal shrugged.

His mother shook her head. "And your brother putting himself in the line of danger. I was so worried all night he was going to get that chemical attack stuff."

"Excuse me?" Cal asked.

"The news said it was a terror attack. They hit that boat with a chemical weapon. Your brother was right there. All night. He could catch it."

"He could." Cal said. "You're right to be worried."

"Are you gonna be working on the terrorist boat case,"

Cal replied jokingly. "Oh, yeah, Mom, I'll be right there leading the investigation."

"Good." She puffed her cigarette. "Just don't catch it either." She put out her smoke gently as she always did to save it for later. "I'll make your breakfast."

She kissed Cal on the top of the head and went into the house. Not only did Cal grab his coffee, he lifted his phone, sending a message to Mark:

'Mom thinks you caught the chemical weapon. How funny is that. Not gonna tell her it doesn't work that way. Chemical weapons don't spread.'

He hit send, chuckled as he did, and sat back.

Although he dreaded being up early on a Friday with such a long day ahead of him, Cal was going to at least enjoy a good breakfast.

What was going on with Mark? Cal had sent him a few texts and without a response, but when an hour went by, he had eaten his breakfast, Cal called his brother.

No answer.

Realistically he knew Mark was probably sleeping or wrapped up in something. But on the far-fetched side he kept hearing his mother.

What if Mark caught this chemical weapon.

As outlandish as it sounded, that actually went through Cal's mind.

But he had to focus on work, not that it would be that busy.

67

He parked up the street from the station and walked inside. Just as he suspected, Mary was at the front desk. Her head resting in her hand, and she was sound asleep.

Cal cleared his throat. "Morning, Mary."

She jumped up and lifted the phone receiver. "Needville Police, how can I help you." After a second she realized she answered out of instinct rather than need and hung up.

"Did you have a nice nap?" Cal asked.

"I wasn't sleeping., I was thinking."

"I'm sure." Cal reached for the messages on the desk. "Anything good."

"No emergency," she replied. "But Buzz called to report a suspicious vehicle parked in the lot."

"Buzz from the Moonlight Motel?"

"That's the one."

Cal paused when he found the message. "He called from the worst motel this side of the Mississippi to report a suspicious looking vehicle in that lot."

"That's what I said."

"Oh, this ought to be good." He set down the pink message.

"Are you going to check on it."

"What else is there to do?" He walked to the door. "Oh, yeah, by the way, Mary. Some of those messages are months old."

He lifted his hand in a wave as he walked out.

The Moonlight was less than a mile away, and since nothing else was urgent, he made his way there.

At first Cal wondered if he'd be able to spot the suspicious vehicle when he pulled up to the single story, twelve room motel. What made it suspicious? Bad plates, a broken window? Maybe even heavily tinted windows. Maybe it was abandoned because it was used in some sort of crime. The moment he pulled into the lot there was no question.

He spotted it right away. Not just because there were only five cars in the lot but because the vehicle stood out.

It was the strangest shade of dark green he had ever seen, there was absolutely no shine to it. The shape was odd, a completely flat front end, with older round headlights. The body was that of a van, but more boxed shape, almost European.

Cal walked around it and noticed the New York plates. He pulled out a small note pad and pencil.

"Can I help you?" the male voice said.

Cal turned around. "Yes, I…" he recognized the man from the night before at Ma and Joe's. The stranger at the bar who was the only one not engrossed in the news.

"You're the chief of police, correct."

"I am. Cal Reigns. You're…" Cal snapped his fingers several times. "Jude. Yes, the scout."

"Correct. Something wrong with my van?" Jude asked.

Cal looked around. "Are you staying here?"

"Yes, I am. I'm parked right in front of my room."

"Hmm, did you tell them when you checked in this was your car."

"I didn't think I needed to. He didn't ask."

"Damn Buzz. Sorry about that." Cal put the pad away. "He reported a suspicious vehicle in the lot."

"Well, I do get a lot of glances about it."

"To be honest I never saw one like this."

"Not here you wouldn't," Jude said. "It was my grandfather's, he bought it in Moldova."

"Moldova? Never heard of it. Is that in New York."

"No." Jude said with a smile and shake of his head. "Eastern Europe. Sandwiched between Romania and Ukraine."

"Ah, no wonder I never heard of it. Well, I'll let you get back to your day. If you're in town long, stop by the station and say hello."

Jude nodded. "I'm sure I will."

"I hope you find what you're scouting for."

"I'm confident."

"Good. Just…Scouting Needville?" Cal questioned.

"My law friend, you wouldn't believe what will come out of Needville."

Thinking, he was right. About the only famous thing to come out of Needville was Margorie Jenkins winning the National Cross stitch competition two years earlier.

Maybe that was it. Maybe he was scouting a really good cross stitch champion for some world stitching thing, because Cal, for the life of him couldn't figure out what a big time New York scout could be scouting in his town.

NINE

HOMEGROWN

Quarantine Bay, Galveston TX

"Everything okay?" Lawrence asked Mark as they stood in the monitoring hub.

Mark figured he asked that because he was staring at his phone. "Yeah," Mark answered then finished texting. "Just my brother driving me a little nuts."

"Your mother's okay, right?"

"Oh, yeah." Mark put his phone in his pocket. "My brother worked a double yesterday and is getting on me about coming over his house tonight to finish the…finish something we were working on, you know when the yacht business started."

"I'm sure he understands you've been busy," Lawrence said. "He's a cop."

"Oh, he does."

"Mark there is no reason you can't go tonight. Forty-eight hour mark, we have to let these people go. You read that court order. Skyna's lawyers worked fast."

Mark grunted. "I get that. But we still don't know—"

"You don't know, Mark. Heck, even I don't know, but we know it's not viral and we know these people aren't contagious. We can't hold them here, unless we find probable cause in the next eight hours, then like that judge said, after forty-eight hours we are violating their fourth amendment."

Mark grunted. "CDC can supersede—"

"The CDC are with the FBI on this one. Chemical weapon of unknown origin. It's not viral. No indication. And don't...don't play the CDC card, you are an independent agency for the state of Texas. You don't play well with them."

"You're right. You're right. Just my gut, those bodies."

Lawrence held up his hands. "I know. FBI is saying it was a weapon, like an acid."

"Results aren't back yet."

"Doesn't mean we can hold these people."

"Their red blood cell count is still unfathomably high," Mark said.

"That's medical. That's what her lawyers argued. They can seek private medical treatment. They aren't a threat or contagious. No virus. We can't hold them. We are infectious diseases. That is where our authority ends. Look," Lawrence lowered his voice. "Off the record. Something is up. I think it's a mistake to release these people until we know. On the record our hands are tied. They filed an injunction; the FBI has a suspect and it's reasonable. We all thought he was some college kid. But that same kid was on the FBI watch list for when he was in Turkey. He has ties."

Mark sighed out. "You're right."

"We keep working. We have samples. You and I will work our agencies on the side. Tonight, after you release everyone. Go see your brother."

"I will. Thanks. I just hate not getting it right."

"Ninety-nine percent of the time you do," Lawrence said. "This just might be the one percent you don't."

He gave a swat to Mark's arm and Mark nodded.

He grabbed his phone, shooting a fast text to Cal to let him know he'd be by late, then Mark went to the quarantine section to let the two people there know they would be leaving soon.

Martie smiled as she stared at her daughter's face in the video call on her phone. Her daughter, however, seemed more engrossed in Brick who was behind Martie during the call.

"Are you being good for Daddy?" Martie asked. When she didn't receive a response, she repeated the question. "Rose."

"Yes, Mommy."

"Are you being good?"

"Is he coming home with you? I like Doctor Danger," Rose said.

Obviously, she was referring to the latest super villain role that Brick had played.

"No," Martie said. "He is not. He's going to his home. Now can we talk. I miss you."

"I miss you too. When are you picking us up?"

"All goes well," Martie replied. "A few hours."

"I'll tell Daddy."

"I already talked to…" Martie cringed when Rose yelled out for her father.

After finally getting her attention, Martie spoke a few minutes more and ended the call.

"Quite a handful you have," Brick said. "Two kids."

"It's not that bad, their Dad is very active in their lives."

"That's good."

"Yeah, it is."

"So …" Brick paced about. "What are you plans after this?"

"Go home."

"I mean for work," he said.

"I don't know."

"Wanna work for me?" he asked.

"Where? I won't leave my kids and I can't move them."

"Houston, I live outside of Houston when I'm not filming. I'll keep you on staff all year. Don't go back to Skyna."

"Wow." Martie was slightly taken aback. "I wasn't expecting that."

"I've thought it for a while, but I didn't want to steal you from Skyna. She can be scary. Plus, I wanted to try those lamb chops."

"Then I will make them for you if I accept that offer." Martie shook her head with as smile. "My children are going to start calling me the celebrity chef." She looked up when she heard the clearing of the throat. Standing in the door was Doctor Mark Reigns. "Doctor Reigns."

"I'm not interrupting, am I?" Mark walked in.

"No." Martie shook her head. "How is everything?"

"Well." He flipped open a chart. "I uh…there's a privacy thing. HIPPA and all."

"I'll go." Brick stood.

"No, it's fine." Martie said. "I have nothing to hide and really, he and I are in the same boat."

Brick nodded. "Yeah, and you can pass the privacy thing with me too. She's seen me naked."

"I won't ask," Mark said. "But if you two are sure, then…" He glanced down. "Everything is great. Absolutely one hundred percent normal across the board. My heathiest two."

Brick asked. "As opposed to the others?"

"The others, like you two will be released at the forty-right hour mark."

"Is that because of what the judge ordered?" Martie asked.

"Honestly, I have no reason to hold you two whatsoever. Especially Mr. Goldman, or rather Brick. But just out of the abundance of caution I would prefer to keep the others here." Mark shrugged. "But my hands are tied."

"No clue yet what it is?" Brick asked.

Mark shook his head. "I don't. But it's apparently being called a terror attack, chemical weapon, carried out by the steward, Marshall."

Martie sighed. "I don't get it. I know Marshall, he's a nice kid. It doesn't make sense."

"None of it does," Mark replied. "Few more hours you can go. You have my contact information. Anytime, day or night, if you have any problems, you call me. I'll stop in one more time before I head out for the night."

"Thank you," Martie said.

Mark turned to leave, stopped then faced Martie. "Can I ask you something?"

"Sure," Martie replied.

"Are you familiar with Asian rice noodles."

"Absolutely," said Martie. "Thin, translucent."

Mark snapped his finger. "Yep. That's them. In your professional chef opinion would those noodles go with lamb."

Martie smiled. "Of course, it's all in the preparation and presentation. Anything can go with anything."

"Thank you." Mark grinned. "It's been a subject of debate with everyone."

"Now, can I ask you something," Martie said. "In your professional opinion, is everything really okay?"

"No." Mark lowered his head. "For you two, yes. The others. No. I have no medical basis for that opinion, just a hardcore gut instinct. Unfortunately, my gut instinct isn't enough to challenge a court order. Hopefully, my gut is wrong," Mark said. "And everyone touched by the attack will be one hundred percent fine."

TEN

THE START

Earls Barton, Northamptonshire UK

Five days earlier, Tip Hedwig was drumming in a band, playing at a massive rave in a warehouse in New Charlton. They
played for an hour before the DJ took over and then Tip just
partied. He was having the time of his life, but the party was
cut short when everyone that remained literally dropped.

At first, Tip felt dizzy, weird and he thought it was the ecstasy, then when his nose started to bleed, he believed it was
the coke. When he tumbled to the floor, he didn't know what
was happening. He blacked out briefly then lay there, con-
scious but unable to move or talk. The only noise he made was
a slight whine.

Tip was told they were only there a few minutes before being discovered. One of the partiers, Nelson, had left to get food
and returned to find them. That same partier was detained.

Apparently, it was an attack, a vicious attack. They weren't
sure if it was a terror attack or some revenge.

One thing Tip knew, there was no way Nelson did it. He
couldn't, Nelson just didn't have it in him. He swore it was

drugs, they all did the same ones. Until he found out that a few had been hit with acid. The kind that ate their body away.

It didn't take long for Tip to bounce back. In fact, he felt fine the next day. He wanted to go home, but he was in quarantine until they knew for sure it wasn't something viral.

Finally, they sent him home and Tip just wanted to go out. Take his girlfriend and go out. Not that he minded their flat mate, but he wanted to spend time with Daphne.

They went to their favorite pub in The Square, ate some food and had some drinks. Typically, Tip was not a lightweight, he could drink a couple of pints and not feel a thing, but he started feeling a buzz and he wanted to go home. They planned to stay for pub quiz night, but Daphne understood.

He could drink at home. Usually, he wasn't like that, he'd stay out all night and often not remember it. Something felt odd, maybe it was the three days eating healthy that threw his system into a frenzy.

Whatever it was, he felt the need to go home.

When Daphne met Tip, he was studying to be a professor of music. But his dreams of being a rock and roll star overshadowed his love for the theory of music. He left school, giving himself two years to return. If he didn't become famous, he would go back.

It was one year in. Tip played several nights a week in four different bands, he loved it. His reckless nature drove her insane at times, but being so carefree made her love him more.

Something was different about him this night.

He did laugh, ate all his food and after only two pints, called it a night. He ordered takeaway for Bill their flat mate and asked her if she minded if they left.

He seemed as if he had drunk several pints, he teetered as he walked, fumbling with his wallet to pay for everything. His coloring seemed to grow paler.

They walked back to their home on Tebbutt's Yard, which wasn't too far at all.

He slung his arm around her shoulder, something he rarely did. Tip claimed he was being romantic; Daphne knew it was probably more for balance.

The walk home began with them talking about those in quarantine. How the main doctor was super nice, they laughed the leg of the journey. Then Tip leaned on her more, his words slurred. He still rambled on.

"Almost there," Daphne told him.

"I'm good."

"You're not. You need to go to bed. I'll get you some water."

"You think Bill will like his tacos. Maybe we should have got him something else."

"Bill will love his tacos." Daphne reached for their front door. "He's probably in there playing video games and eating crisps."

Daphne opened the door. It wasn't locked. She could hear the explosions from the game as they walked in.

"That you?" Bill asked.

"It's us."

"You're home early. I thought it was pub quiz night."

"It was. Tip is under the weather." Daphne led Tip into the living room, where sure enough Bill was playing video games. A bowl of crisps set on the table before him.

"We brought you food." Daphne set the bag on the table.

"Thank you." Bill played for a second, then did a double take to Tip who now stood on the other side of the table blocking the television. "You okay? You look ill."

Tip teetered.

Bill chucked. "How much did you drink?"

Daphne replied, "Not enough to be like this. Something is wrong."

"Tip?" Bill snapped his finger. "Are you alright?"

Tip didn't move. He just stared at Bill.

"Tip?" Again, Bill called him.

"Let's go to bed, sweetie, I'll call the doctor if you're still bad in the morning." Daphne reached for his arm to move him, but he didn't budge. "Tip?"

It was as if his feet were cemented to the floor. Just as Daphne tugged him again, Tip's arms went rigid. His back arched, pushing his chest forward, his arms bent behind him as his head flung back.

"Tip!" Daphne cried out.

Bill immediately stood. "Call for help."

Before Daphne could take a step from the room, Tip's head flung forward. His mouth opened wide and with a loud rushing sound, from his mouth came a rush of deep red regurgitation. He flowed like a water valve being release, wide, fast and

80

forceful. Blasting out of his mouth at such a force, it not only hit into Bill, but sent him backwards to the sofa.

All Daphne could do was scream.

ELEVEN

THE SECRET

Needville, TX

Only once in his three years as Chief of Police, did Cal have to pull his gun in the line of duty. That was two years earlier and it as tragic. A rabid retriever, much like Old Yellow, attacked Mary from the station. Cal had to put it down. Poor Mary was in the hospital for weeks and had gone through all the shots.

It wasn't as if Cal didn't know how to use a gun, he was a great shot, went to the range all the time, but it was different when aiming at someone or something alive.

Now Cal aimed for the second time in his Chief of Police career. This time it wasn't a dog, it was a woman. She was around thirty, maybe a year or two older. Her long brown hair was a mess. She wasn't dirty, but she was frantic, wearing all black and a long leather coat totally out of season for the hot summer weather.

She held Pop's wife at knife point.

Cal knew she was nervous, jittery. She wasn't budging in her stance. A stranger rolling through town, like so many others, stopped at the Pop's shop. A local place for groceries, souvenirs and other items locals could use in a pinch.

A few people were in the store when she walked in. One of them was that stranger Jude with the weird car, and Cal was another. He was on the phone with Mark, making plans for the night when it all went down.

"Let me call you back," Cal said, put down his phone and pulled his gun.

The woman was clearly after one thing and one thing only. Pop's pride and joy and bragging item. It was in a framed case above the cash register.

Pure silver, coffin handled Bowie knife. The original used by James Bowie in the sandbar fight of 1827.

Bowie was a relative of Pop's. He inherited that knife and now the woman had it, in her grip, the blade so near Pop's wife's throat.

She came in, bought a can of beans.

Pop said. "Anything else."

After saying, "I'll take that knife." She wailed the can with perfect aim at the frame, the glass busted, and the frame dropped. Before Pop's could react, she decked the eighty-year-old man, leap the counter and grabbed the knife.

Cal had pulled his gun. He would have had her had Pop's wife not walked out.

And that's where they were at.

"Let her go," Cal told the woman.

"I will. Just let me leave."

"No, you assaulted poor pops. Lady, you went from misdemeanor theft, assault to a felony attempted murder. You aren't walking out of here," he said.

"I only punched him. I don't you know how dangerous I actually am. I'm very dangerous. I don't need this knife to hurt people."

Cal stifled a laugh. "Then why do you need it, Miss Danger? You need money? Think selling that will get you drug money?"

"Don't make me hurt you all."

Cal held his aim steady. He thought about pulling a 'Speed' and shoot the hostage, but with his luck, Pop's wife wouldn't survive. "Put down the knife, now," Cal ordered.

"No."

"Put down…" Cal slowed his words when he saw Jude creeping up behind her. "The knife," he continued, all while thinking 'what the hell is he doing, he's going to get Mrs. Pops killed.'

As the woman moved a few inches toward Cal, he saw a clear shot. Her leg. He was going to take it but he had to do it fast. Before he could, he watched Jude step to the woman. Cal didn't know what Jude did, but the woman's arm dropped as if she had no control. The knife fell to the ground and with a clunk sound, the woman, teetered and fell to the floor.

Pop's wife raced hysterically to her husband.

Jude stood holding a beer bottle. "Trust me she's just out. Have to hit in the right place. No hospital needed."

Cal stepped toward them. "Her arm. How did you—"

"Pressure point. It's immediate."

Cal holstered his weapon. "It's impressive." He pulled out his cuffs and crouched down. "Thank you." He rolled the woman over and reached for her arms.

"Don't mention it. One more thing, Chief. You may want to take precaution and isolate her."

"Oh, yeah, why's that?" Cal asked.

"She's infected."

Teddington, Richmond, UK

The home was new to them, even though they had purchased it just two years earlier, Farina and her husband worked so much they barely had time to enjoy it. Finally, they did. She finally left a days long shift at HTD.

She came home and took a long relaxing bath while Brett, her husband made dinner. After they sat together on the sofa, wine in hand, binging on a new detective and hospital show. It was fun for them to pick apart what the show got right and wrong.

In her mind, Farina had great plans for the evening. A few episodes and some long overdue lovemaking with her husband.

The evening was still considered young, and they had just settled into the second episode and second glass of wine. Brett wanted to pause to enjoy a smoke on the back patio when the doorbell rang.

"Who could that be?" Brett paused before opening the back doors. "I'll get it."

"No, it's fine." Farina set down her glass and stood. "More than likely, it's for you."

"Tell them I'm busy."

"I'm sure." Farina smiled, left the room, walking down the hall to the front entrance. The exterior light was on, and Farina took a peek through the windows on the side of the door.

Shocked to see who it was, she opened the door. "Susan?" Farina said with surprise. "Come in."

Susan appeared fearful, almost nervous. "Is your mobile off or on silent?"

"No, it's," Farina paused and cringed. "I left it upstairs. What's going on? Come have a seat."

"There's no time Farina."

"What do you mean?" Farina asked.

"Remember one of the quarantine, Tip Hedwig."

"The musician, yes."

"We have a situation. A bad situation. Authorities in Earls Barton aren't sure how to handle it. They found our information and called. They're securing the scene until we get there with a team. I have the team ready."

"Earls Barton? That's a drive, it will take a while to get there."

Susan nodded. "I know. We have to go now."

"Susan, is it that bad?"

"Worse than you would expect. I'll tell you about it in the car."

"I'll grab my things and be right out." Farina didn't wait and watch Susan leave, she immediately sought out her husband, finishing her wine as she did.

If Susan came to her home, then it was worse than what Farina could possibly imagine.

Earls Barton, Northamptonshire UK

It took a little over ninety minutes taking the M1. There were no flashing lights calling attention to the authorities' presence, but there was yellow tape, a few police officers out front. A van from the coroner's office and one from the Health Unit.

At the entrance they showed their credentials to the young officer that guarded the door and before he let them in, he advises them to 'mask up'.

Farina was expecting such and already had her mask out along with goggles. Susan told her at the car that Tip was dead. That his live-in girlfriend had called for help. That call ended abruptly, and the authorities went to the home.

A middle-aged man approached them before they could step fully in and onto the scene.

"Doctor Ainsworth?" he asked. "I'm Inspector Andy Paul. Thank you for getting here so fast. We found your information on the table and called right away. Especially since you are with HTD. We figured Mr. Hedwig had to have something to do with you."

Farina nodded. "He was at a party where they were all hit with a chemical or drug. He was just released yesterday." She facially cringed. "I wished we would have held him longer."

"You couldn't have known. I don't think anyone would have thought this. This way..." he extended his hand. "It's not pretty." He took a few steps and stopped. "Right here is where we found the girlfriend."

Farina looked at Susan quickly then back to the inspector. "What do you mean found her?"

"She was unconscious, having some sort of seizures, extremely high temperature. She died on the way to hospital."

Farina gasped. "My God, it was viral."

"I don't know," said the inspector. "Not a doctor, but can a virus do this to Mr. Hedwig."

He led them into the living room. It was an almost familiar scene, one Farina witnessed at the warehouse. Only there was more blood, a lot of blood.

A rich, deep red substance, she could only figure was blood covered the coffee table, the carpet and the man who sat on the couch. In his right hand was a video game controller. His head, legs, shoulder and arms were fine. Everything from his mid-chest to his lap was mush. Completely dissolved into a red mess, much like the three bodies in the warehouse. Farina had no idea what was holding him upright.

"The emergency call stated," the inspector said. "That her boyfriend was sick. That's all we got. What kind of illness would cause this?"

"Nothing I know of," Farina replied.

Farina took another step toward the body. "Okay, where is Mister Hedwig?"

"I'm sorry?" the Inspector asked.

"Where's Mister Hedwig? You said he was dead."

"Isn't this him?"

"No, it's not him."

Quietly, Inspector Paul mumbled. "The footprints."

"What was that."

After briefly closing his eyes, Inspector Paul shook his head. "One of my men thought it was foul play at first because of the bloody footprints." He pointed. "They went to where Daphne was and stopped. I assumed they were hers."

Hurriedly, Susan brushed by Farina and went into the small entrance way, she pulled out a small light shining it downward. With a looking of horrified concern, she turned to Farina. "They went outside. Barely seen. If there is a viral infection, it's in him."

"Inspector we need to find him," Farina said. "We need to find him now."

Needville, TX

In an odd twist of music, the band Bon Jovi played on the jukebox. Something different than the country music that usually played at Ma and Joe's. Cal told Mark who the culprit was. The talent scout Jude, and he was there again.

His presence was starting to alarm Cal. Why was he always around. Clearly, other than himself and Glen the bartender, there was no real talent in Needville.

Cal mentioned that to his brother and Mark just blew that off.

"Mom?" Mark sat down next him Cal at the bar and nodded at his phone.

"Yep. She's pissed that you didn't stop by."

"No, she's not. Plus, did you tell her you had me working."

"Hey, our local doctor gave the clear but he's not you," said Cal.

"True."

"So?" Cal asked. "Anything?"

"I examined Ella. Nothing. No signs of virus or illness. No outward signs. I did draw blood, but that's in your fridge and I'll take it back with me tonight, run the standard testing, I'll know more then."

"My fridge at the station?"

Mark nodded. "Yeah."

"Where I keep my lunch?"

"It's fine," Mark said, reaching for the beer.

"Did she say why she wanted that knife so bad. Was it money?"

"No, she believes she is sick, too, has a virus. and she wants to cut the sickness out."

"With that knife?" Cal questioned. "Or would any knife do."

90

"Something about that knife." Mark shrugged. "I don't know."

"Don't you think it's really too coincidental. Maybe something is going on that we don't know about."

"What do you mean?" Mark asked.

"Well, you said about this doctor from the UK contacting you about a similar situation at a rave."

"Yeah."

"Well, she wouldn't know about your case had your sick ship not been full of celebrities. The only reason she knew about it was because of the famous people. And had she not reached out to you, you wouldn't have known about her cases."

"That's true," Mark said. "Where are you going with this?"

"Maybe it's not two linked terror hits. Maybe there are more incidents we don't know about. Ones that don't involve famous people."

"Brother, that's actually really good thinking. We need to look into that."

"I'll bet." Cal paused to take a drink. "If we look up overdose cases at parties and things like that, we will find something. Just too coincidental that the UK has a similar case and this chick, Ella, swears she has a virus."

"You never mentioned how she told you about it. I mean," Mark said. "When I was on my way here you said you have a prisoner you wanted me to look at. That they may be infected with something. How did you find out?"

Cal reached for his beer and pointed.

Mark turned his head and looked in the direction of the point to the man at the jukebox. "Bon Jovi guy?"

"Yep. So, when the chick had the knife at June's throat, he snuck up behind her, did some sort of pressure point thing. It made her arm just drop with the knife, then he knocked her out."

"He did your job."

Cal grumbled. "Aside from that. He said keep her separate because she was infected."

"Odd. Did you ask how he knew?"

"I did and he said he just knew."

"I think I'll go talk to him." Before Mark could get up, Glen the bartender set down two baskets of food before the brothers. Each had a burger and fries.

"Ah, man, Glen, this looks good." Cal took a sniff. "You make the best burgers."

"Thanks," Glen replied. "That's probably why that Food Network show featured them. Need anything else."

Mark grabbed for the ketchup. "So, you're not just a bartender, you're a chef."

"Cook," Glen corrected. "Here. I'm a musician at heart."

"Let me ask you something," Mark said. "Ever hear of them Asian noodles…." He paused when Cal groaned. "What?"

"Are you still going on about those noodles?" Cal asked.

"I'm getting as many professional opinions as I can," said Mark.

"What noodles?" Glen asked. "Like Lo Mein."

"No." Mark shook his head. "Like rice noodles. They're thin, look translucent, like fibers."

"Ug," Glen grunted. "Yeah. What about them?"

Mark chuckled. "That's a weird reaction. I was just asking if you thought they went with lamb."

Glen shook his head. "I would never use them with anything. I can't look at them."

"Why's that?" Mark questioned.

"Because they creep me out. It's me, I'm weird," Glen said. "But when I see them. I think worm or parasite. You guys need anything else?"

"No," Cal said. "We're good." As Glen walked away, he noticed Mark just staring at his burger. "Mark?"

"Parasite," Mark mumbled almost with a revelation. His mind went to that word 'parasite', lost in his thoughts, then seemingly he jumped from his stool when his phone rang. Mark lifted the phone and looked at it.

"Who is it?" Cal asked.

"The UK." Mark answered, recognizing the number. "Doctor Ainsworth?"

"Yes, Doctor Reign, thank God I caught you," Farina said. "I don't have time right now. I'll call you later, but I need to stress how important it is that you do not release your quarantined patients. Under no circumstances, whatever you do, do not let them out. They may be carriers."

"Shit," Mark blurted out.

"What?" she asked.

"You're two hours too late." Mark closed his eyes. "We released them."

TWELVE

EMBED

Earls Barton, Northamptonshire UK

The rest of Farina's team arrived, and she told them to exercise extreme caution in collecting samples. She needed samples of everything Tip could have touched.

Where was he? Was he on foot? Did he drive?

The search for Tip was on. Authorities were out on foot. He was a man that was ill. Farina was confident he wouldn't be too hard to find.

It was going to be a long night. They were going through the home, checking out everything.

Farina looked around the horror scene in that house as much as she could, then took a moment to gather her thoughts and call her husband as they had removed the body of the unknown male to take him to the coroner's office.

"Oh, Brett," Farina spoke exhausted. "I don't know what happened. How did we miss this."

"This has to be a weapon, Farina," her husband replied. "A delayed reaction of some sort."

95

"But why did it kill the girl after seizures and others dese-crated the body."

"I don't know, you're the virologist. Right now," Brett said. "We are tracking down six of those who were at that party. The others are spread out."

"We're looking as well and seeing if any other cases other than the one in America matched. I'm not sure why we didn't think of this before."

"You did. But I'm not sure you had enough to go on to find anything. The only reason you found out about the American incident is because they were famous."

Nodding her head in an agreement that Brett couldn't see, Farina saw Susan walk into the house. "Brett, let me call you back." She ended the call and placed her phone away. "Susan, tell me you have something."

Susan shook her head. "No, we're all looking for him."

"He can't be healthy, and he couldn't have gone that far."

"There are two others in the area, we're tracking them down," Susan said. "What did Doctor Reigns report."

"They released them."

Susan gasped.

"But that was only a couple hours ago so they should be in the same area. So, they're finding them."

"The bright side is they're all celebrities that were caught in a supposed terror attack. The paparazzi will find them."

"True."

"Doctor Ainsworth?" Gil a member of her team ap-proached. "You might want to look at this. It was in a bag on the floor" He handed her a sheet of paper. "It's a receipt for the takeaway we found."

Farina took it. "Signed by Tip."

"Three hours ago. And by the amount of purchase is too high for just tacos. I'm gonna say that he was at that place for a while."

Farina spun to Susan. "We need to go there and track everyone that was in that pub."

"You think whatever this is could be that contagious."

"We can't take a chance until the autopsy comes back. No chances," Farina said. "We flew blind and let these people go. At least two are dead, how many more?"

"That wasn't our fault. They had no symptoms, they weren't ill."

"I know." Farina looked down when her phone rang. It was Stephen, another member of her team. He was labeled the technology guy, research and so forth "Stephen? What's wrong?"

"I didn't want to suit up, can you come out here?" he asked. "To the van."

"Sure." Farina placed her phone away and shook her head. "Suit up, he says as if we are superheroes." She looked at Susan.

"Who was it?"

"Stephen. He needs to see us." A turn of her head to Gil. "Keep things going here. We'll be back."

She and Susan left the house, removing their gloves, goggles and masks once they stepped outside. They approached the van where Stephen had set up his tech lab, keeping a distance at the back open doors just in case.

"What's going on?" Farina asked.

Stephen had several computers set up in the back of the van. He looked defeated as he turned his chair and faced them. "This is a nightmare and one that we all should have seen coming."

"What do you mean?" Farina asked.

"Okay, so bear with me," he said. "An hour ago, I sent out messages to Interpol, World Health Organization, FBI and the CDC, looking to see if they had similar cases to what we had in London. I mean, I did an internet search, and it bred a lot, but I wanted to see what they had."

"And?"

"And I learned no one shares information. I mean this has been an ongoing problem for decades. No one shares because everyone is afraid of someone getting ahead."

"I don't understand."

"Sharing information between agencies," he said. "It should be standard. But it's not."

"It's there some sort of shared database?" Farina asked.

Stephen laughed.

Slightly annoyed, Farina huffed. "Stephen, what is happening?"

"You need to get in touch with Doctor Reigns in America, I am betting his Texas agency isn't aware," Stephen then rambled. "Because Interpol doesn't share with FBI or WHO, they don't share with the FBI either. FBI doesn't share with the CDC and the CDC definitely—"

"Stephen," Farina cut him off. "I get it."

"No, you don't. I heard from Interpol and WHO. Not yet from FBI or CDC, but I'm certain they have information as well. Because what I got from Interpol and WHO were totally different reports. Only one was the same."

Farina shook her head. "Okay, slow down. What is going on."

"Our little warehouse rave incident isn't isolated. Some are classified as terror hits, some just drug overdose parties. Whatever..." Stephen flung out his hand, then lifted a notepad. "Two agencies got back to me and both similar scenarios to our warehouse."

"How many?"

"Interpol reports three. Paris, Dublin and Cairo. They reported one in India, the same one that WHO reported. WHO reported another two. Poland, Africa. Every single one of these occurred in the last five days. And that's what we know about. China could have it. North Korea. Hard to tell. How many local authorities were investigating on their own. Did we share?"

Farina closed her eyes. "No. If all of these were happening, one would think information would get out."

"One would think. Had it not been for the American celebrities, none of us would know," said Stephen. "But in five days. All of this. Too much. Too fast. All of them local. Affecting twelve to fifteen people. Every situation was at an event or party."

"Keep on it, Stephen. Keep trying the CDC and FBI. Search local news stories as well," Farina directed.

"Yes, Ma'am."

"Farina?" Susan said her name softly. "Hold still."

"What's wrong?" Farina asked.

Susan pulled out a small pen light, then reached for Farina. "Something on your shoulder. Stephen? Hold this." She extended the light to Stephen.

He rolled his chair to the open back doors of the van. "Oh, wow, I see it." He took the light.

"Hold it steady," Susan requested.

"What is it?" Farina asked. "What's going on."

Stephen replied, holding the light on Farina. "Looks like a thin noodle."

Susan reached. "I got it. What the heck?" She lifted it up high and into the beam of the light.

Farina turned her head. She saw it gripped between the thumb and forefinger of Susan's ungloved hand. A small wiry thing, that indeed looked like a noodle. No bigger than a few centimeters. "What is it?"

"It was on your shoulder. On the fibers on your sweater," Susan replied. "I thought it was a hair, but it moved."

Farina shifted her eyes. "Stephen, get something to put it in," she requested.

"Shit," Stephen said.

Farina then looked back at Susan's hand.

100

It was gone.

"Where is it?" Farina asked. "Did you drop it."

Susan's shivering and frightened inhale rang out and her eyes widened with horror. She turned her hand toward Farina. Her index finger was illuminated by the light, showing the tiniest droplet of blood.

She groaned slightly then whimpered frightened, "It's in me."

THIRTEEN

WHAT DO YOU KNOW

Needville, TX

First name Ella and last name never given. She sat in the last cell on the edge of the cot, with her feet on tipped toes; her bended knees danced nervously as she crossed her arms tight to her stomach as if she had a bellyache.

"They should be here any minute," Cal walked into the cell area.

"And they know they have to get her to Galveston?" Mark asked.

"Yep. You have that center opening back up."

"Never really closed, we just sent them all home a couple hours ago."

Ella shook her head. "You should have never, never done that. They shouldn't have sent them home. Shouldn't have."

"Anything from her?" Cal asked.

Ella blasted. "I told you I'm sick! I wouldn't be if you let me take that knife."

102

"Look, Ella," Mark said. "I'm a doctor. If you have a virus or something, you can't just cut it out of you and if you could, a silver knife wouldn't matter."

"Yeah, it would, it's the element of silver at the right time. It's coming. I need that knife."

Cal asked. "How do you know you're sick?"

"Because I was at that party in Tulsa."

"Oklahoma?" Cal asked. "And you came all the way here to steal that knife."

"No." she shook her head. "I came here to find Jude."

Mark looked at Cal. "Who is Jude?"

"That talent scout that took her down and said she was infected," Cal answered then glanced again at Ella. "He didn't say he knew you."

"He doesn't."

Cal tossed up his hands. "None of this makes sense."

"My intake team will get more. She definitely is paler," Mark stated. "I just—"

"Are you back here?" A voice called out.

"Yeah," Cal replied. "Must be EMS."

Sure enough, two paramedics with a stretcher arrived.

"Right here." Cal pointed then opened the cell.

"Did you bring sedation?" Mark asked. "She won't let me near her, and I have a feeling she may give you problems."

"We're ready," said the one paramedic.

Cal and Mark left the cell area, returning to the main part of the station. Ella's fights and screams lasted only a minute, then she drew silent.

It didn't take long for the EMS workers to have Ella strapped and rolling out of the station.

"Are you following them?" Cal asked.

"I'll make my way there." Mark sat down. "Just trying to figure it all out. Taking a second, you know."

"Yeah, tell me about it." Cal heard the door open, and he turned his head.

Glen from Ma and Joe's stood there. The forty something man, wearing a tee shirt, jeans and his bar apron, stood mesmerized, rubbing his gray speckled goatee, staring out at the flashing lights. He held a white plastic bag.

"You okay, Glen?" Cal asked. "It's not a seizure or anything is it?"

Mark leaned toward Cal whispering. "If it's a seizure he won't answer."

"Oh, yeah, I'm fine. Whew, I was hoping that wasn't one of you in the ambulance. Who was it?" Glen asked.

"Just someone I arrested earlier that is sick," Cal replied.

"Was that the woman that tried to steal Pop's knife."

"Man," Cal shook his head once. "Everyone knows everything. What's up? Thought you were working."

"My shift is done. You had me worried." Glen walked in and set the bag on the desk. It clunked. "You just up and left." He pulled out two beers. "Left your food. Your drinks."

Mark asked. "Shit, did we not pay?"

"Oh, you paid. Cal's card is in the computer." Glen continued and pulled out two white takeout containers. "I know you guys were having a brothers' night. You got to eat."

Cal smiled. "You brought our food. Thanks."

"No, I brought you fresh stuff. I want some scoop." Glen pulled up a chair. "I mean the chief of police and his hot shot virus doctor brother go running out, I figured something big was happening or God forbid something was wrong with your mom. By the way, how is she. She dating anyone yet."

"No," Cal replied and opened his container. "She's fine and too old for you."

"Age is just a number," Glen said.

"Dude, really." Cal glanced at him from the tops of his eyes.

"So, it's nothing?" Glen asked. "The reason you ran out was because of knife girl."

Mark nodded. "That's it."

Glen rocked back some in the chair, tapping his hand on the desk while he faced them. "Good. It's not the food. I thought, you were in the mood for noodles when you asked about them. Then, and this is the funny part, I thought I got you all squeamish when I said they looked like parasites. I hope I didn't ruin those noodles for you."

Mark shook his head. "Takes a bit more than saying parasite to get me squeamish."

"Not me," said Glen. "I hate parasites. Hate them. People think they're like these mindless organisms, but they're smart. Some are crafty bastards."

Mark paused in taking another bite of his burger.

Glen cringed. "Now I made you squeamish, huh?"

"No." Mark took a bite and chewed, then wiped his hands. "It's an awful passionate statement about parasites coming from a bartender."

"Dude," Cal snapped. "Come on, that's kind of snobbish of you. The man brought you a burger."

"I'm sorry." Mark lifted his hand. "No offense."

"None taken. It's not like I'm an out of work scientist or anything. I was a truck driver that's how I knew about them. They're why I quit driving. Nope. I'll stay put. Going town to town puts me at risk"

"I'm curious," Cal said. "Why were parasites the reason you quit."

"Because I saw what they did to Bostock Ohio," Glen replied. "Wiped the whole town out. Little lake town. Five hosts caught it swimming they say. They passed it on to animals, other people, highly contagious you know. Not tape worms, parasites. I know people say they're the same. They aren't."

"Wait. Wait." Mark lifted his hand.

"You're not gonna insult me again, are you?" Glen asked.

"No. When was this?" Mark asked.

"Twelve years ago."

Cal asked. "Mark, did you hear about this?"

"No." Mark shook his head. "I'll have to look it up. A town was wiped out and no one knew?"

"Wasn't a big town. Like a hundred and fifty people," said Glen.

"A town though," Mark stated. "For sure we'd hear."

106

Glen shook his head and folded his arms. "Not if they're burying it. It wasn't the first one. Or only one. Gone." He snapped his finger. "Nasty business this parasite. Ask Jude."

"Jude?" Mark questioned. "The talent scout?"

"No." Glen shook his head. 'That's a different Jude. This Jude follows a certain type of parasite. There was a rumor he killed the people in that town. But nah, it was the parasite. I think. Probably. He's in town. When I saw him, I thought, whoa, is there one here."

"Shit." Cal stood up.

"Aren't you gonna finish your burger?" Glen asked.

"I will. Mark," Cal faced his brother. "He said she was infected. How would he know."

"We have to ask him," Mark replied. "And why here?"

Glen replied. "Maybe he was waiting on her. Wait, if the knife woman was the one Jude said was sick. Was she in your cell?"

"Yes," Cal replied.

Glen jumped up. "Better check that cell. Then again, what I learned if they don't find someone to go into, they pretty much die off in an hour. That's what I learned on google."

"Thank you. I'll seal it off for an hour," Cal stated. "Right now, I'm gonna go find Jude. Mark, you coming?"

"No. let me know what he says. I'll head to the quarantine center. Just gonna check her," Mark said.

Glen asked. "For parasites?"

"Yeah." Mark nodded. "Parasites. Thank you." He reached down and grabbed his burger box. "You've been a lot of help."

"You're welcome. Just don't ask me to help out much. They scare me," Glen said. "Some people hate spiders; I'm scared of parasites. I wonder if there's a word for it."

"Helminthophobia"

"Wow. You're smart." Glen nodded impressed.

"That's why they pay him the big bucks," Cal told him.

"Really? I missed my calling."

"Actually," Mark said. "I think you did." He walked to the door. "Call me. Let me know what he said."

Glen raised his hand as Mark left. "I will."

Cal nudged him. "He meant me."

"Oh. Say, can I come with you to talk to Jude."

"Yeah, you can." Lifting his keys, Cal walked to the door that led to the cells and locked it. Not that anyone would be going back there. Calls were already transferred to county.

Glen gave Cal a lot of information, Things he and his brother didn't know. Cal was hopeful that Jude the scout could give him even more.

FOURTEEN

COMING TO A HEAD

Kettering General Hospital
Kettering, UK

"Stay with me, Susan, stay with me," Farina stayed right at Susan's side in the emergency treatment area. Other doctors and nurses worked on her.

'Temp forty'

Farina heard that. She didn't need to have a reading to let her know that Susan was fevered. She eradiated heat.

Susan shook, her skin a paler shade of gray.

Through it all, through her ordeal which had only been fifteen minutes, Susan remained a professional. She verbally told Farina everything she felt, as a way of documenting. At one point, when Farina told her to rest, Susan conveyed that she couldn't be the only one.

Farina had to know.

"The pain," Susan said. "It moves."

"Moves where?"

"Chest to head, burning, searing." Her body convulsed and her eyes rolled back.

"Heart rate two forty. I need a beta push," the doctor said.

"Stay with me, Susan." Farina pleaded.

But it was quick.

Too fast.

A single beep and Susan flatlined.

Farina stepped back out of the way as the team moved in to perform a resuscitation. She knew it wouldn't do any good. Susan was gone. Just like Daphne and how many others?

Farina was fearful of the answer to that question. Tip was responsible for the death of his girlfriend, the man on the couch, and Susan.

Tip was also one of over a dozen people they released with this thing into the world.

It hurt to think how many people, how fast it could spread.

The question that kept pounding in Farina's mind was how? How one tiny object could devastate a human body so fast. Was it the same thing that happened to the man on Tip's couch, but instead of going straight to the brain and killing him, it ate him alive?

Was that even possible?

In all of her years, she never heard of such a thing.

Although it wasn't her field of specialty, thankfully the Hospital for Tropical Diseases had a parasitic department, the best in the world. She would have to call the head of the department, Doctor Kingsman, and get him on this.

As she stepped in the hall, sounds of failing resuscitation carrying to her, Farina's phone vibrated. Believing it was her husband, she lifted it.

It was a text message from America. Doctor Reigns.

Swiping her phone, she read the message.

'Looking into this being a parasite.' He wrote.

Farina shivered a breath. 'Look no further,' she replied in a message. 'It is.'

Needville, TX

"Some say he's like a hundred," Glen stated as he drove with Cal in the cal.

"What?" Cal blasted almost in shock.

"Maybe more."

"You're nuts. He's not more than forty. Forty-five with a good skin care regimen."

"You'll see. Ask for his ID," Glen said as they pulled up to the motel and right behind Jude's van. "Look at the ancient vehicle he drives."

"Stop. He's a talent scout with an ability to string people along." Cal put the car in park.

"I heard he's a vampire."

"He's not a vampire. If he was, why would he be chasing a parasite."

"To breed."

Cal laughed. "What are you talking about."

"Create some weird vampiric parasite and end the world."

"Enough. He's not a vampire."

"Ever see him in the day light?"

"As a matter of fact, yeah, I have." Cal opened the car door. 'Asshole." He waited for Glen to get out of the car, and he walked with him toward Jude's van which was still parked in front of his room.

"Ask him," Glen said.

Cal dropped his voice. "Not gonna ask him that."

"Ask him."

"Ask me what?" came Jude's voice.

Cal cocked back a little when Jude sat on a chair next to the motel room door. "Sorry, I didn't see you there."

"Probably was invisible," said Glen.

"He wasn't invisible. He was hidden by his…. his…" Cal saw Glen leaning forward looking at the headlights of the van. "What are you doing?"

"Checking to see if he has a reflection."

"Oh my God." Cal brough his hand to his face sliding it down. "Why did I bring you?"

Seemingly amused, Jude stood. "I'm not a vampire. I'm just a man."

"Over a hundred years old, right?" asked Glen.

"Hardly." Jude smiled. "I just turned forty-eight."

Cal closed his mouth and nodded with an impressed look. "Forty-eight. You look younger."

"I take care of my skin," said Jude.

Cal backhandedly swatted Glen. "See. So, Jude, you told me you're a scout."

"I am."

"But not a talent scout," Cal said.

"No, I'm not."

"I take it you're not here to catch my country set or Glen's."

Jude sheepishly shrugged. "Sorry."

Cal held up his finger to Glen before the bartender could say anything. "I'm gonna ask you something really crazy. I mean it's gonna sound crazy as it comes from my mouth. Are you—"

"I am," Jude replied.

"I didn't ask you anything."

"I know what you're going to ask."

Glen nudged Cal. "It's them powers."

Jude laughed. "You are really funny. I wish I had powers. I don't. I know the question because I have been asked it before. Am I chasing an ancient parasite. The answer is. I am." He reached for the door. "Come on in."

Cal stared down at the hand drawn map of the United States and all the markings on it. The map spread across the table and Cal ran his finger over it. "All these places had the parasite."

"One forty-five in the US, and that's just the US," Jude replied. "It's worldwide."

"And you have been to every one of these sites?" Cal asked.

Jude shook his head. "No. This map is outbreaks over decades. I've only been doing this for twelve years. My first town was Bostwick."

Glen nodded. "I was there."

"Um, yeah, sort of," Jude said. "Outskirts. If you were there, you'd be dead. It was a small town. Bigger cities are tough to contain, but they can be if caught early. Usually the health department, CDC steps in, whoever, seals the infected, quarantines, them, kills it off."

"So, you aren't some lone wolf in this?" Cal questioned.

"Oh, no. We usually contact the health authorities, and eventually they believe us and deal with it," Jude replied. "Never has it been more than four outbreaks globally a year. Never. Because it's actually hard to catch from the paratenic host. But once someone does…" Jude whistles. "Game on."

"I'm sorry." Cal shook his head confused. "A paratenic host?"

Glen explained. "A paratenic host doesn't really do much. Its whole purpose is to grow the parasite to maturity and pass it on."

"Very good." Jude nodded at Glen.

"Thanks." Glen winked. "Google."

"Alright hold up." Cal waved his hands. "Can we start from the beginning with some laymen, cliff notes explanation. I know you scientists like to complicate things."

"Oh, I'm not a scientist," Jude said. "I went to art school."

"How or why is an artist chasing a parasite?" Cal asked.

"It's what my family does. My whole family," Jude answered. "Some are doctors, most are actually. But chasing this, containing it, stopping it from getting out of control, is our responsibility. Because this thing very easily could bring about extinction."

114

"Why?" Cal questioned. "I'm mean why is it your job to stop the end of the world. I appreciate it, but why is it on your family's shoulders."

"Because a hundred and nine years ago, my great-great grandfather released it."

"On purpose?"

Jude nodded.

"I need a drink."

Jude pointed to the dresser drawers with a bottle of whiskey on top. "Help yourself."

Turning toward the dresser, Cal unwrapped a plastic cup, poured some from the bottle and downed it. He repeated his actions once more, wiping the back of his hand over his mouth before facing Jude again. "Okay, I'm ready. Talk away."

Jude moved about as he talked, gathering papers and folders. "It's called a lycanthropic parasite." He paused when Glen screamed.

It was short scream, one that reminded Cal of a sick crow.

Cal shifted his eyes to Glen. "What the hell was that?"

"He called it a lycanthropic parasite. A werewolf parasite?"

"What?" Cal blasted.

"In Glen's defense, he is partially right." He handed a stack of papers and folders to Cal. "Feel free to look through. It's a werewolf, but the parasite originated in a wolf and that's when it all started."

Cal started to flip through the papers. Glen looked over his shoulder.

"Whoa," Glen said with a point. "It was uncovered?"

Jude nodded. "Archeological dig a hundred and fifteen years ago uncovered it. Actually, it was a well-preserved wolf. It was when they were trying to test it that they discovered the dormant parasite. See, in the paratenic host, the parasite doesn't die if the host does. It just waits until it finds a host. Then it starts its paratenic host cycle. Growing the parasite until it can find a definitive host."

Cal asked. "A definitive host?"

"I'll get to that. Let me explain. This ancient parasite is thousands of years old. Scientists were baffled," Jude said. "They discovered as scientists do that it was super contagious to other canine animals. But it wasn't until it jumped to a human that the realized what it did." Jude reached over and took a folder, flipping through it. He returned it to Cal.

Cal and Glen stared at a pyramid style chart. Dogs and wolves were at the top.

"Again, the paratenic host can only be canine. In this instance. My great-great grandfather believed it was a hybrid created for biological warfare in ancient times."

Cal asked. "Same great grandfather that released it?"

Jude nodded. "In Moldova, a hundred years ago, they were trying to break free of the Russian hold and my grandfather allowed for a pack of wolves and dogs to become paratenic hosts and sent them into Russia. What he didn't expect was for it to spread so fast, not just there but in Moldova. They were able to contain it and stop it. My great-great grandfather was executed. But his research remained. When the parasite kept surfacing in Moldova, my family realized the parasite was in

116

the canines and never going away. Hence why all canines and wolves must be cremated upon death. Once Moldova became a spot to travel, that's when the tracing began."

Glen questioned. "Watching everyone who comes and goes."

Jude nodded. "I'll tell you. I don't know how they did it before my nephew invented the app that cross checked travelers with reported matching events."

"Matching events?" Cal asked.

"Always groups of people that fall ill," Jude said. "Pass out. Wake up fine. Usually, one or two dead. Nine times out of ten CDC or whatever health organization labels it some sort of poisoning. That's what we look for and see if someone in the area was recently in Moldova."

"Should be easy," Cal said. "I mean who visits Moldova."

"About a hundred and fifty thousand tourists a year," Jude answered. "But, only a few carry the parasite out and become definitive hosts. Remember when I said it isn't easy to catch it from a paratenic host?"

Cal nodded. "Yeah."

"Only a few ways to catch it," Jude explained. "Touching internal organs or waste. Ingesting the infected animal or intimacy."

"Ah, no." Glen cringed. "What?"

Cal partially closed his eyes. "So, you're saying those who left Moldova with the parasite, touched it's remains, waste, ate or...?"

"Yes." Jude nodded. "Eating dog or wolf is not uncommon over there." Again, he pointed to the chart. "It's a pyramid."

"Definitive host," Glen said. "When the parasite is passed, the next host is definitive?"

Cal held up his hand. "Stop. Jude, I realize you've been doing this. And you Glen are a closet parasite fanatic. But break it down. How many types of hosts are there?"

"As far as threatening?" Jude stated. "Two more. The paratenic hosts passes the parasite to the Definitive host. For about ten days, the parasite multiplies in the definitive host until the point that the host has this drive to pass it on. Almost maddening, they act on this purpose. Pass on the parasite. They don't know why, they just do. Usually, it's through food or beverage or intimacy. But they aim for groups of twelve or more, so unless it's an orgy, which has happened, it's usually food."

"And then?" Cal asked.

"After they passed all the parasites," Jude replied, "The definitive hosts dies. Like a bee that lost its stinger. He or she, with no recollection, goes off and dies. In all instances there is a missing person."

Glen peered up from the chart. "Then the parasite is in a storage host?"

"Yes," Jude answered. "Those are the worst. The storage hosts are the ones that do the most damage. The most dangerous. They ingested it at the same time, they all pass out. Three, four days tops, the parasite is looking to move on. Millions of parasites have formed in gland and they're ready to invade. It's

118

at that point we're chasing them. Ending it. Because if we don't." Jude shook his head. "It'll be bad."

"Explain bad," stated Cal.

Jude did. "Millions of parasites. When they shed them, eighty percent of those who contract the parasite from the storage host will become incidental hosts. Meaning, the parasite does nothing but kill them. They aren't contagious, they just die. Ten percent become storage hosts themselves. For example, here in Needville. Three thousand people. One storage host can kill twenty-four hundred and create three hundred more storage hosts. So, you see how it can spread like wildfire."

"There's ten percent missing," said Cal. "Eighty percent dead, ten percent become storage parasites, the other ten percent?"

"Livestock," Jude said. "The feeding ground. The parasites disintegrate the body like an acid, instantly reproduce, the storage host consumes the desecrated remains and continues on."

Cal's mouth dropped open. "What the—"

"Heck," Glen finished the sentence. "They eat their victims? So how do they die. You said the parasite is dormant."

"Only in the paratenic host," said Jude. "We need to stop the storage host. Either by not allowing them to feed from the victims. Starvation. You lock them in with other storage hosts and they die off. Burn them after projectile or silver. Silver impaled into the body of the storage host will draw them to the silver and kill the parasites and the hosts. Don't ask me why. I don't know."

"I do," said Glen. "Freaking werewolf parasite. Silver."

"I'm still stuck on projectile," stated Cal.

Jude groaned. "It's like a bloody vomit full of parasites."

Cal cringed. "I don't want to know that."

"Cal *listen*." Jude took on a serious tone. "We never had an instance that wasn't contained. It never broke boundaries. I don't know, my family doesn't know what will happen if the storage hosts are able to continue. Historically, one outbreak, the storage hosts were always contained either before, during or after only one projectile. We're not facing that now. There aren't enough of us to stop all the storage hosts. We don't know what happens to them if they keep going."

"I don't understand," Cal said. "What do you mean?"

"I never seen a storage host projectile more than once. We always get them," Jude replied. "Right now, we're outnumbered. There are going to be storage hosts that keep going."

"How?" Cal asked.

"Fifteen days ago, an international pharmaceutical company sponsored a corporate trip to Moldova to watch a football tournament. The CEO's son was on a team. Twenty-eight from across the globe met in London for a chartered flight. Ten days ago, that flight returned to London, and everyone went their own way. We don't know how, we think ingestion, but those people all became definitive hosts."

"So those twenty some people had a wolf banquet," Cal said.

Jude nodded. "We have been tracking incidents since. Never has it been more than one. This is over twenty and all the outbreaks have occurred days apart. London, Paris, Greece.

Its ahead of us. I came to Needville because it was center of a couple outbreaks. One in Tulsa, the other Galveston where a college student was working as a steward on a private yacht. He had just returned from Moldova with his father. Every person infected felt fine, they were just motivated to release the parasite. Unfortunately, I can't contact everywhere, and the new Storage hosts are released."

Cal finally understood. "So, they ejected the parasite into food or whatever to pass it. The celebrity yacht part. All those famous people are now storage hosts. But if the Definite—"

"Definitive," Glen corrected.

"Whatever," Cal continued. "If that host only has the purpose of releasing the parasite, why do we have acid washed bodies being livestock. I thought only storage hosts did that projectile thing."

Jude lifted a finger. "In some instances, the parasitic gland becomes full and the definitive host will projectile. But unlike the storage hosts, they can't ingest it back."

Cal raised his eyebrows. "Parasitic gland. Oh, that's new."

"Bet it forms in the body," said Glen. "Just bet it's a new organ that forms."

With a shift of his eyes, Cal looked at him. "Why don't you go Google that." He shook his head. "Anyhow, it's a wasted banquet, my next question is, Tulsa. Ella came from Tulsa. How did she know to come here?"

"My blog," Jude said.

"What?" Cal asked.

"I wrote a blog, I have a blog," Jude answered. "A lot of subscribers. I talk about the silver, the parasites. If she researched, looked up her event, she'd find it. I made sure I used every incident as a keyword. And I knew about the knife here and used that as bait. I figured here was centered, if anyone came for the knife, they were infected."

"Whoa." Glen sang out. "That is so smart. Have you calculated how many storage hosts there are?":

"I have." Jude nodded. "In the US, forty-four right now."

"And you said burning them, starving them or hitting them with silver will do it?" Cal asked.

"Yes." Jude walked across the room, lifting a long narrow box from his nightstand. He opened the lid exposing what looked like thick long nails. "These are silver. One will do per host. We'll need to make more."

"So, we just need to find these forty some storage hosts and…well, kill them," Cal said.,

"It's not that easy," stated Jude. "Some have already started making more hosts. Its ahead of us. It's a secret now. In two days, it won't be. Four days from now it will be a battle. In a week, we'll go from fighting the parasite to just trying to find a way to survive."

"No," Glen groaned out. "You're saying we have like a day or two and it's over."

Jude nodded. "It's ahead of us. Our worst nightmare. I won't stop fighting to end it. But it will come to a point where we are fighting just to stay alive."

Cal shook his head. "I refuse to believe that." He reached in the box and lifted one of the silver nails. "We know about it right? We can stop it," he said. "We'll stop it."

FIFTEEN

RELEASE ME

Houston, TX

Finally, that was all Martie could think of.

Finally.

She was the last person to leave the quarantine area in Galveston. While technically it was on the outskirts of Texas City, it was right near the end of the bridge.

She left after getting new clothes from a nice worker. She stopped at Skyna's condo to grab the rest of her things, but couldn't get in there. Authorities had closed it off. She had already told her ex-husband, Dirk, she was on her way for the boys. He probably was worried when he didn't hear from her for two hours.

In the middle of the trip north to his home in the Woodlands, her phone died. Fortunately, there wasn't much traffic and cruising slightly faster than the speed limit put her in The Woodlands within seventy minutes.

She wanted to see her boys; Martie rushed to the front door, but no one was home. A neighbor heard her knocking and said they all had left.

"I've been away," she had told the neighbor. "And my phone died. Any way I can use yours."

He was gracious and not only handed her his cell phone, but retrieved an extra charger for her car as well.

Dirk finally answered and told her he left her a message that he and Carrie drove the boys home. They were almost at Martie's house. Carrie thought it might be smart to air things out and check on the fridge since there were power outages reported in her neighborhood.

Martie thanked him even though she was slightly annoyed and told him she would be home shortly.

Three hours and twenty minutes after being released from the quarantine center, Martie pulled in the driveway to her condo. Dirk's car was there. The lights were on in her home, the windows were all open.

More than likely her power did go out.

The fridge was going to be bad, she thought. She parked next to Dirk's car so he could easily back up. After shutting off her car, Martie took a breath and excitedly opened the car door.

No sooner did she step out, she heard the squeal of tires and sirens. Flashing blue and red lights were around her and head-lights, along with spotlights immediately were on her.

"Don't move!" a male voice called out.

"I didn't do anything," Martie said, shield her eyes from the bright lights.

"Mom!" she heard her son cry out. "Mom!"

"Son!" the man shouted. "Stay back."

"What's going on?" Dirk asked. "What has she done?"

125

"Sir," the man commanded. "Stay back with your family. Stay clear. It's for your own good. Ma'am," he said. "You are Martina Morgan?"

"Yes." Martie squinted her yes.

"You are employed by Skyna Lord and were onboard the Talbot?"

"Yes. What—"

"Do not move. Stay in one position."

"Dirk," she called out. "Dirk, I'm scared, I didn't do anything."

"Don't worry, Martie," Dirk told her. "I'll call our lawyer."

"It'll be fine," Carrie told her with a shaky voice. "I promise."

Fine? Martie shook all over. Immediately she kept thinking that she had something to do with everyone getting sick. She was worried. It was like a swat team surrounded her. She couldn't see passed the lights. Her whole entire body trembled.

The she heard a loud crinkling sound, an unraveling of crunch paper. It was followed by a hiss and whispering voices. She couldn't make out what they said.

Another man's voice emerged, much gentler in the way he spoke. "Miss Morgan please stand still."

"I'm not moving," Martie defected.

"Ready?" another asked.

"We're ready. Open the back."

Confused, Martie shook her head left to right and then from the shadows cast from the bright lights four figures emerged.

126

Just like on the Talbot they were wearing biohazard suits with huge hoods. They carried a huge sheath of plastic. It had a tube connected and the tub ran to a case another man carried.

"Step inside please," the one said, pointing to an opening.

"Step inside?" Martie asked.

"Inside now please. It'll be hard to walk, we'll help you."

Martie didn't see anything beyond what looked like a wall of plastic. But two steps forward she had emerged inside. Immediately they sealed her in, not only zippering the plastic unit but taping it as well.

Air immediately filled it, flowing in slowly with a hiss.

She was in a bubble, a protective unit. Her own hamster ball.

She looked over her shoulder to her family standing on the porch watching. Martie moved slowly; it was the only way to do so without tripping. When they loaded her into the back of a van, she realized she wasn't in trouble they let her out of quarantine too early. She had something so severe that they couldn't take a single chance.

They secured her containment unit from roiling around or bouncing and closed the doors of the van.

They told her nothing. She was left to her own imagination.

Kept in the dark figuratively and literally, Martie was scared to death.

Interstate 46 South – Houston, TX

"So, we have what?" Mark asked, speaking to Cal on the phone from his car. "Two more days before the storage hosts turn."

"He said three days, four tops," Cal replied.

"We have to find them now."

"Did you put the word out?"

"I did," Mark stated. "As we speak, everyone that was on the Talbot is being round up placed in personal isolation, just in case one of them isn't infected they don't pass it on.

"Everyone?" asked Cal.

"Everyone. Including that Brick guy who got off the yacht. The parasite had to have been put in the appetizer."

"Yeah, because you said dinner hadn't been served," Cal said.

"No, it could have been the champagne, but I don't see how the crew got that."

"I asked Glen about that. He's the closest thing we have to a catering expert. He told me the employees probably ate up the leftover appetizers."

Mark sighed out. "This is a mess. I'm in control of mine. What do you know about the others?"

"Well, it's not good. Nine of our Moldova soccer enthusiasts came to America. All connected to the Bassen Corporation. Big textile company. Sister Corporation is in Paris."

"Swell."

"One of them, your missing college steward from the Talbot was on the flight. I spoke to a Chief Dawn Bates in Galveston, and she said the lifeboat was missing, the lines were cut. He dropped it and took off."

"Hence the thump the chef mentioned."

"Hence the thump," said Cal. "Wouldn't surprise me if the Coast Guard finds him dead in it."

"The others?" Mark asked.

"We're batting five hundred. Four of them were released, including our Tulsa people. You're playing round up and the other three, haven't released yet."

"That's only eight."

"Yeah, well, Los Angeles refuses to even admit to anything. They said the incident we cited was an ecstasy party gone bad, no casualties, no quarantine, they didn't have names."

"I guess that definitive hosts didn't have a full parasitic gland, whatever that is. When we hang up I'll get ahold of Doctor Ainsworth in the UK and give her the heads up on the new information. Although after just talking to her, she has a good idea." After inhaling, Mark huffed. "I'll tell you Cal, after this is done, I am so filing a complaint with the UN about Moldova and their inability to share this public health concern.'

"Let's settle this first before we look long term," Cal said. "If there is a long term."

"I'm thinking positive." Mark slowed down and turned on his windshield wiper to clear the slight drizzle of rain that formed on it. He could see the flashing lights on the side of the road ahead. "Hey, let me call you back. Looks like an accident ahead. I'm gonna stop."

"Now? Right now, you're picking to be a good Samaritan. Mark, this is Texas, there is no Good Sammy Laws, you can drive right by."

"I'm not gonna do that." He put on his turn signal and using caution because the highway was busy, he eased his way over before he even arrived at the ambulance.

"Be careful, it's night and sixteen percent of all highway accident deaths are people that are on the side of the road."

"I'll...I'll remember that statistic. I'll call you back." Mark disconnected the call and inched up to the ambulance, staying as close to the guardrail as he could. It was as he stopped, he realized that back door of the ambulance was slightly ajar.

No one was around. No disabled vehicle in sight. The sounds of fast-moving cars zipping by was intimidating. "Why are we not moving to the left lane?" Mark questioned out loud of the drivers as he opened his door, knowing that was a courtesy to move over when there was a disabled or emergency vehicle.

After putting on the flashlight of his phone, he stepped out and immediately moved more toward the guardrail. At first Mark thought the paramedics had gone over the guardrail to rescue someone but he didn't see any flashlights in the distance. And the close he got, he saw the ambulance wasn't just right against the guardrail, it had hit the guardrail. The lights were on and flashing, but the engine wasn't running.

At no time in his walk to the ambulance did he give a second thought to where it came from.

Until he pulled out his phone to call 911 and saw the writing on the Ambulance.

Fort Bend Emergency Services.

Mark was in Houston. Harris County.

Three feet from the back of the ambulance, Mark stopped.

Needville was in Fort Bend County. Could it be the same ambulance that came and picked up Ella? They weren't in a rush or a flashing-lights-sirens-blaring state.

They left ten minutes before Mark. It was conceivable but was it possible?

"Hello?" Mark called out, his voice buried in the flowing loud traffic. "Hello!"

No answer.

Using caution, he extended his foot and opened the right door wider.

Gasping, breath taken away for a second, Mark stepped back and covered his mouth. Not from any smell, but to avoid getting sickened from the sight.

The back was in disarray, as if a struggle ensued. The stretcher was overturned and the EMT workers were clearly dead. There was no patient, the straps were released. The legs of one paramedic were on the overturned stretcher and his head was about eight inches from a torso that had been reduced to a thick jelly looking substance.

The other paramedic was gray, intact, but motionless and dead. He lay not far from the desecrated body.

A sight Mark had seen before on the Yacht.

He wished he had gotten a better look at the EMT workers when they took Ella to know for certain if it was them.

Backing up, Mark then turned around and lifted his phone to call for help. It was then, the beam of his phone flashlight reflected off of Ella.

Not far from him, Ella approached him slowly. Her arms extended slightly. Blood smeared on her chin and down her chest.

"Ella." Mark held up his hand. "I'm gonna call to get you help."

"You had your chance," she said with a weeping voice. "I couldn't help it. I couldn't help it. I didn't want to. I tried. But it happened."

"I know. I know. You're sick."

"It didn't have to happen. I begged for the knife. Begged." She sobbed.

"I'm sorry."

"It's not going to stop. I can't stop it. I'm trying."

"We'll get you help."

Ella yelled. "There is no help! I feel it. It's building. It senses you."

"Ella, listen—"

"No. You should have gotten the knife. They would be alive. No more. No more. Tell my mother I'm sorry."

Mark prepared to plead with her, to calm her when Elle shook,

Her body arched, chest forward, head back. She heaved as if gagging or preparing to vomit.

"Tell her…" Ella said with a sputtering voice. "Sorry."

Before Mark could say anything, Ella ran into the highway.

The first car hit her instantly, sending her up in the air and bouncing from the roof of the SUV, the moment she landed on the road, a car ran over her, then a second, a third.

Tires screeched as drivers came to the realization of someone on the highway, all trying to stop without causing another accident.

But it was too late.

Mark couldn't even scream. He was utterly horrified. He dropped to his knees, crying out in a silent scream, as vehicles shred her poor body to pieces like she as roadkill.

Of her own doing, she was roadkill. Ella was aware of what she could do and made the sacrifice.

That didn't make what he witnessed any better.

It was the most traumatic thing he had seen in his entire life.

He hoped she felt nothing and that what she did wouldn't be in vain.

SIXTEEN

INCHING FORWARD TO THE APOCALYPSE

Teddington, Richmond, UK

Farina went home.

Following Susan's death, shuffling through calls and texts, Farina was done.

She fought about keeping those ravers in isolation for a week, but was ridiculed and in return they all left. She didn't want to hear anymore, Susan was dead.

Farina questioned her purpose.

In the brief exchanges she had with Mark Reigns, she knew it was over. Not that she would stop fighting, but on the night of her friend's death, Farina was done.

Unless a dire emergency she didn't want to be disturbed.

Brett had wine waiting for her even though it was the crack of dawn, she shut off her mobile knowing that anyone that needed to get a hold of her knew her home number.

Curled up with a blanket, Farina fell asleep nuzzled against the corner of the sofa. It wasn't much sleep, enough to revitalize her. After waking, the reality came back, and things were worse.

Sitting at the breakfast counter in her kitchen, Farina stared at her open laptop, a map of the UK on the screen with Stephen in the corner.

"We can't worry about the rest of Europe, we have our own problems here," Stephen said. "We have not located Tip. Maybe he died somewhere after tossing his load."

"No." Farina shook her head. "That's only the definitive host. The others?"

"Out of twelve, we located three."

"And?"

"They were bloody, and we sealed them. The others, we're looking."

"In the meantime, its spreading."

Stephen nodded. "Every place we checked there are deaths, and mutilations. Every day that goes by—"

"I know." Farina closed her eyes for a second. "Keep me posted and if you get a chance, look at that data from the Moldova man in America."

"Will do."

"Thanks." Farina disconnected the call, staring out for a moment before a fresh, hot cup of tea was set before her. She glanced up to Brett. "Thank you."

"This is insane," he said.

"I know."

He sat down next to her. "A part of me wants to run to somewhere isolated and wait this thing out."

"Can we?"

"You're the doctor, but if I think about it, listening to what you say, and the data you share. Eighty percent die, ten percent of all people become feeding vessels. From the body condition, they're not reusable."

"They'll run out of food."

"You need to learn them, Farina," Brett said.

"The inquest for Susan is today. I'll be attending."

"That won't tell you anything, I read what the Moldovan American said. When they are part of the eighty percent, they aren't contagious. Although I'm kind of thinking that the feeding vessels may be contagious."

"Why do you say that?" she asked.

"How did the parasite get on you? Susan picked it from you. Where did you get it from? Do we know if the storage hosts shed them? From what I learned, they projectile into the body of the person, ingest that to start the cycle again. Maybe there are leftovers."

Farina cringed. "I don't want to think about it. I do know if they don't ingest the regurgitation they die."

"What happens if they don't projectile."

"Brett, this is the investigator in you. Do me a favor."

"You're not going to tell me to stop, are you?"

"No, I'm going to give you the number of the law officer that send this information. He's Doctor Regin's brother, speak to him, get him to find out more, but give it a couple hours it's only about two AM there. In the meantime. We have three storage hosts contained. As you suggested." She lifted her tea and faced her computer. "It's time to learn them."

Quarantine Bay, Galveston TX

It was a nightmare.

Martie had been moved from her hamster bubble to a room that wasn't much different. It was even smaller than the one she had been in not ten hours earlier. The room, no bigger than eight by ten, had see-through plastic walls, a single cot, nightstand and rolling hospital tray table. There were no privacy curtains between units. The only privacy there was the shower stall with a toilet inside of it.

Almost barbaric.

A prison of sorts set up in a circle around a large lab area with computers and people wearing hazmat suits.

Unlike before, Martie wasn't scrubbed down or cleaned, she was just placed, clothes on her back in one of the quarantine cells. There were a lot of them and only a few had people in them. The ones next to her on both sides were empty.

"Martie," her name was called. She recognized the voice.

Stranding at her door, fully suites was Lawrence from the health department. Had she not known his voice, she wouldn't have known it was him.

She walked over the plastic door.

"How are you doing?" he asked.

"Confused. What's going on?"

"We released you all too soon," he replied.

"I figured as much."

"I'm sorry."

"Can you tell me what's going on?"

"I'll try," he said. "You know I've always tried to be transparent."

"I do."

"So, know that," Lawrence said. "As you figured out, we released you too soon. We know this because the Talbot was not an isolated incident. Many others happened the exact same way in the days before and after. It's the earlier ones that told us we let you go early. Not sugar coating, it's highly contagious and deadly. Like nothing any of us has ever seen."

"How long do I have? Are you going to run tests?" Martie asked.

"We don't know if you have it, and we cannot run tests. It's too contagious. There are two types we are facing. One kills you within minutes, the other makes itself know in four days or less."

"Any early symptoms?"

Lawrence shook his head. "None that we know of, but we are leaning it."

"In four days, I'll know," Martie said.

"Four days, yes, and then we will keep you until the sixth to be sure."

"Okay." She exhaled. "No arguments from me. Especially if this thing is that bad."

"It's that bad. It's so bad, that if we can't stop it, then when we release in six days," Lawrence said. "There may not be a world to release you to."

When Cal got the call, it wasn't from his brother. It was from the state police stating that Mark needed him. Immediately his mind when to one of the final things he said to his brother. Warning him about the high percentage of highway fatalities that occurred when people pulled over.

Every part of Cal's insides shook. He had a horrible gut feeling something happened to his brother. Mark didn't listen, he pulled over to help and WHAM, a car hit him.

The state trooper said, "Is this Chief Reigns. There's been a horrible accident on the highway and your brother asked if we'd get you here."

At least if he was asking for Cal then he was still alive.

A part of him was afraid to ask anymore questions. But Cal did call his mother.

"This can't be good, it's two in the morning," his mother said.

"Mom, I don't want you to worry."

"Oh, now I'm worried."

"I got a call to get to I-45. State Police called and said Mark needed me there."

"Oh my God!" his mother exclaimed. "Oh My god. I'll get dressed."

"Mom, listen, I'm on my way to the highway. I know he pulled over to help someone."

"Doesn't he know that sixteen percent of all accident fatalities are those who pull over to help? My Markie, my baby,"

139

"Mom, I'm the baby," Cal said.

"Still. Just…please let me know what hospital to go to. If he's asking for you, he's not dead."

"My thoughts exactly. I promise to keep you posted and call you as soon as I know anything. I'll send a car for you, okay?"

"Thank you, baby," his mom replied.

He exchanged 'I love yous' and drove like a bat out of hell. Sirens blaring, passing every car he could.

Then traffic slowed down. Cal knew it had to be bad. If things were backed up at two in the morning, things were shut down.

They were.

At the exit, police cars closed off the southbound lanes of the highway and an officer wearing a raincoat directed traffic to exit.

Cal pulled to the blockade, and they approached his car.

"You can go through," an officer said. "But only as far as the next blockade then you have to pull over."

"Thank you." Cal pulled around the squad cars., He could the flares lighting up the wooden horses set up as a block. Another officer stood there when Cal pulled over and parked. His wasn't the only car there. Two coroner vans a fire chief vehicle.

He stepped out and the officer called to him.

"Sir," the officer said. "Please walk on the shoulder. A lot of remains out there."

"Thank you." Cal nodded and as soon as he did he saw not ten feet from that second blockade, the ambulance against the guardrail and Mark's car.

Immediately Cal grew sick. His stomach twisted and turned. He hoped he wasn't there to identify the body. He could imagine Mark laying there, broken and bloody, grasping for the policer officer and saying, "Get my brother. I need my brother."

A few more steps, his legs wobbled in weakness. He couldn't do it. No way. It was his brother. He felt his heart breaking before he even received confirmation. How was he supposed to do it? How was he supposed to go on without Mark.

The he realized his overactive imagination took off when he heard Mark's voice.

"I told you guys," Mark blasted. "Do not go near without PPE. You wanna be next?"

A huge, heaving breath of relief blasted from Cal and in the after moments of that, he trembled. He took a second and headed toward Mark. It was as he walked, he took in the scene. Several cars and trucks were stopped on the road. A few had collided. He could hear sobbing. Several officers spoke to different groups of people on the side of the road and the median.

In the northbound lane, cars slowed down to a crawl to peek.

But they would see what Cal did. Some collision and officers interviewing people. What was going on that Mark called for him?

"Cal." Mark yelled out his name.

After a grunt, Cal raced to his brother and embraced. "Oh, thank God, you're alive."

"Why wouldn't I be?" Mark asked.

"The state police called me. They said you needed me."

"Yeah."

"I thought, you know, needed me because you were in an accident."

"What? Why would you think that?"

"Dude, you pulled over to the shoulder. People get killed doing that."

"I'm sorry, brother. I am. I dropped my phone when it all happened, and it wouldn't work."

"I'm just glad you're okay." Cal placed his hand on his shoulders.

"Not sure about that. I have to say in all that I witnessed in my life, this was the most traumatic thing."

Cal tilted his head with an inquisitive looked. "What's going on?

"I wasn't ready. I wasn't expecting this."

Just about as Cal was about to ask him what he meant, he watched them carry bodies from the ambulance and then he got a good look at the vehicle. "Hey, Mark. That's my county. Is that?"

"Yeah," Mark replied. "That's the ambulance that came and took Ella. The paramedics are dead, Cal. One just dead the other decimated."

"Where's Ella?"

"She knew what she did. I guess it's better to ask where isn't Ella?'

"What do you mean?"

142

Mark stepped closer to the road. "She's..." He huffed then shouted, turning his head. "Hey! Hey! Come on! Four feet away or wear masks and gloves."

Confused at first, Cal then watched Mark move quickly in the direction where a man in a white medical suit crouched down toward the road.

"Watch your step," Mark told Cal. "You don't want to step on her."

"Step on—" Cal cringed. "No."

"Most parts are flagged," Mark said. "Cal, it was bad. It was just one car after another that ran her over. I hope with the first impact she was gone."

They arrived at the man.

"Doc Garrison," Mark said. "I told you four feet. She has a highly contagious parasite"

"I think we're safe," Garrison replied. "And she had more than one. Haven't found one or seen one alive. Then again, nothing can survive this."

Upon those words, Cal saw the body., It was the single worse thing he had seen in his life. It literally broke his heart to see the suffering she endured and hoped that, like Mark stated, she didn't feel the massacre that occurred to her body.

It was evident that like roadkill she had been shred apart from the wheels of fast-moving vehicles that ran over and dragged her thinking she was probably an animal. With each passing car that hit her, she grew smaller.

Some drivers realized what happened. They pulled over, speaking to authorities and obviously distraught.

They didn't know. How could they?

Little flags with flares nearby marked pieces of her body, they extended far up the road.

Cal stood by what was the largest remains of Ella. It was hard to distinguish if the body was male or female. Both her legs were gone below the knee. It was just stumps, they had been torn from her. The same happened with the left arm, but her right was completely gone. There was skin on her face, it looked turned inside out. Everything about seemed turned inside out.

"This," Garrison said. "Has got to be the worst case of suicide by traffic accident that I have ever seen."

"She just stepped into the road," Mark stated. "No warning, right into the flow of traffic."

Cal could visualize it. Ella stepped out. The first car plowing into her, breaking very bone in her body, sending her flying down for the other cars and trucks to do their thing.

"You saw the parasites?" Mark asked.

"I did," Garrison answered. "There were a lot on the first car that struck her. None alive. They're everywhere, but I honestly think whatever kind of parasite this is, it needs an immediate host to stay alive."

"Doc, this is gonna sound insane," Mark said.

"I doubt it," Garrison replied. "But go on."

"It's a possibility that they are nesting in the body."

"You're right." Garrison nodded. "That does sound crazy. But I won't dismiss it. I saw the body of the paramedic. Not sure what could do that. Do you?"

"Unfortunately," Mark replied. "It appears that once the multitudes of parasites are mature, they eject or projectile from the host onto the victim."

Cal continued, "But it doesn't infest the victim, just tenderizes them for ingestion."

"Only the mid-section," Mark continued. "And um, supposedly this is how the host is able to keep growing parasites. I'm still learning."

"Better let me know about that," Garrison stated. "And I'll keep my eye out. I can tell you that there were a lot of those dead parasites. Like maggots in bunches, all dead. I'll never eat rice noodles again."

Mark asked. "Do you think you can tell by looking at her where they could have nested."

Cal added. "Our source that is familiar with this parasite, called it a parasitic gland."

"So, they take over a gland," said Garrison. "I'll look back at the office, but here." He shook his head. "I can't tell anything. I mean, damn, her blue jeans are tangled in her intestines."

That was it.

Something about that statement hit the 'I'm done' button in Cal. Suddenly, it just made him sick. "Can you guys excuse me." He walked away finding a safe spot away from the gore behind his brother's car.

News of the closed highway spread fast. Beyond the barricade Cal saw reporters, the lights on the cameras acted like spotlights. Cal wondered how they got through. The probably

145

parked on the other side of the highway or the grassy median strip and made their way over.

"You okay?" Mark asked

Cal peered over his shoulder. "I am. It's just…Mark, that's pretty horrific and I have seen a lot."

"Me, too."

"She did this to herself; did you talk to her? Did she say anything?"

"Yes, I did. She was angry that we didn't let her have the silver. Angry that this happened and said she felt as if it was going to happen again."

"So, it's never-ending cycle," Cal stated.

"I guess. We have a lot of storage hosts out there. We'll find out one way or another."

"So up to the second projectile they are in control of their faculties," Cal said. "They know right from wrong. So, there's a way to reason."

"Brother, the only way to get them to stop is for them to die."

"We don't know that. You're on this right?"

Mark nodded. "I am. I also want to figure out a way to use the silver to test. I passed the silver information on to Farina in London. Her hospital has an extensive parasitic research lab."

"That's great news."

"It is," Mark said. "Speaking of news." He pointed to the reporters. "Thank God it's late and Mom's asleep. Or else she'd see this mess on the news and flip out because she knows I come this way."

"Shit."

"What?" Mark asked.

"I have to call mom and tell her you are alright. I may or may not have told her you were in an accident."

"Cal!" Mark blasted. "What the hell. You know how she is."

"I know. I know."

"Call her, my work is done here. We have several people now at quarantine bay, I want to go and start setting up some tests. If we can figure out the incubation, this gland thing, we may be able to stop it without killing the hosts."

"You really think so?" Cal asked.

"No. But it's worth a shot." Mark gave Cal a quick hug and walked away.

Cal just knew he was going to hear it from his mother about allowing her to worry for so long. At least Mark was fine, he was going to give her good news. At least he thought so. Just as he was about to dial, Mark called him over. Cal put away the phone figuring he'd call her as soon as he found out what Mark needed.

John F. Kennedy Airport., New York

It didn't happen often, but when it did, Transportation Security Administration Office, Evan Johns got annoyed.

When it did occur, usually it was early morning hours as it was then. Just before five am, when business executives and gamblers to Vegas, took early flights crowding the TSA checkpoints. There weren't that many checkpoints open and at that time of morning, few officers were on duty.

The rich and famous typically used the VIP service for private and smaller TSA, utilizing a side entrance to avoid the public eye. But on days like this one, that area was down. An infrequent inconvenience. Those who were accustomed to using that service always exclaimed their dismay when they had to use the public terminal.

Skyna Lord was no exception. In fact, she was bad. Not vocally, but her body language screamed that she as annoyed.

She drew attention to herself. Evan did get it. She caused it, not her celebrity status. She wore tight designer clothing no normal person would wear on a plane, she had people lifting her purse and carry on, not to mention sunglasses indoors. Dead giveaway.

Evan was certain that most of the people flying at five in the morning hadn't a clue who she was. Nor did they care, until she acted too good to be in the line.

He had the advantage of watching her wait in the long line. At first, he was working the 'check ID' podium and they moved him to screening.

He begged in his mind for her to get in his line. There were two areas she would go to, he hoped she would use his.

The other TSA agent was in agreement that they'd make her to the full body scanner instead of the simple metal detector. Lifting her arms in the air in that tight outfit would be uncomfortable.

They'd get a good laugh.

Evan saw her head to his checkpoint and he hid his excitement. He couldn't wait to hear her gripe.

After taking off her shoes, as if it was the most irritating thing she had to do all year, they waved her to the full body scan.

"Seriously?" she snapped. "In this outfit do you think I can hide anything?" She spoke of the tight white pants and short cropped clingy shirt.

The female TSA agent wasn't sympathetic and waved her through. "Hold still," the agent said.

Evan looked. Something was off and it wasn't a joke or his desire to inconvenience her. "Have her stay put, we're going to run it again."

"What's going on?" A supervisor, Clinton, approached.

"A mistake. Has to be a glitch." Evan nodded for Skyna to lift her arms again. "We'll scan again."

When they scanned, it was still there

Clinton signaled the other agent to pull Skyna aside.

"What is that?" the supervisor asked.

Evan had seen thousands of scans, never had he seen anything like it. There was something odd inside of her. Two of them. One looked like abag to the right of her esophagus and another bag, just above the stomach.

"Two," Evan replied. "Two of them. She had to ingest."

"Is she smuggling?"

"Looks like it."

"Awfully big to swallow," the supervisor stated. "Why would someone like that need to smuggle. If I didn't see something in those sacs, I'd worry about her health. Let's go talk to her."

Evan and his supervisor walked over.

"Hello," Skyna barked. "Can I get to my flight? It's bad enough I had to be pulled through here."

"Ma'am," Clinton said. "Just hold on." He lifted a wand and waved her over. No metal noises. "Ma'am are you carrying anything you are not disclosing."

"Excuse me?"

"We'd like to search you. We can have a female agent pull—"

"No!" Skyna blasted. "You are not searching me. There's no…" Skyna stopped, her body swayed left to right. Her entire tone changed as her color drained some. "I'm sorry. I think, I think I'm going to be sick."

"This way." Clinton reached for her.

Before his hand could rest on her arm to guide her, Skyna's arm shot back, her chest protruded outward as her head flung back.

"Ma'am," Clinton called.

Surely something was wrong, Evan saw it. She was having a seizure or something. She looked possessed. "I'll get help," Evan stated.

He took a step back and it was the step that saved his life. Not far from his boss, Clinton, he watched as Skyna threw her head forward at the same time, her mouth widened in an unnatural way and a blast of red vomit projected from her mouth. It was looked like a fire hydrant the way it blasted.

It hit Clinton with a force, sending him back and to the floor.

People screamed; chaos ensued as other agents rushed over.

Evan froze, he couldn't move, he just watched.

What he witnessed Skyna do was beyond comprehension. Those after moments of the violent blood regurgitation, would forever be etched in Evans mind.

SEVENTEEN

Prepare Ye

Ma and Joe's – Needville, PA

The forks and knifes clanked loudly on the bar as Diana 'Di-Di' Reigns, Cal's mother emptied the felt case into the already large pile. "My mother's good silver," she said. "I also have my father's silver quarters."

Glen nodded impressed. "I have my mother's as well." He looked at the large pile on the bar. "We should have enough if we barricade."

"I agree. Unless we're going out hunting," Di-Di replied. "We may need more."

"Did you get the borax?" Glen asked.

"I had some in the basement when I tried to make soap. It's only a box. How much do we need?"

"Not much."

"What about the other stuff you found on the net?"

"Got it. Crucibles, tongs, kiln, blow torch," Glen replied.

"Okay, where are we doing this?" Di-Di asked.

"Kitchen will be safer. I put the small kiln in there. I have the directions and I think Jude knows how as well."

"How did you get the stuff?" she asked.

"Oh, Maryanne makes jewelry. I called her and asked if she had what we needed. I couldn't find it anywhere to pick up, and that just clicked about her making rings and stuff."

"Good thinking. Did you wake her because it's only eight-thirty now."

"I did," Glen replied. "She was fine especially after I told her why and made her look."

"I can't believe this is happening," Di-Di said. "Okay so what are we making it into?"

"I thought of that." Glen lifted his finger. "You're gonna love it. We're going to take—" he turned his head when there was a knock at the door of the bar. He could see Jude standing there. "Hold on."

"I was wondering when he'd show up."

Enthusiastically, Glen hurried to the door and unlocked it. He pushed it open. "Hey, come on in. We're ready to start."

"You have everything? Jude asked.

"We do. I'll tell you I have been self-educating all night. Being my own McGyver with inventing a delivery system. But then again you know more about the silver melting process."

"Not really," Jude replied. "My brother does that."

"Swell."

As he was about to close and lock the door, Glen heard Cal call out.

"Hold it. Don't shut it. Or I'll shoot my way through," Cal said.

"Well, that's extreme." Glen held the door open. "What's going on Cal?"

"My mother's here, right?"

"Yeah, she's…" Glen turned around to face the bar but didn't see Di-Di. "She was there."

Di-Di popped up. "Sorry. Found the good stuff. Oh, hey, honey." Di-Di poured a drink.

Almost mocking her, Cal stepped in. 'Oh, hey, honey. Mom! I was worried. I went to the house. You weren't there."

"No, I wasn't." She sipped her drink. "I was with Glen all night."

"Wait. What?" Cal snapped a view Glen's way.

Glen held up his hands. "Not what you think. She called me at four to see if the bar was still open. She needed a drink."

"You have booze at the house," Cal said.

"Drank it all." Di-Di down her drink. "I was horrified thinking my baby boy was dead. Dead on the road. Which he wasn't." she poured more. "He wasn't even in an accident. I would have known that if you called me right away."

"Your mother was in hysterics," Glen told him.

"Wait she called you at four," Cal said. "I talked to her and told her Mark was fine before that."

"Still." Glen shrugged. "She was upset and man, I never knew how well your mother could hold her liquor."

"You went and got her?" Cal asked.

Di-Di answered. "I drove."

"Drunk?" Cal questioned.

154

"Buzzed. Barely." She waved out her hand. "I haven't felt a thing. Strange." She poured another drink. "Why are you so upset?"

"I was worried. I went to the house to talk to you, and you weren't there."

"Worried about the end of the world that's at hand?" She sipped. "It's the apocalypse. Not in the God way. Maybe it is."

Jude shook his head. "No, it's not."

"They told you?" Cal swung a point to Glen and Jude.

"After," Di-Di answered.

"After?" Cal asked.

"Cal." Glen stepped to him. "I know you're the chief of police and all. But have you not been online."

"No. No I haven't. I have been too busy helping my brother with a woman that was in my custody that is now roadkill spread out between four exists."

Di-Di gasped.

"Was she hit by a car?" Jude asked.

"Many times."

"Oh." Di-Did gasped again. "Her poor mother. But at least she's spared the end of the world."

"We're not gonna let that happen." Cal shifted his eyes "Why are there all these forks on the bar?"

Jude replied. "You know we need silver. Even more now. It's out of control."

"You haven't been online?" Glen asked again.

"No!" Cal blasted. "I was busy with my brother then busy looking for my mother."

"Then maybe you should. Open your phone," Glen told him.

The sudden switch to a very serious tone in Glen made Cal pull out his phone.

What had he missed?

It was the third time Cal watched the video that had been plastered everywhere on every news source in a short period of time. He imagined people like his brother, Mark would analyze it, break it down. Maybe even some would call it a hoax, though he didn't see how.

He'd pause the video, look, tilt his head, trying to do a frame-by-frame thing. Which was impossible.

A man out of New York, captured the video from start to finish. At least until he was told to 'move back and clear the area'.

The news identified him by Jasper and gave a warning that what viewers were about to see was graphic and disturbing. He had been standing in line at TSA when he noticed Skyna several people behind him. He went through first and played it coy with his cell phone.

The video was obviously taken from the other side of TSA.,

"Okay, see her?" Jasper narrated. The video showed Skyna showing her ID to the TSA agent. "That's Skyna Lord, reality show queen and leaked sex tape porn star." Jasper giggled. "Look how annoyed she is. Dudes, I seriously wouldn't have given her a second thought if she wasn't wearing those big ass sunglasses and

an outfit you wear out to the club. At not even five in the morning."

The video showed Skyna putting her purse on the belt.

"Dudes, they're making her go through the body scan and take off her sunglasses. Look how annoyed she is."

He zoomed in and the camera started to shake from his laughing.

"They're making her do it again. You know they're just messing with her."

The unstable video showed Skyna being pulled aside.

Laughing, Jasper said. *"She's arguing. It's a pat down. I love it."*

Then Jasper laughed no more.

When Skyna arched back and red vomit blasted from her mouth, Jasper at first commented on, *"What did she eat?!"* then he freaked out. *"This is real. This is real. Oh my God, what is happening?!"*

The bloody regurgitation hit and knocked over the older TSA and without skipping a beat, Skyna hovered him, one leg on each side of his body. She looked down. Her jaw dropped at least six inches and everything that she had projected from her body, shot back into her mouth as if the video was played in reverse.

People screamed and ran. She turned and looked, face bloody.

"What did I do?" she cried out. *"Oh my God, what did I do? Help me. Please help me."*

The video went from Skyna to the TSA Agent's mutilated body.

"Get back, clear the area," another voice said.

Bang. Bang. Bang.

Jasper moved his phone in just enough time to show Skyna jolt from a gunshot and fall to the ground.

Cal couldn't believe what he watched.

Jude spoke up, "They can't explain it. They'll try, but this is the start." He touched Cal's phone. "Never in all the years that my family has been chasing this has it happened on this scale. It's done, Cal. I can promise you eighty percent of all those exposed to her were dead within an hour. At least one of them is infected as a storage host."

Glen added. "Once it is in the storage host, it's like highly, super contagious. Authorities already know this. Ask your brother, he probably is just getting this information."

"They're probably figuring out," Jude said. "What they can do and tell people."

Cal lowered his phone. "What happens if they don't die?"

"What do you mean?" Jude asked.

"I mean, the storage host, say they didn't shoot her. What would happen?"

"She'd feed again. Restart the process."

"How many times?"

Jude shrugged. "We've never had anyone projectile more than twice. We've always caught them."

"So how," Cal stammered in the aftershock of the revelation. "How did an entire town die if you guys catch them before they do this shit the third time."

"They shed," Jude answered.

"I'm sorry what?" Cal tugged his ear. "You said they shed?"

"About an hour before they erupt the first time, and only the first time, they shed parasites," Jude explained.

"So, anyone around them stands a chance of picking one up?" Cal questioned.

Jude nodded. "It doesn't always invade their body. And the shedding happens only before the first time. As if they have an abundance or the parasite has a back up plan to keep going."

"But they don't survive," Glen said. "After an hour, at the most, without a host, they die."

"And you got this from him or Google?" Cal asked Glen.

"Him." Glen pointed.

Cal faced Jude. "You have some really in-depth answers for someone that isn't a doctor."

"We had a hundred years to figure it out. Right now," Jude said. "This is new on this scale. My brother said it was bound to happen and it did."

Cal ran his hand down his face and glanced at his mother behind the bar. "I have to get my mother somewhere safe."

"There's nowhere safe, Cal," Jude told him. "It's everywhere or it will be in a matter of days."

"So, what do we do?" Cal asked.

"Hunker down." Jude pointed to the massive amount of silver on the bar. "And get ready to protect your town."

Teddington, Richmond, UK

"With the death of American television star, Skyna Lord, authorities have shut down John F. Kennedy Airport and are asking all travelers that departed or arrived in that time frame to report to health officials—"

Farina shut off the radio in her car. She turned on the wipers to clear the rain that started to fall. She was tired and it had been an unbelievably long day. Even though they were in the thick of things, she wanted to go home, just for a short period of time.

Nothing made sense.

It was a parasite. She understood the passing of the parasite through the projectile, yet so many of those who had been at the pub with Tip were now dead.

Too many.

Her phone rang and she looked at the dash to see who it was. Briefly, she closed her eyes and hoped it wasn't more bad news and then she answered. "Stephen, what's going on?"

"Several things," Stephen replied over the call. "The inquest found nothing in Susan, but it's still pending other results."

"No parasite?"

"None that they could find."

"So, we don't know where it embeds in the victims it kills."

"No, but I would venture to guess the brain."

"Me, as well," said Farina. "I'm waiting to hear from Kingsman."

160

"On a positive note, that may be a while. We located Myrna Phillips from the rave party. She had projectile once and she's been killed. He's examining the body now. He wants to know more about the parasitic gland."

"What about the agent in New York. The one isolated and claiming he saw something in the scan."

"We're looking into that," Stephen said. "Farina, if that's true it could be a first line of defense."

"I know. Listen, Stephen, I'm pulling into the drive. Can I call you back?"

"Yes, but after you watch the video I sent."

"A video?" she asked.

"Of Tip."

Farina exhaled. "He's been located and apprehended?"

"Located, yes. Video surveillance. Apprehended, no. You need to watch it. It's frightening."

"I'll do that and get back." Farina ended the call as she stopped her car and turned it off.

It was early evening; the lights were on, and she knew Brett was there. Oddly, the garage door was open, his car was inside, and the boot was open. That worried her for a second. Until she saw Brett.

He approached the boot with a box and placed it inside.

Farina gatherer her bag and keys and stepped from the car.

"Hey." Brett walked over to her. "Are you alright?"

"No. But I will be," she replied. "What's going on?"

"We're leaving. I spoke to my parents. We're going to their house. Swayfield is secluded, very few people. They have enough supplies to last."

Farina laughed in disbelief. "You want to run to the hills."

"Yes," Brett replied. "Farina, a virus, we can't really run from. A parasite, we can. We go and wait it out."

"We both had an obligation to the public."

"Really?" Brett asked. "Does that obligation mean telling them the truth. Screw my job, It's just a job. I've been watching the news. Nowhere has it been mentioned that a third of Earls Barton is dead."

"That would scare people."

"Yeah, it could save people," Brett replied. "Tell them what they need to do."

"We can't do anything until we know more."

"By then, it'll be too late. In fact, it's already too late. We need to go somewhere and wait it out."

"I can't leave. Not now," Farina said. "I have too much work to do."

"What would that be?" Brett asked. "Find a cure? You can't cure a parasite. You kill it or remove the hosts. You and I are potential hosts."

"Millions of others are as well."

"Then tell them what they need to do."

"Brett, I don't know what that is yet," said Farina.

"I do. Stay away from others and stay alive. Farina, we have to go."

"I can't."

Brett tilted his head in frustration, taking a long blink. "Fine. Fine. I'll unpack."

"No." Farina stopped him reaching in for a box to remove it. "Go to your parents. Give me a week, two tops. I'll be there."

"I'm not going without you."

"I think you should. Go first," Farina told him. "Watch your parents. I'll be there."

Brett shook his head. "I don't know. I don't want to leave you, but staying here is suicide." He closed the boot and walked away.

Deep down inside, Farina knew staying away from everyone was the answer. But it was something she just couldn't do. Not yet.

It wasn't that she wanted to stay behind to see it to the end. She just needed to stay behind long enough to learn if indeed, it was the end.

Quarantine Bay, Galveston TX

Mark was in his makeshift office at the quarantine center, it wasn't far from the bay where over the course of several hours had success in getting ninety percent of those on the ship. Two were still unaccounted for. Six people called when the video of Skyna went viral.

He had just learned he had a conference the next morning in Washington DC with leaders in the public health sector. Mark wanted to know all he could before that meeting. For the time being he sat with Jason, the young doctor that was his assistant, he had been with Mark since the first reports came in about the Talbot. They sat next to each other, viewing the TSA scanner footage Lawrence had sent him. Images from Skyna when she walked through security.

Jason pointed. "It's not any gland we know of. It's new."

"Hence why they call it the parasitic gland."

Jason nodded. "Looks like it's forming just above the pancreas."

"To me it's attached to the pancreas. Did the medical examiner do a scan?" Mark asked.

"I guess you didn't get the memo?"

"No. An actually memo?"

Jason shook his head. "No. The coroner's office isn't touching her until they know for sure that the parasite is done in her."

"I guess the word of a parasite hunter from Moldova isn't good enough."

Jason laughed. "Would it be for you?"

"It is now." Mark rocked back and forth in the chair. "I should do the autopsy. I'm worried that we won't get the information we need if we wait too long."

"As if the gland may vanish?"

"Yes," Mark replied. "If it formed out of nowhere. How do we know it doesn't work like a fluid filled cyst? It doesn't regain its parasite nourishment or release again, it bursts leaving no trace."

"Tell me about the silver thing," Jason asked.

"I'm not sure how that works." Mark folded his hand in a praying fashion, bringing the tips of his fingers just under the chin as he stared. "We need an autopsy or testing. Because we have nothing."

"We know some stuff," said Jason. "We know incubation, the basic two types of hosts we're looking for. We know thanks for Farina, they grow stronger. Which I find hard to believe. How much stronger can the host be?"

"She said it wasn't strength as much as fast and has a lot more stamina."

"Any physical changes that she noted?" Jason asked.

"She didn't say. She hasn't sent me the CC footage yet," said Mark. "I think she is still reviewing it. How is it possible? I mean does the parasite create other glands that make them stronger. We need answers and this is out of our league. I mean we can't test them. I wish we could."

"Can we scan those in quarantine," Jason said. "I mean we know scanning shows at least later stages, right. If it gets to an exodus point, they can use scanners at checkpoints."

"Exodus? That's extreme." Mark cringed. "Where are the people going to go?"

"Maybe figuring out how to use silver as a test?" Jason suggested. "I'm just tossing out ideas."

Mark shook his head. "No matter how little, I know it kills the host. Scanning is best but how?"

"What about passive terahertz screening? Would that work."

"I'm sorry, what?" Mark asked.

"It's a mobile screening developed by the British. About the size of a laptop. Totally passive, it scans people without knowing and looks for hidden objects. I mean if the walk-through scanner caught the abnormal growth in Skyna, this might."

"Can we get one?"

"I don't know. It's not something we've looked into before."

"Well, you heard about it, so you have a better start than me." Mark stood. "I'm gonna go check out our people in the bay." The second he reached the door, his phone rang.

It was his brother.

He answered the phone, "Cal, I don't have time if you're calling to bitch about Mom."

"Oh, she's finally sleeping. I'm done bitching."

"I wanted to see if you had anything," Cal said.

"Not yet. I think I wanna do an autopsy. Can you double check with Jude about the life span of the parasite?"

"So, you don't run into any?" Cal asked.

"No, I need one."

"Dude."

"No, Cal, listen. I can't beat this if I don't know what I am dealing with," Mark explained. "Killing them is unacceptable. There has to be another way other than poking them with silver. Did he even say what exactly is the series of events with the silver?" Mark asked.

"No," Cal replied. "I can ask."

"Please do. I need all the information I can gather for this conference tomorrow."

166

"Wait, a conference?"

Mark huffed. "I don't want to go. They're bring the heads of CDC, WHO, TDCW and other doctors that work with contagions and parasites."

"Wow, the meeting of the acronyms," Cal stated sarcastically. "So, is it like a Zoom thing?"

"No, I have a five thirty flight to DC in the morning."

"Mark, you can't leave town," said Cal. "Not now. You said you want to do an autopsy to get a parasite and learn it. How are you going to do that from out of town? This isn't something that is spreading slow."

"I know. I have to go. Maybe together we can figure something out."

"With an incubation period of three to four days, this thing can steam roll while you're there. You really should think twice about going."

Mark laughed. "The world is not going to end in three days. I promise to make it home."

"Fine. I also promised to keep you posted about Mom and her desire to be a parasite exterminator. I will bitch."

"I don't get why. She wants to help. What's the big deal."

"Because I know what we're up against and it's not pretty. I want to lock her way," rep0lied, Cal. "I saw the video of that Skyna person. I watched the CC footage of super parasite man jumping—"

"Wait. Stop. What? Super parasite man?" Mark asked.

"Yeah, the dude on the London train."

"Cal, what are you talking about?"

"You've been talking to the doctor over there; she didn't mention the CC video of someone infected?"

Mark sighed out. 'She did but she said she'd send it to me. That he had grown stronger." He paused when he heard Cal laughed. "What?"

"That's an understatement. I'll send you a link, you might want to watch it before you go meet with the disease people."

"I will." Mark stopped at the door that led to the bay. "I'll call you back. I have check on something. And Cal, be nice to Mom." Mark hung up the phone as he approached the bay door.

It wasn't a typical quarantine area. He didn't 'suit up' because all of the quarantine were in plastic, self-contained units.

They were a circle that surrounded a station with doctors, nurses, computer and monitors. A camera recorded events in each unit. It wasn't enough, though. Mark thought about that scanner and hoped Jason could pull through with it.

He lifted a chart as he walked by the station. It listed each person quarantined, where they were on the ship and if they were showing any symptoms.

One of the things Mark wanted to bring up at the meeting was the high red blood cell count. That had to be something important. He looked at the patients, they all looked fine, so he made his way to Martie the chef. She was speaking to the woman in the next unit. Talking to her through the sheath of plastic.

Mark looked down. The other woman was Kelly. A server on the Talbot. He was curious about Martie because she had locked herself in the galley, which had fire doors.

"Doctor Reigns," Martie said when she saw him approach. She walked away from Kelly and to him.

"How are you?" Mark asked.

"I feel fine," she replied. "I am so worried about my kids. Did I expose them to something?"

"I honestly don't know if you were exposed," Mark replied. "Plus, my reports tell me you weren't near your children that we were able to take you into quarantine before you breached contact."

Martie nodded. "You did."

"Well five days, Martie," Mark said. "After that, we'll let you out and clear you."

"What about me?" asked Kelly.

"How are you feeling?" Mark questioned.

"Fine," Kelly responded. "Other than anxious and feeling really irritated."

"That's to be expected, No one wants to be in a glass box," Mark replied. "Or plastic rather."

Martie questioned. "Can you run tests to see who is infected?"

"No blood test will show. However, we are hopeful…" Mark stopped speaking when Martie turned her head and attention toward Kelly.

"Kel," Martie walked over to the wall. "Are you okay?"

Mark lifted his eyes. In a snap of a finger Kelly had gone from fine, to making her way to the plastic sheath, staring at Martie with confused look. Kelly's hands lifted to the plastic.

Immediately Mark looked through the chart. Who was Kelly? He knew she was a server. What was she doing on the Talbot at the time of the event.

When he saw she had been one of those who were found unresponsive, he immediately made his way to the doorway of her unit to use the speaker. "Kelly are you okay?"

Only once Kelly looked over her shoulder to Mark. She said nothing but the expression on her face was fear.

Her body trembled, she instantly turned pale and in a matter of seconds, she was up against the plastic wall between her and Martie. Kelly's head went back, her chest arched and when she brought her head forward, she released a bloody regurgitation that plastered and painted the entire wall between her and Martie.

Martie screamed.

She screamed long, loud and in horror, stepping back away from the blood mass that covered the plastic between her and Kelly.

It was instinctive. Kelly saw Martie, A potential recipient. The parasite controlled the ritual. Project, cover, feed, repeat., The parasite didn't know plastic, it didn't know that the projectile would hit nothing.

As horrifying as it was, it was a moment for Mark to learn.

The scientist in him was in awe.

He knew the host hit the victim with the projectile. The projectile acted like an instant acid and breeding ground. The host then inhaled it back in. The ingestion and inhaling restored the parasite in the host and started the process again.

Only Kelly didn't hit a person or animal, she hit nothing.

Mark watched her heave in, as if trying to retrieve the parasitic substance that was empty calories.

Nothing retracted into Kelly's mouth.

Three times. Kelly looked demonic, determined, her jaw dropping unnaturally longer and wide.

Heave, wheeze, nothing.

When she failed, Kelly fell to the floor.

While Martie continued to scream, Mark absorbed what he witnessed. He learned so much in those moments.

The parasite needed that 'feeding' to survive and thrive. Without it, did they starve instantly?

Is that what happened to Kelly?

How many parasites were shed in that room? Was Kelly alive, dead or in some sort of hibernation. All questions Mark needed answers to.

Mark would get them.

He would give it an hour like Jude had stated and then Mark was going in.

The old saying was if you wanted something done right, do it yourself. Mark believed if he wanted the right answers, he was the one that needed to find them.

Kelly's body held answers. Mark would get them.

EIGHTEEN

THE WAY

Ma and Joe's – Needville, PA

It looked a lot easier than it actually was. Di-Di was frustrated as she held the crossbow. But it wasn't any normal crossbow. It was a mini. Designed to shoot large toothpicks from a desk, the object was no bigger than ten inches and worked with a trigger like a handgun.

Maryanne, the jewelry maker in town was creating the mold that would make the actually nail size ammunition. Once she found out what was happening, she was all in.

In the back of Ma and Joe's. Di-Did practiced. Surprisingly, the mini crossbow had a forty-foot range, but for accuracy, Jude said she needed to be around twenty feet from the target.

Jude heard her grunt as she shot again. "Di," he said her name and walked up to her. "Calm down."

"Good thing we're not wasting the real ones," she replied. "Maybe because these are nails. They're heavier."

"We'll be practicing with the real ones," he explained.

"Oh, I'll lose them."

"How you're hitting the target every time."

"Not the head."

Jude calmly placed his hand over her mini crossbow and lowered it. "You don't need to hit the head. Center mass is what we aim for that is the quickest way," he explained. "You can hit them anywhere and the parasites will flock to it like metal to a magnet, it's just quicker hitting center of the body. That's your biggest target."

"Oh, okay, I'm good then."

"Yes. Yes, you are."

She lifted the mini bow and looked at it. "How creative of Glen to think of these."

"Yes, it was. When he told me, I thought for sure we would have to make them. I also wondered how we were going to make the ammo. But he figured that out."

"How did he put this all together so fast?" Di-Di asked.

From behind, Glen's voice answered. "I'm a bartender in the only place in town."

Jude turned around. "I will never doubt the skills of a bartender again."

Glen smiled as he walked to them. "Look. I listen to people, hear them talk. I talk to them. When I thought about melting the silver, I remembered Maryanne the jewelry maker, double gin and pineapple juice, great tipper. When I wondered how I could get the most out of the silver, I thought about silver tipped arrows. But that would use more than making nail size arrows."

"And you thought of mini crossbows?" Di-Di asked. "But how did you get eight so fast."

"Malcolm Davidson," Glen replied. "Comes in for Happy Hour on Tuesday and Friday, gets only the drink specials and an order of nachos. Okay tipper, but he has like nine kids. I feel bad for him."

Di-Di looked at him confused. "Okay, why Malcolm."

"He talked about how he collected mini cross bows. Didn't think much of it, filed it in the back of my brain," Glen replied. "And it hit me. Melt the silver make mini crossbow ammunition. I reached out to Malcolm, offered him two hundred and fifty bucks for each one he could give me. Dude, was quick on the draw, gave me a third of his collection."

Di-Did walked to him. "You are so resourceful."

"I listen to people; everyone is a resource."

Impressed, Di-Di folded her arms. "What will you think and get next?"

"A scanner," Glen replied.

"What?" Jude asked.

"I need a truck though, it's heavy. An oversized pickup," Glen said.

"I hate those," said Di-Di. "They always block me in, park next to me and I can't see in a parking spot to back out. You don't know anyone with a truck?"

"Oh, I know lots. I'm just gonna run out of money soon. Then again." Glen shrugged. "If the world is ending, money is useless."

Making an entrance from the rear of the bar, Cal stepped into the back lot and into the conversation. "The world is not ending."

174

"He's right," Jude said. "It may not be the same. But it's not ending. At least not Needville."

"Cal, sweetie," Di-Di said. "Doesn't the police department have an oversize pick-up truck."

"No." Cal shook his head. "What do you need a truck for?"

Glen answered. "A scanner."

"Like a printer?" Cal asked. "Can't it fit in a car or is it one of those big office ones."

Glen chuckled. "No, a full body scanner, like TSA. That's how they say they saw it in Skyna Lord. I figure use one in town."

"And then what?" Cal asked. "We find someone infected, and we kill them?"

"Yes." Glen replied.

"No!" Cal barked. "You can't just kill sick people. Give Mark time to find a cure."

"No offense," said Glen. "Jude's family's been at it for a hundred years, I don't think Mark is gonna find a cure that fast. For every storage host we put down, that's how many lives we save."

"It'll get under control," Cal replied. "Where did you get a TSA body scanner anyhow?"

"Lane Airport," answered Glen.

"Why do they have one?" Cal questioned. "They don't need one."

"Exactly."

Cal tossed out his hands. "That's explains it all."

"Glen is brilliant," Di-Di said.

Cal curled his top. "Mom, please. Glen how did you know they had one."

"Jeff Lane," Glen replied. "Last year was bitching that his father got a TSA body scanner because someone told him they'd need one. Which is not true, but Old Man Lane refused to sell it because they may need it."

Cal asked. "If he refused to sell it, how did you know he'd give it to you?"

"I paid his overdue property taxes. Yeah, Jeff was talking about those just last week. I called him and used that. Told him if they gave me the scanner, I'd pay the back taxes. I maxed out my credit card after my savings hit zero. Of course, that's with everything else I bought."

"Why are you doing all this if you're so convinced the world is going to end?" Cal asked. "What happens if you save it."

"Then I start again," Glen replied. "Debts can be paid. Bankruptcy files. Lives can not have a price tag."

Cal scoffed. "And this is coming from a man who wants to kill every storage host."

"Because it saves lives," Glen said. "Look, the best way to do so is keep it out. Keep an eye on people."

Jude who had been silent spot up. "Cal, if this thing gets ahead of us, which I think it has, we need to focus on your town. You need to focus on your town. Save them. That's three thousand lives."

Cal exhaled. "How?"

Jude shrugged. "Pull a town meeting, get people together, get ideas."

Glen interjected., "Scan them when they walk through the door."

"We're not gonna get three thousand people crammed in Ma and Joe's," argued Cal. "Protect the town. You know how spread out everyone is. It's cattle country with a major roadway running right through."

"Cal," Di-Di called his attention. "They aren't saying it's gonna be easy. But if anyone can do it, you can. You save this town and how many people two years ago when the killer bees came."

"Mom," Cal scoffed. "That was different."

"Is it?" she stepped to him. "Is it really?"

Cal brought his fingers to the corner of his eyes and squeezed. He lifted his head and looked at the three them before exhaling and turning to Glen. "Call Lane, we're coming to get the scanner."

Finsbury Park, London, UK

London had gone on lockdown upon the discover of three mutilated bodies and nineteen dead inside a pub at Camden Town, which made it easier for those chasing the contagion. Farina hoped it would put things under control. People were still on the roads, some walking the streets.

Maybe they didn't get the 'shelter in place' warning, or maybe they didn't care.

She hoped the Prime Minister would take time to address the nation, but he probably didn't have enough information that made sense.

Nothing made sense.

It spread fast. No longer was it just some wayward drummer who went to a rave.

There were more. There had to be. Earls Barton was his doing, but Camden and Poplar? Now she had reports Tip was in Finsbury. With that information, she didn't care how fast he moved, he wasn't hitting all those places at the same time.

How many more were storage hosts?

With her husband safely tucked away with his parents in Swayfield, Farina focused on her problem at hand.

She was in the thick of things and despite her superior's disapproval, dispatched with a task force of London Metro police and SCO-19 to the Finsbury Park underground station where they believed Tip was taking refuge.

They had been chasing Tip for a while. CC footage showed an agile man that moved quickly and defied death. It wasn't that he wasn't cornered or even shot at, but he didn't die.

She didn't understand that.

They had eliminated several storage hosts with ease, but Tip defied those odds in a supernatural way.

Sergeant Toby Billings led the SCO-19 team. He was a younger man fresh out of the military and he was the only known survivor of a projectile attack.

He accredited his survival to his body armor, something the parasite projection couldn't penetrate.

He removed it quickly, stepped back and was able to execute the host.

Because of his experience, Farina wore body armor.

She needed to see Tip. Doctor Reigns in America told her that if they were unable to inhale projection, they basically starved because the parasite wasn't able to restart the cycle. Something he had learned from an expediated autopsy that he performed himself.

All of it was new and information everyone was piecing together. Shared information between agencies that singularly didn't make sense.

What did she know?

The storage host need to regenerate. It did so by projectile and inhalation.

While Farina had never seen a projectile firsthand, she believed from witness accounts that the storage host didn't projectile randomly, that the presence of a human source was a trigger. Just like the smell of a wonderful meal could make one hungry.

She based this on the fact that not once had they found the projectile without a victim. It wasn't like a drunk vomiting on the street after drinking too much, the storage host needed a target.

Farina moved with the team toward the underground station. Security footage showed Tip was down there. The last image was of him crouched on the tracks as if he were hiding.

But why would he hide. Yes, he was being pursued, but for some reason he was gaining strength.

"It's a trap," Toby told her. "I believe he's leading us to him. We've got him cornered. All trains are stopped, and another team is waiting at the next station."

"Why would he do that?" Farina asked.

"Your guess is as good as mine. Maybe he wants to die."

"Maybe." Before they took the stairs, from her vest, Farina pulled out a silver knife. Small, rounded edges.

Toby glanced down. "Is that a butter knife."

"A silver one. It was my grandmother's."

"A butter knife and we're armed with rifles."

"Parasites are attracted to silver, impale once," said Farina. "It will draw them from the body in a violent way and kill them."

"You need to get close to do that," said Toby. "That's suicide."

"I'll do what needs to be done."

"Doctor, if I may, save self-sacrifice for a grander scale. Stay close to me," Toby instructed. "Stay quiet."

Quietly, in a group and in formation they ascended the stairs to the underground station.

The lights flickered some, but it was quiet. No sounds of trains or automated announces.

They made it to the platform and the leader of the team swung out his arm, directing soldiers to different areas and positions.

"I hear you," a raspy male voice called out from the darkness. "Noises get…loud at this point.

"Where are you?" the leader asked.

Toby stepped in front of Farina.

"In the darkness. On the ledge."

"Come on out," the leader ordered.

"No, not yet," he replied. "I need to speak to Doctor Ainsworth of HTD. She's working on this."

Farina stepped out from behind Toby. "I'm here. Is that you, Tip?"

Toby immediately have her a scolding, 'what are you doing' look.

"Yes," Tip answered.

"We want to help you, Tip."

"Help me in which way?" Tip asked. "You can't cure me, and you know that. The only thing you can do for me is kill me. Find a way to kill me. I want to die."

Farina looked at Toby because he had said that was why Tip led them there. "There is a way," she said.

"It can't be guns. They don't work. I've stepped into the line of fire and these things inside me just create new skin."

"if you don't continue the process," said Farina. "If you don't inhale the remains. I believe you will die. At least that's what I have been told."

"We'll see. But for all the death I caused, I want to help you."

"How?" Farina asked.

"Ask me anything. What do you need to know?"

"Are you in pain?"

"Right now, yes. It's a hunger pain that controls me more so when I am around the scent. I can not control what happens to my body. How I release this vomit that dissolves my victim, fills with more and I consume it. I've grown stronger, faster, all of my senses are off the charts. But I'm not only killing my source of regeneration, am I?"

"No," Farina answered. "You infect others, and they die."

"Some become like me."

"Yes. Have you seen others like you?"

"Yes," he replied. "But it isn't like a family. We do not hoard together. Or hive." Tip grunted loudly and in pain. "This hunger, this thing in me needs to grow. I have tried to avoid people. I have. Like now, but," he grunted and cried out loudly. "It becomes a maddening search. It is taken everything I have not to emerge and target."

"You talk about scent. Is there anyone or anything alive you don't smell?" Farina asked.

"Sick people. I went to see my mother. She has cancer. I stared at her, never once felt the hunger."

"Is it only cancer? Is it other diseases?" Farina asked.

"I don't know. Figure it out, you're the doctor. I can't do this anymore doctor. Any minute I will emerge uncontrolled. I need you to be ready in case I don't die using my plan."

Farina looked down at her butter knife.

Toby laid his hand over hers. "Don't think about that."

Farina nodded then called out. "Is there anyone here that has an illness. Diabetes, something. Anyone unwell?"

Toby spoke through clenched jaws. "What are you doing?"

"Testing him," Farina replied. "We need to know defenses."

"I'm diabetic," a woman's voice called out. Then the female soldier stepped forward. "I'll be bait."

Tip's grunts and cries echoed in the tunnel.

Toby stepped toward the female soldier. "I have your back. Once he prepares and releases his substance I will pull you back," he told her. "If any gets on you remove the vest."

The woman soldier nodded.

Toby gave the 'okay' to Farina.

"Are you going to kill me?" Tip asked. "I need to die."

"We will kill you. I promise." She looked down to the knife.

The female soldier stood near the edge of the tracks with Toby ten feet from her.

Tip emerged from the shadows into the light and his appearance took Farina aback, causing her to gasp.

He didn't wear a shirt and parts of his chest were covered in a red, rippled, burn looking patches. His face was pale, his hair splotches and falling out. To Farina he was the poster child of death. How was he so resilient in that state?

Tip looked at the soldier and immediately his chest heaved out. "You..." He grunted. "Can rule out..." Another painful grunt as his body jerked. "Diabetics."

Tip had been facing the female soldier, his arms flew outward, and he trembled slightly as his head went back. Just as he flung his head forward, mouth opening wide and large, Tip turned his body, and the bloody projectile went onto and across the tracks.

A raging blast of infected substance came from his wide-open mouth, rushing out with some hitting the wall across from him.

When he was done, he glanced over his shoulder. "Kill me if I don't die." He inhaled but it was in vain. He was able to retrieve nothing. He kept trying, wheezing in such desperation.

After four or five attempts, he gasped loudly. His body dropped lifelessly to the edge of the platform, bouncing off and landing to the tracks below in a puddle of his own immortality.

Every soldier hurried over with weapons engaged, ready to shoot.

Tip didn't move.

He was dead.

The storage host was the most dangerous. They created more, they also caused so much death.

As Farina stared down to Tip's lifeless body, she was grateful for the information he gave her, but it also frightened her.

The only way to end it all was to starve out and kill every storage host.

With every hour that went by it became more and more of an impossibility.

Washington, DC

There are moments in life when a man realizes that he isn't all that he was built up to be. Mark came to that revelation as he headed into the conference.

He was supposed to be the guru, the man that knew all. The doctor that could figure out any disease. Yet, the contagion was beating him.

He had information but it was depressing and not what they wanted to hear in the conference. Actually, Mark didn't know what they were going to talk about other than the parasite. He came armed with all the information he could.

Photos as well.

That final phone call from Farina gave him some insight. Some information was new, other was a confirmation of what he suspected.

Almost as if he were some novice, Mark fumbled with his folders and tablet as he entered the conference room at the pentagon. He passed information to everyone.

It was somewhat unnerving. Mark didn't expect it to be there in such a high security facility, a hotel maybe, or even a hospital.

It was the largest conference room Mark had ever seen. More people than he expected were there. The head of CDC, a representative from World Health Organization, generals, Secretary of health, several virologists, but the strangest was an emergency room residence from Spokane.

Mark quickly learned that he was the attending physician for the first event, which occurred three days before the Talbot about the same time Farina was brought in with the Rave party.

"Moldova?" a General asked after reviewing the documents Mark handed him. "Doctor are you sure?"

"Positive," Mark replied. "My source and his family have been following this for a hundred years. It's ancient. Moldovan authorities are aware of existence."

"What the hell?" the general gasped. "That's a violation of everything I can think of. They knew of this and never let it out?"

Mark shook his head. "But that's the least of our worries. This is here and everywhere now." He faced the Spokane doctor. "You were first. What was your reaction?"

"We believed it was carbon monoxide poisoning," Spokane said. "We let them go. It was a ten people, two of which had died."

"No mutilations?" someone asked.

"No." Spokane shook his head. "None that I was aware of."

Mark spoke up. "I'm learning that's not the case in every situation. Which is why it is so easily dismissed as carbon monoxide. Doctor, can I ask what the situation is now in Spokane?"

"No increase in the emergency room," he replied. "The morgue is another question. We're getting dozens a day. Groups, families, mysteriously dying."

"It's everywhere," the CDC director, Collins said. "It's spreading and we are clueless how to stop this. If it was a normal virus, we have resources we can try, but this is a parasite. One that, from my understanding," he looked down at his notes. "Kills or replicates. Doctor Reigns, can you explain that."

Mark nodded. "I'll try. Um, the parasite does three things. But it's easier just to say Storage host or victim. Ten percent of the time, the parasite will find a very viable body to create a storage host. The parasite does this. Not the human host, he or she has no knowledge who is chosen. It kills eighty percent of those it enters. It seems to me that the parasite is looking for something specific when it turns someone into a storage host. Not sure what those qualifications are, and we have not found a common denominator in any of the storage hosts. Like I said storage host or victim. The parasite is shed at maturity two ways. Through the skin and through a projectile regurgitation. Which is bloody in nature. Typically, it is intended for a human or animal victim, the regurgitation breaks down the core of the body implanting parasitic eggs which the storage host then ingests to refuel."

The CDC doctor sat back. "Almost unbelievable. They're feeding on people."

"Well, no," Mark replied. "They're shedding mature parasites that create more in an ingestible way. The more the host does this the stronger he or she becomes. Almost indestructible. Doctor Ainsworth in London has provided photos as you can see. The Storage host in the picture was shot several times and was healed by the parasites. The storage hosts need to be our main concern, they are the ones spreading the death."

Another doctor asked, "How do we find them? And when we do, do we contain them."

"At this time there is no cure for the parasite. There's no drawing it out like a tape worm. Once inside the host they create a new gland. It is between the pancreas and stomach, extending to the esophagus. I did an autopsy on a storage host after she had projectiled and I found the empty gland. She passed away because she wasn't able to ingest the parasitic eggs."

Collins from the CDC nodded. "So, they die if they don't feed."

"It appears that way. The parasites reach maturity and leave the body, if they do not have a target, the host dies."

"And it can be anyone or anything?" Collins asked.

Mark shook his head. "According to Doctor Ainsworth who was able to speak with a storage host before they expired. Not everyone. They have to be healthy. The parasite will not target someone ill, like with cancer."

Another had a question. "You said the host in London was shot and didn't die, yet celebrity Skyna Lord was shot at the airport and died."

Mark nodded. "According to my source they are only vulnerable to death in conventional ways if they are exterminated before they projectile and ingest a second time. Otherwise the only way to put them down is to trap them into a projectile where they can't ingest or kill them with silver."

"Silver?" someone asked.

"It draws out the parasites, but I have yet to test it, I just hear it's not a good way to go. It's minimal silver impaled into the skin."

Mark was taken aback when everyone laughed.

"What?" Mark asked, "What's so funny?"

"Do you hear yourself?" Collins asked. "Selective infections and silver. World War Z and The Werewolf. Sounds like a fiction movie with very little hardcore facts."

"Yeah, it does. But we can't dismiss its fiction qualities," Mark said.

The General asked. "What do you suggest we do. I mean that's why we're here."

"Go into lockdown," said Mark. "Everyone stays in their homes. Does not leave for any reason. Any water that comes from the tap must be boiled and set for an hour before consumed. A shed parasite has a one-hour lifespan. We can beat that."

The Secretary of Health who had kept quiet, stood. She paced some before speaking. "You realize history has placed this country and many others in a weary state when it comes to stuff like that."

"I know. I get it. I do. But it's not two weeks. It's one," Mark replied. "There's no test other than make everyone get scanned. Keeping people locked in and away from others will stop it."

"How?" another Doctor asked.

"Because eventually, if the storage host can't find anyone to infect, ingest and start the cycle, the storage host will die," Mark stated. "The parasites it sheds die. The goal is to starve them out. If there is no one to projectile on, the mature parasites leave the body, and the host is done. No one gets infected, no one dies."

Wearily, Collins sighed. "It works in theory, but not everyone is going to lock down. We know this. As longs as people don't listen, there will be a breeding ground."

"We have to try," Mark said. "At the rate this thing is spreading globally, in four days we are looking at a different world."

Audible sounds of scoffs filled the room.

"Four days?" someone asked. "Really."

Spokane doctor spoke in Mark's defense. "You guys aren't paying attention. I'm not a virologist or expert by any means. But in four days that means it been ten since storage hosts have landed and since been creating more, flying from one city to another. It's out there. Seems to me the parasite knows no boundaries. It's not only making more hosts it killing people left and right."

With a closed mouth smile, Mark nodded at the Spokane doctor. "We need to unify and come up with something because as I see it there are only two outcomes to this situation. We get people to stay inside and away, and we starve all storage hosts. Or we don't and the storage hosts starve," Mark said. "Because there's no one left alive to infest."

NINETEEN

SPLITTING ENDS

Alexandria, VA

He had made it across the Potomac, but in three days that was as far Mark got. At least he got a room for a couple days, but they told him in the morning he had to go.

No guests were permitted to stay, the hotel was closing down, like every other business across the county. They allowed him to stay in the lobby until he secured things. Mark spent his time, with his phone attached to the charger, trying to find a rental or even a car for sale. Something that will get him home.

He did locate one car, but the guy didn't take credit cards, nor would he take a check. He wanted cash.

That wasn't happening.

The parasite arrived in DC, the day after the conference. The day after they pleaded with the president to shut things down. He said no until the parasite showed up. If it hadn't, Mark believed the president would not have signed the executive order for everyone to stay inside. Everyone on Boston bound train car three was dead. That started the panic.

Websites broke the news before actual news organizations did. Word that London had been on lock down for days started to spread.

The executive order went into effect at four PM, by midnight it was chaos.

The police were enforcing the shelter in place rule, but they were overworked and over their heads. How long, Mark wondered would it be before they just got tired of fights and injuries and walked off post. People voiced their concerns about having enough water and food for a week. Authorities released a number to call if someone was in need of food and volunteers were supposed to bring it, but it wasn't being distributed fast enough and people went out. What choice did they have. They opened the stores themselves if they were closed.

That was twenty-four hours after the order was give.

According to Mark's calculation, the next day, day four, would bring unsurmountable deaths, which is turn would cause more panic.

There was already enough death to do that, and the news didn't shy away from reporting.

American journalist Alfred Henry Lewis once said there were only nine meals between mankind and anarchy.

Three days.

Mark could see that happening.

He had to make more phone calls and find a way back to Texas, the near fifteen hundred mile journey might as well have been ten thousand.

No buses, cabs, ride share, trains or planes.

It was even tough at times to get out a call. He was unable to reach Lawrence or anyone at the quarantine bay.

He spotted another listing for a car and just as Mark was about to call, his phone rang. He didn't recognize the number, but he answered it anyhow. He left a lot of messages.

"This is Doctor Reigns," he answered.

"Doctor Reigns, hi," the man sounded rushed and nervous. "You gave me your number a couple days ago in case I needed anything. My name is Dirk Morgan, my ex and mother of my kids is Martie."

"Yes, yes, I know Martie. She's in the bay. What can I do for you?"

"Doctor, I can't get a hold of anyone there. I'm trying to find out what's going on with her. To be honest I don't have a good feeling about the situation, and I just want to pack up my family and leave."

"If you can, that's a great idea," Mark replied. "Someplace away from the city to hunker down. Heck, go camping. But go."

"I agree. I don't want to do so without letting her know. I mean, I can leave a voice mail and a note but, I just need to find out about her for our kids' sake."

"I wish I could help. I can't get a hold of them at the bay either."

"Can you just go there?" Dirk asked.

"It's not that easy. I'm trying to get home myself which is an impossibility. I'm stuck in Alexandria."

"Virginia?" Dirk asked.

"Yes."

"My sister lives in Alexandria. Maybe she can help you."

"Oh my God, if you could do that, I would be grateful. Give her my number please. I'm at the Comfort Inn and they pretty much kicked us all out," Mark said. "I'll tell you what I'll do, I'll call my brother. He's the Chief of Police in Needville, I'll get him or our buddy Glen to take a ride to the bay."

"Sir, seriously, I appreciate it."

"Call it an exchange of favors via siblings."

They spoke for a few seconds more and Mark ended the call. He was hopeful and optimistic about Dirk's sister. Maybe he would finally get out of town. As he lifted the phone to call Cal, he glanced out the lobby window and knew he didn't have much time to leave.

Woodlands, TX

Carrie ran her hand over her extended pregnant stomach and exhaled slowly through her parted lips as she watched her husband Dirk finish his call. He hung and looked at her.

"Carrie, tell me you aren't in labor."

Carrie shook her head. "No. I'm fine. What did he say?"

Dirk shook his head. "He can't get a hold of the facility either. He is stuck in Alexandria."

"Alicia's there."

"Yep. I'm gonna call her and see if she can help him. In the meantime, he's contacting his brother to head to the facility."

194

Carrie exhaled. "That's good. Did he say anything when you mentioned leaving?"

"He thought it was a good idea, encouraged it. So, finish packing up. We're leaving."

"Dirk, I'm scared. I'm days from giving birth."

"Yes, I know. But we can't have the baby here. We have to get away from the city. This Doctor is the famed knows everything guy. He suggested to the president to lock people in. If he's telling me to leave now, he knows something."

"It'll get worse."

"This thing," Dirk said. "This parasite is not stopping. You heard the news. They need to stop it by stopping available hosts. You also saw the news and how many people are out there. No." he shook his head. "We need to go someplace rural and hide out."

"Where?"

"Needville."

Carrie stepped back and squinted her eyes. "Needville. That was a sudden answer and pretty specific. Why?"

"Because he." Dirk lifted the phone. "Has family there. Doctor Reigns isn't gonna keep anything from there. Like me, he's gonna do all he can to keep his family safe. We want a safe place? We go where his family is."

"Okay," Carrie spoke nervously.

"I'm gonna call Alicia."

"I'm gonna call James. I'll tell him where we're headed."

After getting a 'sounds good', Dirk immediately called his sister and as his conversation started, Carrie walked from the kitchen to find her phone. She didn't just call her brother, James, she made a video call.

"Hey," he answered.

Carrie immediately saw the background. "Tell me you are not at work. No one is buying life insurance right now."

"I was getting things. I have the pistol old man Sanders gave me. I want to have it. And I had extra food. If I have to lock down, you know."

"I told you to come with us. James we're leaving town."

"What do you mean leaving?" James asked. "We're supposed to be locked in for a week."

"And you're doing that?"

"I will when I leave here. Carrie, you guys can't leave. It's crazy out here and safer to stay put."

"That doctor. Doctor Reigns, who is heading all this, he thinks we should.'

James laughed. "I don't think that's a good idea. Did you see the CDC just released a list of things to do if you run into anyone with a parasite."

"And did they tell you other than blood vomit how to tell if they had a parasite?"

"Well, no."

"Well, time to go. Find a rural place. Hit the hills," she said. "You always say you have no wife or kids to worry about. Leave soon or come with us."

"I don't think it's a good idea Sis."

"I know. But we're leaving."

"Do you know where?" James asked.

"Yes. We're headed to…" Before she could finish her sentence, the phone went out. Connection lost and the words. 'No service' appeared on the screen. Carrying her phone, she walked back to the living room. "Dirk, the phones are down."

"Yeah. I know. I got the information to Alicia though. She's gonna find him. You?"

"We got cut off, but I told him we're leaving."

"We're leave a note in case him or Martie show up," Dirk said. "Right now. Phones may be down, but there's still power. Once that goes, people will go nuts. We need to go and go now. The sooner the better. Let's just hope. For the kids' sake." He kissed his wife on the forehead. "Doctor Reigns got a hold of his brother."

Needville, TX

The volunteer fire department on Richmond Street was being called the distribution center. Cal was proud of his EMS, Firefighters and police force. Once the lockdown order came through, they went door to door making sure everyone had enough to make it through the week, if not, Cal would get it to them. They also took donations.

Of course, Cal had a heads up on the lock down and was able to come up with a plan to pull everyone together. Including information sheets created by Jude.

They passed them out.

The TSA scanner was temporarily located at Ma and Joe's. Right in the entrance. Glen insisted it be there with the

197

meeting they planned on having in two days. Then again that wasn't the only test Glen had to check for parasites. He created a thin silver needle and had no problem poking someone with it if he thought they slipped through the scanner.

Jude told him it would work.

So far all Glen got was a bunch of 'ows' and cursing at him.

Cal invited people to be scanned not poked.

No one really was too worried about it. Most of Needville was spread out.

There were several people organizing items at the distribution center. Cal was one of them.

With a 'huh', Cal started down at his phone after he lost connection. His head sprung up when he heard a holler.

"Ow. Damn it Glen," one of his firefighters yelled. "I hope you sterilized that thing before you went and poked me."

Cal shook his head. "Glen, quit poking people."

"There's no scanner," Glen defended walking toward Cal.

"Then take them to the bar, scan them and get them a beer."

"Why are you staring at your phone?" Glen asked.

"It's dead."

"Charge it."

"No, I mean, no signal."

Immediately, Glen pulled out his phone. "I don't have one either. Can the towers be down."

"Maybe."

"Dude, they are supposed to be the last thing to go in the apocalypse."

"Well, apparently not. Anyhow," Cal put his phone away. "That was Mark. He may finally have a way home."

"That's good."

"And we need to go. He needs a favor."

"We're not his way home, are we?" Glen asked. "I really don't want to go to DC."

"No. No." Cal shook his head. "Just grab your needle and gets us a couple of those mini crossbows."

"Okay," Glen sang out. "Are we going somewhere for supplies."

"No."

"Then where are we going?" Glen questioned.

"Mark can't get a hold of his people and we're headed to his Quarantine Bay."

Glen shrieked. A short, high-pitched shriek.

"Did you just scream?" Cal asked.

"I did."

"Why?'

"I am not going to parasite city. Not paradise city like the song. Parasite city. Quarantine bay is where they have all the infected."

"They aren't all infected."

"Wanna bet?" Glen asked. "They aren't answering. He can't get a hold of them. All dead. That place is a walking talking parasite paradise. Everything buried in parasites."

"Oh, stop, it is not. Go get your stuff," Cal told him. "We'll take the squad car. I'll let you play with the lights."

"That makes it better, but why me?" Glen asked.

"You're the parasite expert."

"I never claimed to be the parasite expert," Glen snapped. "Okay, maybe I did. Once."

"Get your stuff we're headed out."

"Fine." Glen turned to walk away.

"And Glen. I promise you," Cal said. "Nothing is buried in parasites."

Quarantine Bay, Galveston, TX

Martie didn't look at her watch at first, so she didn't know the exact moment it happened, but it hadn't been an hour.

An hour, that was the important time frame.

That's what she had been told.

In a bay that held thirteen people other than herself, she watched ten of them expire, including Kelly over the course of a couple of a few days. All suffering the same violent outcome. Expulsion of a power blasting bloody projection from their bodies and then they dropped to the floor of their plastic sheath cell.

Only one had been removed.

Kelly.

That was when Doctor Reigns was there. But he left for a conference leaving Lawrence and another man in charge. The others that died just remained in their quarantine cells, never moved, always observed.

She spoke with Brick who was next to her. He hadn't been infected, but like her he worried that it was going to happen.

Every hour that passed they both wondered, would they be next? Were they infected.

More than anything Martie wanted to go home, see her children, but she knew, if she were in that bay, something was wrong with her.

Unlike everyone else in the world, Martie was kept in the dark.

The workers, three women and a man, along with a male security guard were center of the bay. They didn't want to be there any more than Martie did. She could hear them gripe and complain.

She didn't blame them.

"I figured a way," said Brick through the plastic wall between them. "Got the screw off the bed." He sneakily showed her it in the palm of his hand.

"What are you going to do with that?" Martie asked.

"Already did. I poked a slight hole in the plastic. I'm gonna rip my way out."

"You can't do that," she said.

"Martie, what are they gonna do? Shoot me?"

"Considering the security guy has a gun."

"Please," he scoffed. "They aren't. They're about a day from just leaving us here."

"They wouldn't do that, would they?" Martie asked. "They wouldn't just leave us."

"They could. Then again, worst case, they could all die."

"What?"

In the back of Martie's brain, a youthful mentality stayed hidden. It emerged and she wanted to blast at Brick that he jinxed everyone by saying that.

Whether he jinxed it or not, if that was even possible, things took a turn neither of them expected.

Especially Brick. He created that hole, then ripped through that plastic. He bravely emerged, looked at Martie. Was he thinking he was going to be some sort of hero? Bust them both out.

The workers stood from behind the circular counter. Their voices were muffled but they yelled at him, then the security guard rushed over.

The five of them were huddled together. The three female workers, one man and security guard. Martie shifted her eyes from them to Brick. He looked ready to make a run for it and they looked ready to rush him.

Just as the male attendant reached for something under the counter, one of his female coworkers stumbled some in her balance. Almost immediately her body started shaking and her arms shot back.

Martie knew that that meant and by the look on Brick's face, he did as well.

She made eye contact with Brick, certain the look she conveyed was horrifying. "Run!" she screamed at Brick. "Run!"

He hesitated.

"Brick, run." She smacked her hand on the plastic.

Brick bit his bottom lip, again hesitating before he yelled out to Martie, "I'll be back."

The workers, like Martie were familiar with what would happen next. The workers bolted, from behind their workstation. The male worker raced to Martie's quarantine room.

What was he doing?

Martie panicked. He was coming in.

She shook her head, begging him not to come in as she pressed her hand to the plastic door. He reached for the keypad to open it.

The infected worker spotted him and pivoted her body.

Martie's focus was on it all. The infected worker was four feet from her the man who desperately tried to get in.

The keypad beeped.

Access granted.

Martie screamed trying her best to hold the plastic closed when the infected worker released her load.

It was something Martie had seen a dozen times only this time, close.

The bloody projectile hit into the man, knocking him back against the plastic. He slid down to the floor leaving a bloody trail on her doorway as more and more regurgitation poured from the woman's mouth.

Martie made sure the door was sealed and she inched back.

She had seen an infected expel the blood fluid, but because they were in sealed cells, she never saw what happened next.

The female worker hovered over the fallen male and widened her mouth. It looked like a snake's mouth consuming an animal, abnormally extended, then as if in reverse, a thick bloody substance shot from the fallen man and went back into her mouth as fast and at the same force as it came out.

Screaming, Martie jumped backwards

When the infected worker was finished, she turned from Martie and stopped.

It was hard to see what she was doing; the blood smear blocked her view.

She appeared as if looking around, confused, maybe searching for another victim. She glanced over her shoulder at Martie, turned and walked her way.

Martie knew what she was doing, especially when the worker extended her hand for the keypad.

Martie tried to grip the plastic, to stop her from coming in and as it beeped, once again, fate saved Martie.

The worker repeated her actions, body shaking, arms and head back. She sensed Martie, spotted her, but the plastic was deceiving.

She hurled forth blasting the plastic door covering it completely in the bloody substance.

Martie didn't need to see what happened next, she had witnessed it many times before. The infected doing that desperate inhaling to ingest something. An act that was futile. As Martie stepped back, she stopped when she saw it. Tilting her head she got a good look at the bloody substance, and she moved closer.

The substance that adhered to the plastic swirled some and upon closer look, standing nearly against the plastic, Martie could see it wasn't just blood. It was multitudes, hundreds of thousands if not millions of small thin worms that were delivered in blood.

As they slid down on the plastic until they sensed Martie. Suddenly, they became energized moving quickly, multiplying, all with a hive like mind and unaware that they couldn't get her. They spread out, leaving the bloody delivery system, showing their colorless true form. It was as fascinating as it was terrifying. Within minutes, it happened so fast, her entire plastic cell was encompassed with those things. The made their way through Brick's open side.

Her room grew dark as the three plastic walls were covered like a fresh layer of snow. Only it moved, causing the plastic to creak.

She hoped the weight of them didn't cause her protective room to collapse or that there wasn't a default, a pin hole somewhere.

They wanted her, she could feel it.

It took her a while to look at the clock she had at her bedside.

She didn't know how long it had been since the worker expelled them but Martie knew from Doctor Reigns that the parasites could only live an hour if they didn't find a host.

An hour.

Five minutes seemed like an eternity. Martie kept shifting her eyes between the clock and the plastic walls.

Finally, when it hit forty-two minutes, she heard something against the plastic.

Certain they had found a way in, her heart-pounding, Martie moved as far away from the plastic walls as she could.

The bloody area by the door was first, the parasites slid down, instantly dropping dead. She thought she really miscalculated time until she saw the white blast hit the area to her left.

A small section cleared. The parasites there fell as well.

It happened in sections. Allowing her to see what was beyond her captive area.

The infected lay there along with other workers, the body of the male attendant, desecrated was against her plastic door.

About the fifth blast she realized someone was hailing a fire extinguisher. She thought at first it had to be Brick, until all the parasites cleared, and the security guard stood by her door, holding the extinguisher.

"Are you okay?" he asked.

"Yes," Martie shouted in response, racing to the door. "Thank you. Thank you…" her words trailed when she spotted it. A parasite on his top lip. "It's on you. One is on your lip. Get it!"

He felt it crawling there. His hand shot to his mouth, but he was too slow. The parasite slithered quickly up his left nostril.

The security man panicked, rubbing his nose hard and fast, chasing a bad itch that wouldn't go away.

His eyes held so much horror when he came to his own realization the parasite was in.

Shaking his head left to right, he stumbled back and reached for his gun.

He knew what would happen to him. Just as he drew his pistol, his eyes rolled backwards, and he dropped to the ground.

A puff of white from the extinguisher rose up when he landed.

There was nothing Martie could do but watch with heartache as he convulsed in a mound of his own heroic endeavors.

He had saved her at the cost of his own life.

It was in vain because not only was Martie still in her quarantine cell, she was alone and surrounded by nothing but death.

TWENTY

FIN

London, UK

The weather wasn't hot, but Farina broke a sweat because she was continuously in the plastic suit. Once and a while when the oxygen ran low, and she needed to exchange the cylinder, she'd take off the hood and breathe, feeling cooler, but otherwise she was covered and protected.

Less than an hour before hand she was plastered with the feeling of being alone and scared. She wasn't technically alone, there were team members and other health professionals out on the streets with her. But she had he last conversation with Brett. Her husband pleaded with her to just leave the job and join him,

He left his job without a second thought, sitting nicely in a secluded him with his parents waiting on Farina.

Brett had been following the news and was scared. Long before anyone else, he was the first to mention to Farina about starving out the storage hosts. His thinking was reinforced by experts now that said to stop everything and go. Just leave. If a person was unable to leave a crowded area, seal up, stay put wait seven to ten days.

Those people, the disadvantaged, the ones that didn't have transport were the reason Farina stayed on the job.

She still believed telling people to leave their homes was counterproductive. Sending people out to crowd the country was just taking the problem out there.

Farina became a doctor to help people. Especially those who couldn't afford the high-end treatment. She never expected to be working with viruses and parasites, along with other tropical disease. She was a bit removed from helping people, now as she carried a box, she was helping a different way.

Strapped over her shoulder was her medical bag, if people needed help, she would give it.

He job, like all others out on the street, was to check homes and deliver food. The boxes and its contents reminded her of the food bank boxes her family would get in India. Rice and grains. Tins of soup and vegetables, a carton of milk, cereal, peanut butter and usually two types of protein. Exactly what was in the box Farina carried.

They were on a residential street with row homes. Farina and nine others had that neighborhood. A clipboard from the health service let them know the last persons that lived in each house and how many there were.

As she approached the home, Farina paused when she heard the familiar sound.

Spray paint. Glancing over her shoulder she watched two workers spray a red X with the number three under it.

The death team, as Farina called them. When a volunteer like herself didn't get an answer, the death team would break the lock, go inside and check. There were too many bodies to remove at that moment, it was a matter of registering them.

Looking down to her sheet, she approached the Rogers' house. Five people. It looked like a mother, father, grandmother and two children.

She knocked on the door then rang the bell.

A few seconds went by she repeated her actions. Knock then ring.

Three times. That was protocol. On the third time she called out identifying herself.

Still no answer.

Leaving the walkway, she peeked into the front window and didn't see anyone. Perhaps they had left like so many others. She waved for the death team. It was their job to check on the Rogers family and then Farina moved to the next row house

The Parsons, three people.

Balancing the box, she knocked on the door and as she did, the slight force of her knock caused the door to open.

She pushed on it, calling out. "Hello. Health Services. I have food."

No answer.

Her heart pounded and she widened the door stepping into the small entranceway.

Please don't let there be bodies, she begged in her mind, *please no bodies.*

When she stepped in, Farina knew she didn't need to call the death team to search for deceased. The home was in slight disarray, items on the floor, kitchen cupboards were open. She would have feared looters but there wasn't a single photograph anywhere. Ghost markings were visible where frames once hung on the wall, telling Farina, the family had taken the pictures and left.

Looters wouldn't do that.

She would tell the death team to check anyhow, but Farina knew they were gone.

Relieved that she didn't discover bodies, she stepped out with the box and stood on the stoop.

Glancing to her left, she saw the death team paint an X on the Rogers' home along with the number five. Unlike the Parsons they didn't leave town.

It was depressing and increasingly defeating.

The truck with supplies was still full.

On a street with thirty residences, not a single box had been delivered. Those living in the homes had either left or were dead.

By the multitudes of Xs on the doors, Farina lost hope by the second.

Quarantine Bay, TX

Glen enjoyed a good apocalypse thriller movie., He would be the first to admit it and start naming off films or televisions shows that he found cool.

There was always one thing he never got or understood.

Why the highways had stranded cars.

In the one series about zombies, there were cars everywhere, with bodies in them.

The virus in the television show rejuvenated the dead making them walking, gnawing corpses, so why were their bodies in the car?

Glen never understood that nor why so many cars were just left on the road. Until he headed to the quarantine bay with Cal.

It hit him like a prophetic vision.

So many cars driving way from Houston and while traffic moved slowly and steadily, there was bound to eventually be one that broke down. One car would slow the flow of traffic, bringing it to a crawl. Impatient drivers desperate to get out of Houston would try to go around the inching vehicles, hence causing wrecks, and finally bringing everything to a grinding halt.

Then as the cars sat there, people stepping out to find out what was going on, someone would be infected.

Crammed in and unable to leave, people would either run or smash into cars trying to clear them.

Glen imagined in a few days highways would be impassible.

"You okay?" Cal asked him as they neared the exit.

"Yeah, why?"

"You've been quiet."

"I was just thinking about the traffic."

"Me, too,"

"Really?" Glen asked.

"Absolutely. We have to take a different way back. Maybe a ferry."

"A ferry? Yeah no. There's not one that goes west." Glen shook his head.

"Well, obviously you're thinking about it."

"I'm thinking about how all that slow moving traffic will eventually block the highway all together. It's a death trap, Cal. The parasite is running rampant. We don't know who has it and who doesn't. All it will take is one stalled car and one infected to caused mayhem."

"Wow."

"What?"

"I wasn't thinking anything like that."

"Well, you should. Because highway traffic passes right through our town," Glen said,

"Not if it come to a halt before us. Here's our exit." Cal pointed and pulled off the ramp.

Glen leaned forward, closer to the windshield as Cal took the first right then ended up a road that ran parallel to the bay.

The quarantine bay compound was easy to spot, it was lit up and looked like a large warehouse surrounded by a tall security fence.

They drove up the driveway to the security booth where the entrance was blocked by one of those arms that lift and lower.

"Dude," Cal said. "Something is up. I don't see anyone."

"Yeah, me either. Is there supposed to be security?" Glen asked.

"Lights on in the booth." Cal put the squad car in gear and opened his door.

"Whoa. Wait, where are you going?"

"We have to get in there somehow. Obviously, something is wrong. Right? No one has been answering."

"You think they're all dead?"

"Um, yes." Cal walked from the car.

Glen watched him. He approached the booth, gun pulled and with a sideways slant peeked inside. He looked back out at Glen and gave a thumbs up before reaching into the booth.

The security arm went up and Cal trotted back to the squad can, slipped inside and as he closed the car door pulled forward.

"So, he abandoned post?" Glen asked.

"No."

"What?" Then as they passed the booth Glen saw the security guard slumped over in the chair. "Dude, he's dead."

"Yes."

"You gave a thumbs up."

"I did."

"About a dead man?" Glen asked. "You can't give a thumbs up when someone is dead."

"It wasn't because he was dead, it was because everything was all clear."

"Still."

"Still?" Cal shook his head. "Let's just head into the building."

"And again, why aren't we wearing any of those fancy, rubber protective suits?"

"For what?"

"To protect us. Obviously, the parasite broke the boundaries."

Cal shook his head. "And it's been hours since my brother called. Those things only live an hour. Trust me," he said. "I doubt we'll even see one."

Glen held his mini crossbow as he crossed the threshold to the actual holding area of the quarantine bay.

Then he stopped cold. "No. Nope. No way." He shook his head.

"What?" Cal asked.

"I saw eight dead bodies," Glen replied. "Eight on the way here. You were right not a single parasite until this. Look at that Cal. There has to be a million."

Cal glanced into the bay. A million was not an exaggeration, they were everywhere, but they weren't moving. Thy appeared dried out like long strands of rice. "Hey," Cal said. "See that by that one room?"

"No."

"Come take a look."

"No."

"We have to look to see if anyone is alive."

"And infected, no?" Glen said. "They're dead, Cal. I don't need to go in there to look."

"We can learn."

"About what?"

"Something else that kills them." Cal stepped in. It was as if the parasite remains were by the door, they were over by the body of what looked like a security guard.

There were four other bodies there, withered and on the floor. Some of the cells had dead bodies. He inched toward the mound.

"I am checking you as soon as you step out," Glen called. "You heard Jude, they go right in you."

"I'll be careful," Cal stated. "It looks like they're dead and…" He pointed to the one cell. "This person cut themselves out."

"You sure it wasn't the parasite?"

"Positive." Cal reached down.

"Ug!" Glen cried out. "What are you touching."

"This white stuff." Cal glanced around and then saw the red cylinder on the door. "Fire extinguisher. Someone blasted them with a fire extinguisher. "M. Morgan."

"Okay, M. Morgan blasted them."

"No. M. Morgan. The name on this cell. That's who we're here to check on. She's gone. Someone let her out."

"Maybe it was the cut-out man," Glen suggested.

"Probably. Security guy blasted the parasite, took one himself, died." Cal shifted his eyes to the quarantine cell with the cut and ripped plastic. "I. Goldman probably released her when it was all clear."

"You think they're alive?"

"I don't know. We can only…" Cal turned around and his eyes widened. "Glen." Cal rushed his way. "Behind you. RUN."

For a split second, Glen thought Cal had some sort of super vision and spotted a parasite. His felt the twitch of a scared stomach as he turned around and saw what Cal did.

A woman, older, stood about three feet from them. Her face pale, head back, arms arched while her chest protruded.

Glen had watched the Skyna video enough to know that standing slight seizure was a prelude to the eruption that, if landed on Glen would turn him into parasite feed. He didn't know if it would make a difference, if it would work or if he even had enough time, but he held out his mine cross bow and fired the small silver.

It landed right smack center of her torse under her ribcage. Glen backed up, racing into the bay and at a distance just in case she regurgitated on him. Then he saw firsthand what Jude meant.

The area around the small silver sliver swelled and she stopped looking as is she built to a heave out. Instantly the swelling grew, larger and larger, as if a basketball was under her shirt, pushing the material to its limits.

The woman dropped to her knees. She glanced down to her stomach, then her arms, The veins in her arms were predominantly black and spread out down her arms eventually making everything under the skin purplish black. She lifted her head to Glen and made eye contact.

"Thank you," she said, then fell to the floor on her side.

Eyes wide, mouth agape, a thick black substance slowly oozed from her mouth.

Glen was at least six feet from her. She didn't move. Her stomach didn't explode as he was expecting. Everything inside of her, just turned vile and she died.

Scared. Glen fumbled as he reached to his tee shirt pocked and pulled out the silver pin. He poked himself. Leaving the pin in me. He hurriedly looked at Cal. "Check me. Do you see any. We know they shed."

Cal pulled out his flashlight looking at Glen. His face, his hands, any area exposed. "I don't see anything. You can take that pin out."

"I'll leave it in, thank you. You never—Cal," Glen's voice dropped. "There's one of you cheek."

"Shit. I feel it." Cal's hand shot to his face.

He missed it. Glen watch it slither fast toward his eye. "It's moving to your eye."

The pin. He knew it wasn't the most sanitary, but it had to be the only way. Glen pulled the needle from his arm as Cal frantically tried to get it without a mirror.

The parasite had a mind of its own. It arrived at the corner of Cal's eye, curved back, readying to go it.

Glen wasn't fast enough. The head of the parasite went into the pink corner of Cal's eye, but before Glen could poke Cal, the parasite withdrew.

It slithered out, then fell to the ground by Cal's foot.

"Where'd it go?" Cal asked.

"There." Glen stepped down on it, twisting and turning his boot, grinding it until he knew it was dead. He lifted his foot. "I don't see it."

"It's dead." Cal took a lighter from his pocket and flicked the flame over it. "Well, fire shrivels the dead ones."

Glen stomped his foot a couple times. He stared down to the dead woman on the floor, stepping over her, looking for more parasites. "Can we go."

"Yeah. Let's keep a look out for more though. Man," Cal put his hand on his chest, as they walked out. "I'll tell you I was worried. I felt it go in."

"I saw it."

"Was it the pin that stopped it. The needle?" Cal asked.

"No, it stopped and came back out."

"Guess it didn't like me."

"Guess not." Glen replied. He honestly didn't know the reason Cal was spared. It was close. Cal was either the luckiest son of a gun or maybe he had something about him that made him immune. Whatever it was, they dodged a bullet and Glen couldn't have been more grateful.

Woodlands, TX

Martie couldn't thank Brick enough when he came back for her. It took an hour, she supposed he waited to be safe, and during that time he found a car for them. He did so by going through the purse of one of the bay's dead employees and using the key fob to find it in the parking lot.

They were careful when they left especially when they saw one or two people moving around. They didn't want to take a chance of being shot for escaping quarantine or setting them off to do that vomit thing.

The car he found was a mess inside not to mention older. Old take-out bags, crushed empty packs of cigarettes and Starbuck coffee cups littered the front and back seat. Martie had to clear an area to sit. But the car had a full tank of gas.

Ten miles outside of the city of Houston, traffic moved slow, crawling down the highway.

All those people leaving.

Martie wondered if leaving was actually the thing to do. If so, many people were 'running for the hills', that meant the city could be safer.

Then as they drove nearer there was a mile or so when they didn't see a single car.

Martie saw the reason for it, a massive pile up. Completely blocked traffic.

"Gotta be something." Brick pressed buttons on the radio.

Each press of the button brought a partial sentence of someone talking. Martie hadn't a clue what he was searching for. It couldn't be music?

DJ after DJ, voice after voice.

'I'll tell you folks if you are going toward—'

'Yesterday I went to the store, it was busy, but now—'

'Police are reminding people to not just shoot someone you think might be—'

'And the Lord said unto them—'

Martie shut it off. "Brick, what are you looking for." Her hand hovered over the radio.

"Just, I know it when I hear it." He reached down for her hand.

Martie shook her head and sat back. "Just pick—Brick! Watch out!"

A drove their way on the wrong side of the road.

Brick jolted the wheel narrowly escaping a head on collision. The car didn't slow down, in fact that driver laid on his horn as if Brick was in the wrong.

Then came another car, followed by a truck.

Hand oner her chest, Martie breathed heavily. "They're coming over the median. What are they running from in such a hurry."

"That's what I was trying to hear." Brick pulled over to the shoulder. "An exit is ahead. We'll just ride this until we get there."

It was a scary several minutes. Watching cars fly by and as they pulled off the exit, nearly being hit again.

"This is insane," Martie said.

"I know. Let's just try to find something on the radio. Check my phone again."

Brick turned on radio. It was the religious station and he flipped through.

"No signal." Martie looked at the phone. She felt anxious listening to the partial sentences of people speaking on the radio. Then Brick stopped when a low staccato buzz rang out like a Morse Code version of an amber alert.

"There it is." Brick withdrew his hand.

"What?"

"What I was looking for. Emergency system." He reached down again and pressed a couple buttons. "Yep. It's every station."

"So, you knew that would happen."

"A real emergency yes. This tells me it's not some hyped toilet paper emergency."

"We know it's not hyped. We've seen it," Martie said.

"How many of those people on the highway." His finger tapped on the window. "Have?"

A text to speech sounding male voice spoke over the radio.

"*This is the federal emergency alert system. With an advisory on the current contagion situation. Level is reported as high. The contagion has been identified as parasitic in nature. It is spread through an alpha carrier. An alpha is highly contagious and dangerous. The parasites are passed through their skin and bodily expulsions.*"

Martie shook her head. "Bodily expulsions. To put it mildly."

"*Infection is through close contact with the alpha and bodily expulsions. The term 'shedding' is used to define the contagious period of the alpha,*" the alert system continued. "*There are periods of alpha shedding episodes. If you believe you have been infected by the parasite, seek immediate medical attention. Symptoms include high fever, loss of consciousness and seizures. The following at steps civilians can take to minimize exposure and ensure survival. Stay inside. Secure all windows and doors for a period of no less than*

222

seven days. Avoid contact with anyone outside of your home. If you must leave, be vigilant of your surroundings. Shut off all water intake valves to the home. If bottled water is not available, water must be boiled for ten minutes. A shedding episode of an alpha will be proceeded by rigid body movements and slight convulsions which last thirty seconds before expulsion. Should you be around an episode it is advised to create distance as quickly as possible. The Centers for Disease Control advised the only to way to stop a parasitic outbreak is to stop the parasite from finding their hosts. Stay indoors. Stay safe. This message will repeat in two hours."

Static.

"No number?" Martie asked. "No website? Nowhere to call for help. That wasn't very informative."

"It doesn't sound real," said Brick. "I mean if I didn't witness if firsthand, I wouldn't believe it."

A female DJ voice came over the radio. "If that wasn't scary enough, right?"

Brick reached for the radio.

Martie stopped him when she heard the mention of the words 'Alpha Hosts'. "Leave it. We're almost at Dirk's. Just let it alone. Maybe we'll hear something."

"I doubt it."

"Originally," the DJ continued. "Was about four days from exposure to full blown symptomatic or shedding. That was the original ground zero wave, and what I am hearing from others is that is cut now. If you are infected, you either die or become an alpha and go full blown in less than two days. Maybe even one. These are people that watched loved one get infected. And if it isn't science fiction enough. The ground zero drummer guy in London turned almost superhuman. The more he shed, the stronger he grew. Again, rumors."

Martie glanced at Brick. "Incubation period is shorter. See we did learn something."

"Doesn't matter, Martie. Anyway, you look at this thing. We as a human race," he said. "Are screwed."

"Please don't say that," Martie whispered. "I have children. It's not what I want for them. I'll do everything I can to protect them."

"I'll do what I can to help," said Brick. "Are we close to your ex's house."

"Actually, yeah two more blocks and turn into the housing plan on the left."

He followed her directions, but Martie knew things were off the moment she pulled into the housing plan. She didn't see any cars, any movement. People were either inside or they had left. A lump formed in her stomach when they pulled to Dirk's house. Carrie's car was in the driveway, the blinds were drawn.

"I can't." she shook her head. "I can't. I have a bad feeling."

"I'll go check. Stay here."

"Thank you. The extra key is under the garden gnome by the porch bench."

"Are you sure?'

"Yes, I just, I can't be taken by surprise."

Brick opened the driver's door and stepped out.

Martie watched him walk up to the porch. He searched out the spare key, holding it up when he found it to show her. Her heart beat faster as he walked to the door.

She hoped, she hoped for her children's sake that if God forbid something did happen, it happened fast, and they didn't suffer.

Brick pushed open the front door.

It seemed like an eternity that he was inside, her mind imagining the unimaginable. Then when he emerged, she couldn't read his face.

Was it sadness, sickness, shock?

Brick had a fast pace as he made his way back down to the car, and he opened her door immediately causing her heart to skip a beat.

"They left," he said. "There's a note up there for you."

Martie wheezed out a sigh of relief.

"They left things for you to take, like supplies and stuff. There's a whole note."

"Thank God."

Brick looked at his watch. "It's four now. I think we should regroup, maybe shower, rest up and plot a way out of the city. The main roads and secondary are gonna be jammed. I don't know the area."

"I do." Martie stepped from the car. "Did they say where they went?"

"The note said Needville. Needville, Texas."

"Needville specifically?"

Brick nodded then must have noticed the confused look on her face. "What's wrong."

"It's just odd. Needville," she said. "Why?"

Needville, TX

In all the years Jude had been chasing the parasite, it was the most insanely brave thing he had witnessed a person do. Not a single person in his family or anyone that chased them every attempted it. Well, they did, just not in the way Connie Reigns did.

She responded that she didn't think about it, that it was only instinct.

She captured one. Connie captured a parasite.

They had been at Ma and Joe's, talking, doing an inventory. Jude went over what he wanted to discuss with everyone at the meeting the next night.

Connie insisted on making index cards as reminders for what Jude had to discuss. She had one in her hand along with the cocktail size plastic cup, when they heard the close and loud sound of a car crashing.

No sound of brakes, just crash.

Racing out of the bar, Jude saw the crash at the edge of the parking lot. It slammed into the metal dumpster and by how smashed the front end was, it was full speed.

The female driver slumped forward, her eyes facing Jude. They were lifeless.

A man had been ejected. His body was upside down, bent nearly in half with his back against the dumpster, head on the mangled front end.

"Oh my God," Connie gasped.

"Call for help," Jude instructed. "If there is any."

"Right away."

"Connie. Stop." Jude watched the man untwist himself, stumble to the ground and stagger his way to the driver's side using the car as leverage.

From the corner of his eye, Jude saw Connie move forward and he pulled her back, because something seemed off. No one got up and walked away. He was determined to get to the driver and it wasn't to check and see if she was alright.

He reached through the broken glass, pushing her back. Jude watched his shoulder's heave back and he knew what the man was about to do. The second the man's jaw dropped and his mouth widened, Jude pulled out his pistol, aimed and fired.

One shot. It hit the man right above his ear and he dropped to the ground.

"I thought you said you can't shoot them," Connie commented.

"You can if they haven't fed twice. He was about to feed. Somehow," Jude said as he turned walking toward his van in front of Ma and Joe's. "I think this was his first projectile or he wouldn't have been in the car with her." He opened up the back of his van and hurriedly reached inside.

He pulled out what looked like an exterminator's spray tank and from the side of the door a flame thrower.

"What are you doing?" Connie asked.

"We need to burn this now." He carried the items over toward the car, go close enough to spray the gas, then set down the canister. His eyes widened when he saw them. Multitudes of parasites, like an eruption, oozing out of the car and over the driver's door. "Shit. Shit. Shit."

Moving forward only a foot or so, Jude blasted the flame thrower starting with the driver's door and then he moved it to the man.

"Will that do it?" Connie asked.

"I hope."

"You hope?"

"I have never seen that before."

"Happened so fast," Connie said.

Jude nodded and then he saw them. He didn't know how he spotted them, luck he supposed. Three right by Connie's foot. "Watch out. Parasites by your foot." As he raised his foot to stomp, he saw Connie drop the over them. It tipped over, flipped once and landed perfectly on top of the trio.

Her foot immediately rested on the top of the cup. "Are they in there?"

Before crouching down, Jude checked for more, then peeked. "Yes. They're crawling up the side. Why did you do that?"

"I don't know. My instinct was to catch them."

"Why?"

"Because they sensed us, right? That's why they came out?"

Jude nodded. "Has to be."

"Well, they live an hour," Connie said. "We have an hour to find something we can put on or eat that they can't sense."

Jude saw the index card still in her hand. "This is insane." He took the card. "Promise me you'll hit me with silver if one of these go in me."

"Promise the same."

"Deal," he said, then bent down to try to get the parasites.

TWENTY-ONE

ONE WAY ROUTE

Teddington, Richmond, UK

The blisters on her feet were real. Farina couldn't recall every having blisters before and she walked a lot as a child with bad shoes, if any shoes at all. Maybe it was age, it wasn't as if she pampered her feet. On this day she abused them. Farina never really bought shoes that were for walking distances.

When she removed her socks, she could see the bubbled blisters. Some of them had popped. Unlike the others who were on duty, Farina went home. She'd go back the next day at the rate everything was happening, she'd be joining her husband in a few days.

Farina didn't even know how he was. The phones were down. Internet had gone down several hours earlier, and while the power was still going, she heard it wouldn't be for long.

What a mess.

She knew the story of how it started. On group of men going to Moldova, feasting on something that was infected, all carried it back to different parts of the globe. The ultimate natural biological weapon delivery system.

It spread so fast., Instantly killing almost everyone and those who were carriers fed on others in order to keep going. Not for food but to create more parasites.

Eventually, as Brett suggested, they'd run out of food source.

One thing Farina hadn't learned was how long it would take for them to starve out?

Would animals suffice? Would they weaken or grow desperate. In the days that had passed, she only spoke to three storage hosts. Tip was one of them. He gave such helpful information. Another host had stood outside the police station, screaming for help. For someone to stop him. He said he felt invincible until he was near people, then the hunger grew painful.

Only one had never fed or projectiled. *That* storage host came to Farina, she wanted to be checked out and was certain she was infected. She initially passed out, woke up to find two others dead and a body so mutilated she vomited. She felt fine. and Farina did a scan.

The parasitic sac was just forming. Had they not been looking for it that may not have seen it. They gave her treatments for parasites, even a dose of chemo. Make her blood like poison. Nothing worked, the sac grew. Farina knew from the Americans that silver did work, but even the slightest prick from a silver needle, killed the host. She couldn't take that chance. Farina needed data.

Camilla was her name, she appeared fine, acted fine, but within a day of being at the testing site, she spoke of a 'full'

231

feeling in her gut. A slight pain just above her stomach as if she swallowed something too big. Within hours of reporting that sensation, she projectiled in her quarantine room. But it was out of nowhere. It was when one of the nurses was checking in on her through the plastic panel.

Camilla caught her human scent or rather the parasite did.

It was the people controlling it, it was the parasite in them.

The problem was, Farina didn't have enough information to know what they were dealing with in the long run.

Tip had actively searched out people, an instinct he fought. The more the parasitic carrier rejuvenated its parasitic sac, the more they needed it. How many times could they rejuvenate the sac before their entire system was taken over. What would happen if people or animals were readily available to find? The streets were clear already. Those who hadn't died were hiding.

Businesses were closed, no mass transportation.

In theory, the parasite would eventually destroy the storage host if left in the body too long. But what was the time frame.

The scientist in her wanted answers, the woman in her just wanted to think about survival.

More than anything she wanted to go back to her lab the next day, learn more. But there were no patients. Unlike any other sickness or flu outbreak, people didn't line up to see a doctor. They stayed away. Surviving or dying in their homes.

At that moment, Farina thought about her feet. She needed to make them feel better for another day on the streets.

She couldn't rub them, so Farina thought about soaking them. Not feeling like sitting on the side of the tub, she opted for the plastic dish pan. It was in the kitchen pantry. Maybe some warm water as she sipped on a glass of wine.

She stood from the sofa and as she made her way to the hallway that led to the kitchen she heard it.

The turning of the doorknob. But the door was locked.

Was Brett trying to open the door.

Cautiously she inched to the door, and she crept close.

The jingling handle sound stopped, and Farina exhaled. Back against the door, she peeked carefully on the window panel next to the door. It wasn't Brett. There was a man there. At first, she through it was a looter, until he spotted her.

His face was pale, blood stained around his mouth and jaw, and his shirt was saturated with blood and remains.

Farina stepped back, then jumped when she heard the bang of the door. Trying not to scream, she knew she had to make an escape. In a run to the back door, she swiped up her keys, aiming for the kitchen. As soon as she stepped in there, she saw the man at the double glass doors to her kitchen patio.

He was a host and had reached that 'fast' stage. There was no way she could outrun him, the only thing she could do was hide, and Farina had the perfect place.

The safe room.

It wasn't any high-tech room and Farina never thought she'd have to use it, but it was a selling point for her. A false wall in the back of the pantry that opened to a small room. That wall locked along with an interior lock on the pantry door.

Double protection.

She just needed to find a way to seal the cracks of the archways in case the host got in.

Duct tape.

The utility drawer was at the end of the counter, next to the pantry.

Perfect. Convenient.

Keeping her eyes on the man outside, she backed up only looking behind her quickly and a few times.

He pulled at those doors focused entirely on Farina.

Arriving at the counter, she pulled the drawer, grabbed the roll of tape and opened the pantry. She glanced once more to the back doors.

He was gone. Maybe he gave up.

Crash!

At the archway of the pantry, Farina watched the man blast through the windows. He jumped on her island counter and lunged her way. She slammed the door and locked it.

He must have slammed his body into the door because it jolted. Tape in hand, Farina opened the false wall, slipped into the small safe space, closed the wall and after locking it, immediately began to place the duct tape on the creases.

She didn't know if it would work, but she had to try.

It was insane. Her fingers trembled, making it so hard to hurriedly pull and rip the tape.

Farina did the best she could, as fast as she could.

That was the best she could hope for.

Connie tapped her finger on the top of the clear plastic cup as it set on the far back table. An index card separated the cup from the table top but the three parasites captured in that cup seemed focused on getting to Connie's finger. If she pulled it away, they dropped.

"Fascinating," she said.

"Insane," Jude replied. "My father would kick my butt into next week if he heard I had done something like this."

"Your family never captured one?" Connie asked.

"Oh, sure my crazy great grandfather did when he tried to use them as a biological weapon for genocide."

"But they never caught one to see if they find something that they couldn't sense."

"No, because they only live an hour," Jude replied. "These guys are gonna die in…" He glanced to his watch. "Seventeen minutes. Not enough time to learn anything. I mean, alcohol doesn't hide our scent, garlic, salt. Mr. Whatever his name was…"

"Tenner."

"Him, yes, he was on that blood thinner. He put his finger on the cup and they came for him."

"There has to be something," Connie said.

"Yes, there is. Disease," Jude replied. "From the mouth of a storage host that was trying to help before he died. Disease. He didn't know what kind, but he knew he would not hunger for a sick person, and the parasites wouldn't invade a sick host."

"Sort of like that movie."

Jude shook his head. "No. That movie was any illness. I know these infected a town with malaria in 1963. So not all diseases. The UK doctor said diabetics were sensed."

"Obviously."

"What do you mean?" he asked.

"I'm diabetic," Connie answered.

"And you drink that much?" Jude asked shocked.

"Listen. Don't judge." She wagged her finger then replaced it to the cup. "I'll never eat those rice noodles again. So, what kind of sickness."

"I think anything that lowers the red blood cell count or destroys it because these things thrive on it. My opinion. All cancers, Leukemia, Anemias, like Sickle Cell or aplastic. Cirrhosis. Certain HIV medications, Chemo."

"Mark said the last communication with the doctor overseas, they tried Chemo."

"To destroy the parasite. Not to see if it works as a protection. Then again. Chemo means cancer."

"No, it does not." Connie shook her head. "We ought to get Henny Rollins here to test this out. She gets Chemo for her lupus. She's getting treatments now. Put her finger on the cup. If they don't go for her, we know that's a possibility and you don't have to be dying to be safe from parasite invasion."

"Can you get her in…Fourteen minutes?" Jude asked. "If we can that might help."

"That'll be tough, she's a good ten miles out." Connie turned her head when she heard the door open.

Cal walked in. "What happened outside. A car is blazing."

"Oh, honey, you're alive and safe. We were so worried," Connie said. "Glen." She smiled when he walked in behind him.

Jude replied. "Accident. The one was infected. We had to torch it. Let it burn."

"Wow. That was close to home," Cal said.

"Exactly what I was saying," Glen added. "All that traffic out there. Too close."

"What are you guys doing?" Cal stepped to the bar. "I need a drink. It was hell getting back here."

"Yeah," Glen agreed and walked behind the bar. "Like a video game through traffic. Those storage hosts or Alphas as the radio is calling them, they'll leaving a death trail." He grabbed a bottle. "We need that meeting soon to come up with a way to protect this town."

"Fire extinguisher kills the parasites. Cold. But that's all we have," Cal said, then accepted the shot from Glen. "What we need is a way to make people invisible to the parasites. Make them unable to be invaded so they can fight and eliminate the storage hosts."

"We could find those PPE suits," Glen said. "They seem to work."

Connie spoke up. "That's what we're working on. What can someone ingest that makes the parasites not sense them. Nothing we thought of works."

"Really?" Cal asked. "How are you testing this?"

Connie tilted her head down.

"Mom, what do you have?" Cal walked over.

Glen walked from behind the bar. "Connie? Jude? What's in the cup?"

"Mom, are they…. Parasites?" Cal questioned.

"They are."

Glen shrieked.

"Dude." Cal snapped. "Enough with the screaming. Mom, why do you have parasites in a cup in this bar."

Connie replied. "To know your enemy—"

"Yeah, yeah," Cal cut her off.

"Look, Cal," Jude said. "No matter how much alcohol we consume or whatever we put on our fingers. The moment we do this," he placed his finger on the top of the cup. "They sense us. If they were free, they'd invade."

"Unless you're Cal," Glen stated. "They didn't want him. One went right in his eye and came back out."

All expression on Jude's face dropped. "What?"

Glen nodded. "Yeah, it was scary. Hey, Cal put your finger on that cup."

"You," said Cal.

"No way. I hate them." Glen bodily shivered.

"It was a fluke," Cal stated. "I got the one that didn't like me."

Jude lifted Connie's hand from the overturned cup. The parasite dropped down to the index card.

"Why did you do that?" Connie asked.

Jude faced Cal. "Cal, would you?"

"Fine." Cal huffed and stepped to the cup. He placed two fingers on the bottom.

The parasites squirmed but didn't go after his finger. They were completely oblivious to his presence.

"Huh." Cal nodded then smile. "Looks like I might be able to front line fight these bastards. I'm immune."

Connie was stunned, she couldn't move or speak. In fact, she felt an instant sickening feeling in her stomach.

The parasites didn't go after her son. From what Jude said that only happened when the potential host was seriously ill. Either Cal was immune, or something was wrong with him.

As a mother, a part of her just didn't want to know.

TWENTY-TWO

CLOSE CALLS

Teddington, Richmond, UK

Farina was well aware of the time frame. It had been confirmed over and over.

A parasite, outside of the host, would only live one hour, after that it died. It ceased to exist and even if it had any life left in it at all, it wasn't enough to invade a human body.

Even with that knowledge, Farina waited. She waited longer than an hour.

The infected host banged on the door of the pantry and as Farina finished sealing the outline of the false wall, he had broken through the pantry door, tearing things from the shelf and trying to get beyond that false wall that separated him from Farina.

Then he went silent.

She didn't know if his silence meant he left or died, but she wasn't taking a chance.

Once there was no noise, Farina waited two hours. She couldn't rest or do anything; fear had consumed her. Frozen her in one position. That back area behind the false wall was dark. She finally snapped to enough and found the dim battery-operated light, at least ten minutes had passed. Enough time for her to have missed any parasites that had come in.

Just because she was still alive didn't meant they hadn't invaded her.

She very well could be like the man that crashed through her windows in a desperate attempt to rejuvenate,

Farina waited hours. Scared in that dark hidden room, until finally she mustered the courage to leave. She was cautious. Trying her best to be silent, she unbolted the lock on the false wall and slowly opened it. Immediately the stench hit her. It was a sour metallic smell. Her first step back into the panty told her she didn't want to look down. But she did.

She fell it. Beneath of bare, blister covered feet, the slippery, thick substance. The host had caught her scent and couldn't hold back. Not only was his projectile all over the floor, but tens of thousands of the parasites as well. They mixed in with the bloody substance. They were dead. And she was stepping on them.

In the archway of the broken pantry door lay the storage host that sought her.

His body lay on his side in a fetal position, mouth open, pale, and withered. Farina had seen many people who had passed on from viruses, parasites, and the man looked as if he died an agonizing death.

Farina passed, almost frozen, looking down to his body, feeling pity on him. Sorry she couldn't help him. Who was he? Did he have a family? Did he even know what he was doing when he came for her or was he driven by the hunger of the parasites to replicate?

Finally, she stepped over his corpse and walked into her kitchen. She looked about for more of the parasite remains. She knew they'd be dead; they didn't last longer than an hour outside of a host.

There were so many of them, her escape was narrow, and she was in a dark room. Farina was uncertain if she was infected and there was only one way to find out. Tip toeing her way across the kitchen she made it to the box that set on er counter. A brown box, lined with felt. Her grandmother's silver. Actually, it was her husband's grandmother. Her own grandmother wouldn't have been able to afford a single piece. She lifted the life and pulled out a knife.

It was the only way to find out.

If one had made it into her, the silver world draw it and it would kill her. Farina was more fearful of not knowing than dying. After a few breathes of courage, she pressed the knife to her forearm and then added pressure.

It wasn't easy to cut her own skin. She held back, just pushing down enough to make a painful dent. Then she did it. She gave enough pressure and watched her own blood seep out from under the blade. She even held it there for a few minutes.

When no parasites came from the silver, Farina dropped the knife, gasped out with a sob and fell into the counter. She wasn't infected.

She made it through that ordeal. One instance. One battle. But the war against the parasites was far from over. At that moment Farina felt like a lone soldier. The last one left. She wasn't sure how much longer she could trudge on.

Bellville, TX

This is how it ends, Martie thought.

Noisy and quiet. Insanity inside the cities, humanity outside. She stared out the passenger window while waiting their turn in the line at the small-town gas station. It was manned by police officers keeping order while drivers were only allotted two gallons of gasoline.

A woman walked down the line of cars informing people as such and because it was a national emergency there was no charge. Martie couldn't see how that would work with people in the city. Tensions there were high. In fact, Martie was surprised how calmly people handled being told they could only have two gallons. She supposed it wouldn't be like that for long, eventually someone would get angry and make a scene, causing a chain reaction.

Two gallons was all Martie and Brick needed, Needville wasn't more than sixty miles. Although had they been able to get through Houston, they would have already been there. But they had to take the long way, backroads and out of the way routes.

Not only were people trying to leave, but there was so much panic. So many hosts that would just step from their cars, turning on a dime in the midst of waiting to move forward. And it

243

wasn't just the recipient of their bloody projectile, it was those near or around when it happened.

Maybe even before because it wasn't just hosts she had seen. There had been cars, some blocking the road, some crashed as if driven out of control. The were bodies in the cars. It was disheartening and sad.

Martie worried about her family. There was no way to get in touch with them to get reassurance that they were fine. The phones had gone down.

Those who spread it, it wasn't their fault. They were ill, their instincts taken over by some half an inch worm that looked like a noodle.

The authorities, government or whoever was in charge of creating those repeated messages were warning people not to leave.

Seal in.

Stay in.

No one listened.

It wasn't like an invisible virus, one without a cure. The cure to the parasite was to stop giving it hosts.

"We're next finally," Brick said referencing the gas pump, then cleared his throat. He tilted his head and cleared his throat again.

"Are you okay?" asked Martie.

"Yeah, that peanut butter sandwich feels like it's stuck."

"Told you not to eat it without anything to drink, especially without jam. You loaded it on that bread."

"I was hungry."

"It was too much."

"Is this the chef talking?" he asked jokingly.

"The mother in me."

"I think I'm a little too old for you to mother." Brick moved the car forward, put it in gear and opened the door.

"Two gallons, Buddy," the officer said as Brick stepped to the pump.

"Yes, sir."

Martie watched. She felt bad for Brick. He looked exhausted, but still flashed that Hollywood smile when he noticed her staring at her.

It didn't take long for him to reach two gallons. He thanked the officer and got back in the car. The flow of traffic moved steadily at a slow pace down the southbound road until it turned int TX 36 South. The road they needed to be on. A two-lane road that transformed into a four lane highway divided with a narrow concrete median strip.

Not even two miles into the new leg of the journey, traffic moved to a crawl and Brick stopped.

"Brick?" she called his name with concern.

His hands tensed and release on the wheel as he stared forward.

A barrage of honking rang out, one car tried to pass him but ended up hitting the slowed car left lane, bringing everything to a grinding halt.

"Brick?" she called his name again.

He slowly turned his head to her, his face was pale, a mustache of sweat formed on his top lip. "I gotta go." E put the car in park.

"Are you sick."

As if he didn't have control of his left hand, he reached to open the door. His hand slipped a few times.

Martie was convinced he was having a stroke or was sick from the peanut butter. She exited the car at the same time as him.

"Brick, what is it?" Martie stood outside of her door. "Let's pull over."

The honking continued.

"Get away from me," Brick shouted.

Before she could respond, she saw a man get out of the car behind them.

"Hey Buddy," the man snapped harshly. "Get in your car!"

Brick didn't respond.

Martie noticed the baseball bat in the man's hand.

She rushed to the back of the car to stop him.

"Buddy! Get your car or I'll make you get in your fucking car!"

"Stay away! Please!" Brick held up his hand.

With concern for her new friend, Martie rushed to the man. "I'll get him to move."

"Bud—"

"Back away!" Brick shouted.

Martie just wanted to deescalate the situation. They didn't need another reason for traffic to back up. Standing behind the bully man at the driver's window, she saw the parasites covering the seat.

"Oh my God," Martie gasped in revelation, reaching for the man.

He shrugged her off, sending her back a foot.

"I said…" Brick pushed him. "Back away!" Brick stepped back, trying to flee, obviously too sick to move much.

"Oh, yeah," the bully man puffed out his chest, so focused on fighting Brick he didn't notice what was happening. He reached out pulling Brick toward him.

Martie grabbed the man. "Please get away from him. Back away."

The man shoved Martie back. So hard she spun back first into the passenger door, before tripping over her own feet and falling to the ground.

She glanced up as she climbed to a stand, screaming out, "He's infected!"

But the man registered it too late. He looked at Martie and before he could turn his head back, Brick's jaw distortedly extended and he projectiled straight on to the man.

Bully man screamed and Martie scooted away, knowing the parasite were going to be everywhere. Splattering out, she supposed. That single instance caused people to actually get out of their cars and run.

They ran screaming.

Bully man dropped to the ground and Brick, enraged like some sort of monster, stood over the man, one foot to each side of his body. A body that looked like steak tar-tar.

It was obvious that Brick wasn't in control. He saw nothing but a way to replenish.

Even at a distance, Martie could see it on his face. Her friend was missing.

Arms still extended back, and jaw dropped so low he looked like a Picasso painting, Brick began to reverse vomit. Inhaling and ingesting his way to continue on.

Just as the last drop entered his mouth, he slurped a few drops before his jaw returned to normal. For a split-second Martie saw the look of remorse and hurt on Brick's face as he realized what he had done.

He didn't get a chance to say anything.

His eyes made contact with Martie before three shots rang out and Brick dropped to the ground.

Martie didn't see who shot him. It didn't matter. She was stranded on the highway, alone, in a highly contagious situation.

London, UK
10 Downing Street

It was truly the first time Farina really looked at the home or even been so close. It wasn't that extravagant for a placed that housed someone so important.

She stood outside, staring at the door, waiting. There was no guard, Farina stood in that position. Only she wasn't keeping guard, she was waiting on her team member. He seemed to be taking a while. Maybe it was just her imagination because she was overly warm and tired.

Farina couldn't recall a time since her residency days ever feeling so exhausted. So tired she could sleep in anywhere. Getting rest the night before was a bust. She didn't bother cleaning the house, she just grabbed what she needed and went back to work after the attack.

Catching a few hours in the lab, she expected the team of ten to show up to finish sweeps. Only one person did. Stephen.

He went from computer guru to search and rescue. But they found very few people to rescue in the days after everything began to fall apart.

It wasn't hopeful for them as they ventured out on this day.

The streets were quiet. No sounds of people, motor cars, buses. She knew that the UK was a day ahead of most countries in the outbreak. She wondered how the others across the globe were faring, if they were doing better than she and her team were.

Farina couldn't see how. It spread so fast, so many dead. There was no way to bury them all or even burn them. Those who were healthy and avoided the parasite had fled.

Fifteen years earlier, a freak blizzard hit London, bigger than the one in 1963. Farina was stranded at work and made house calls. Power had gone out in thousands of homes and the snow had given the impassible streets a sound-proof, deadened effect.

It felt that way to her now. Except there was a slight echo to everything.

They'd drive some then park, getting out of the car to walk and search.

On whim, they headed to Downing Street since nothing had come out from anyone in authority in over thirty-six hours.

Finally, Stephen emerged and shook his head.

"Gone?" Farina asked.

Another shake of his head. "No."

"My God," Farina gasped.

"There's no reason to do this anymore," Stephen said as they walked toward the car. "It's time for us to go. Yesterday we passed out food boxes to dead people."

Farina glanced down to her watch. "It's still early afternoon."

"It's time to stop."

"For the day?" Farina asked.

"For good."

"Someone may need our help," Farina replied. "We can't just abandon them."

"Abandon whom?" he questioned.

"People. Here or on another street. They may need help or be hungry."

"Farina, if we continue to walk these streets. We're going to be the food. The whole purpose to lock in or leave is to starve out the parasite, right? What happens when they starve. We don't know how they can get.'

But she did.

She experienced desperation the night before. A stranger, not a neighbor or someone that knew her, stalked her home, sensed her inside and came for her.

"Okay." She nodded. "You're right. So, we wrap up?"

"We head back to hospital. I think we need to find a way to secure items for when this is over. Medication and other supplies. You're a doctor, you should travel with items you need. Someone is Swayfield may need your help."

Stephen was a good man, smart and quick. She had known him since his early days on the job, coming in to work after a night at the pub, smelling like ale and downing power drinks for his hangover. That was ten years earlier and he had since outgrown that, or at least handled it better.

They drove back to HTD and after double checking the area, went inside, locking the doors behind them.

It was so empty and quiet.

After ditching the protective suits, they headed to the lab. There was something scary about the emptiness. Farina's heart beat fast, scared to death something would jump out at her at any corner.

There was a feeling of sanctuary when they entered the lounge area of the labs. That was where she had spent the night. It was more like an employee break room with a couch, table, small refrigerator and microwave. Once in there, Stephen locked the doors and pulled the blinds. "We'll gather what we can from the labs," he said. "Then hit above in the morning. After our scent has cleared."

"Scent." Farina chuckled. "Like animals are tracking us. They're humans."

"What's inside of us is not." Stephen checked his watch. "It's only a couple hours until evening. No use traveling unless you think you want to leave now."

"No. One more night won't hurt. What about you?" Farina questioned. "What are you going to do."

"I thought, if it is fine with you, I'd go to Swayfield."

"What about your mum?" Farina asked.

"She was visiting family in Scotland. So, I will search for her when it is done."

"I understand," Farina said, walking to the sink and reached for the cupboards. There were several food items in there. "Crisps for now? We have stew in a tin for dinner."

"Crisps work."

"Crisps it is." She grabbed two bags from the box then closed the door to the cupboard. "You know what's scary?" Farina handed him a bag.

"What?" Stephen asked.

"The not knowing. Not knowing if our family is fine. If what is happening here is this bad everywhere."

"We're so used to popping on our computers and getting information at our fingertips." Stephen opened his bag. "We've gone backwards in time."

"We have. No radio, tele, phones. Nothing. No communication. No leadership." She sat at the table with him. "We're in the dark about everything."

As soon as those words came from her mouth, with the sound of a power surge, all the lights went out.

Stephen chuckled. "And with that we're in the dark quite literally, as well."

Bellville, TX

Had it not been the apocalypse, Mark was certain that he would seriously love to date Alicia. It wasn't just gratefulness that she showed up at the hotel to give him a ride home to Texas as he stood on the sidewalk outside the hotel with his suitcase.

She was Dirk's sister. The former husband of one of Mark's patients. It was kind of crazy. Dirk needed to know about Martie. Mark sent Cal. Dirk sent Alicia to help Mark and then the phones went down.

Everyone was in the dark.

Mark hadn't a clue if Cal made it to Martie, had her or what.

He did know he had a ride back home.

Mark wasn't a snob by no means, but he was slightly reluctant when the tiny car pulled up. It was one of those 'smart cars', and the woman inside asked if he was Doctor Reigns.

Upon first meeting her, there was no way, no how that Alicia was his type. Alicia was a couple years younger than Mark and was on the thin side. Mark liked his women with some meat. Her hair was one cut away from a mullet and she chain smoked.

After a hundred miles, he was laughing forgetting every few miles that the world was actually falling apart. She was funny, an artsy type and explained the weird hair by telling him that she was trying to grow out her pixie cut and now she didn't have a choice but to grow it out because her hairdresser was probably giving up the craft in light of the parasites.

The smart car was just plain smart.

It was ridiculous how many miles per gallon it got. Alicia knew her car well. She knew when to stop. Most gas stations were backed up or limiting what customers could buy.

Thankfully she estimated only had to fill up three times to make it to Needville.

They took the long way, the back roads that brought them through smaller towns that had less confusion and traffic. The last fill up was two hundred miles from Needville and after twenty hours of driving.

Eventually they did come around to the topic of the parasite, that was when Mark learned not only was she funny, possibly talented, but she was smart.

He was right in his assumption that her knowledge of the current event was limited to only what was said on the news and the emergency alert system. But Alicia seemed to have a natural understanding of things and a different way of looking at everything. A view that a scientist just didn't have.

"And I am gonna assume," she said. "You guys tried the Ivermectin?"

"Yeah," Mark replied. "How did you know about that?"

"My mom was a nurse. She hated parasites."

"Yes, well, I do, too. And it's killing me."

"Because you made the book of world records for always being right?"

"No." Mark shook his head. "Yes. It's killing my confidence. I mean before this thing. Ninety-nine percent of the time I could diagnosis from symptoms, touching and sniffing. Didn't need a blood test or imaging."

"Sniffing?" she asked.

"People that are sick give off a certain scent. Not everyone can pick it up."

She asked. "Is it the same scent per person."

"No. Not all illnesses give off a smell nor do all people. It's complicated."

"Like this parasite." She lit another cigarette. "What?" she looked at him.

"Nothing." He shook his head. "You and my mother are gonna get along great," Mark commented. "Not sure how you're gonna keep up the habit if the world falls apart."

"I'm sure I'll find them and honestly," she said. "I'm not worried about the consequences of smoking now." She exhaled. "Back to the parasite. I've been waiting a thousand miles to talk to you about this."

"Why did you wait?"

"Thought maybe being the 'know all' guy, I would be beneath you with the conversation."

"Please." Mark scoffed. "I am so down to earth. Plus, I know very little. Granted, I understand it's been less than two weeks, and that's not a lot of time. But we know nothing. We don't know how many times they are able to recycle."

"Recycle?" she asked.

"Regurgitate the parasite and ingest what it does to the person they get. We don't know how many times a day, how often."

"Then start with what you do know. Where did it originate?"

"Moldova," replied Mark. "It's been there awhile the parasite that turns people into storage hosts is very hard to get. It really is my new friend Jude and his family have been tracking this thing for a long time, keeping it under control. Unfortunately, a soccer team and their families ingested the infected animal."

"Which was?"

"A wolf or dog. It's called a lycanthropic parasite."

"A werewolf parasite?"

"No."

"Yes." She nodded. "Myths and legends have them come in all shapes and sized and have different effect. A duh…silver attracts and kills it."

"Werewolf." Mark shook his head. "No."

"Not the Lon Chaney, furry kind. Just saying," she said. "What else are you certain of."

"If you get the parasite, more than likely you die fast. Or you become a storage host or Alpha as the radio calls them."

"Do you know how they are able to, for lack of better word, vomit the parasite on to people."

"I do," Mark answered. "They parasite actually forms a new gland between in the digestive system. It burrows a new hole in the esophagus that's how it ejects or projects. It's pretty interesting, you can actually see it on a body scan. I'm not sure what causes the acid effect. How many times it recycles. I mean, really, I know feasibly, hide out, don't give the parasite a host and they'll implode with parasites…theoretically. But how long? I mean, how long can a storage host last."

"Three weeks," Alicia replied, very matter of fact.

"Excuse me?"

"Give or take. How long does it take the human body to starve or even die of thirst. Not long, right. If they have a hole in their esophagus, chances are they aren't eating and if they do, it's hard. I'm going to say they are digesting or absorbing anything they eat. They're not dead. They need to eat and not just flesh they regurgitate."

"That's a brilliant theory. I wish we knew," Mark said.

"We do know this. Whether it's stopping them from finding a host or letting them starve, they aren't undead, they will die Let's hope that it doesn't end because the parasite has killed so many people, there's no one left to be a host or food."

"That would be devasting."

"You think?"

Mark was taking a moment, he looked out the window as Alicia drove around cars. There were so many dead. On the road, in cars. He didn't spot any signs of projectile. Then again, he may have missed it. He and Alicia were engrossed.

"All this." Alicia pointed. "This is scary. Look how fast we as a human race died."

"Alicia, slow down."

"Why?"

"Look," Mark said. "Someone walking."

"Uh, Doc, you said not to stop. Even the radio says don't pick up stranger."

"I know," Mark stated. "But I think we know her."

I'm gonna die, Martie cried as she had those thoughts.

She would die somehow trying not to destroy another human being, more than likely on the side of the road, never seeing her children again.

Several people stopped and offered her a ride, but she didn't think it was fair to accept a ride. Martie didn't know if a parasite entered her or not. Brick tried to stay away from her, but he shed them.

She heard another car slow down behind her. People were so kind to offer a ride and she felt so bad turning them down. She'd do it again if the current stranger offered. They were stopping, she could tell.

"Martie," the voice called to her.

She stopped then slowly turned and looked over her shoulder. She gasped emotionally when she saw Mark get out of the truck along with her former sister-in-law.

"That is you." He rushed to her and looked relieved. "We were so worried. Dirk and the kids are out of their minds sick with worry about you. I'm sorry. I am so sorry I had to leave town. I sent my brother to find you, but the phones went down."

She stepped back. "Doctor Reigns, Brick is dead."

"Brick?"

"Goldman."

"Oh." Mark nodded and cringed. "I'm sorry." He reached for her.

Martie shook her head. "Please step back."

Alicia tried as well to reach for her. "Martie, please."

Martie shook her head. "Please stay away."

"Martie, did one get in you?" Mark asked.

"I don't know."

"What do you mean?"

Martie whimpered. "I don't know. I didn't feel it, but Brick had…there were a lot in the car."

"When was this?"

"An hour ago."

"Martie, get in the car. If it's only been an hour or even half a day, you're fine. You're safe. We know that. We can test you with a scan."

"But you can't cure me?"

Mark shook his head. "I'm sorry."

She sobbed once. "I just wanted to see my kids. That's all I wanted was to see my kids."

"That…I can do." Mark opened the back door. "Get in, Martie. Even if you have a parasite, there is still time to see your children."

Martie was reluctant. "Are you sure."

Mark reached out placing his hand on her arm. "I'm sure." He locked eyes with her. "Get in."

TWENTY-THREE

ALAS HOPE

Needville, TX

When Cal saw Glen stomping his foot and moving in circles, admittedly he was worried. He was pounding those clod hopper boots to the ground.

"Did you see one?" Cal asked as they walked down the small side street from the car.

"Huh?" Glen asked confused.

"See one. A parasite?"

"What? No! Why? Did you?"

"No. But you're over there stomping."

"Oh, yeah, sorry, my foot is itchy."

Cal shook his head. "Good. Because I was going to be surprised."

"I wouldn't be. It won't be long."

Cal stopped walking. "They aren't coming here."

"How can you be so sure?"

"Because no one leaves their houses or land anyhow. Telling them to stay inside is meaningless to them. Most of them

261

barely leave but to get supplies and when they do, they stock up."

"We don't know how long," Glen stated.

"Long enough that we can do this," Cal replied. "Long enough that you can't keep scanning yourself every hour. You're gonna radiate yourself."

"Maybe it will protect me," Glen replied.

"No. Jude said that doesn't. work. Everything is alright. Trust me. I took a ride, it's fine outside."

But Cal knew it wasn't. He had taken a ride out onto TX 36 and saw the maze of abandoned cars, the carcasses of not only animals but people. He didn't tell Glen or even his mother. He told Jude who didn't seem surprised. Jude was the battle-weary warrior who knew he lost the war. Still in the mode to never give or surrender.

"Don't worry. We got this," Cal reiterated as he approached the modular home just on the edge of the business section of town. It had been for sale, but now had occupants.

Cal knocked.

Dirk opened the door. "Hi Chief."

"Hey, Dirk. How's the family?" Cal asked.

"Fine. The boys are worried about their mother. Any word?"

Cal shook his head. "No, but she was gone so she's more than likely finding her way here. Roads are bad out there so travel is not going to be easy."

"I understand."

"Do you need anything?" Cal asked. "How's your wife."

"Stressed, but you'll have that."

"Not that you have to, but…we're having a town meeting tonight at eight for anyone that wants to come. Discuss what we can do as a community to beat this. Glen here." Cal pointed back. "Has a TSA body scanner at the door, so you can rest assured no one is going to be carrying a parasite in. There will be food. We're wanna cook things off before the power hoes out. And it will."

"Thank you, Chief. What happens if someone walks through, and they have a parasite."

"The parasitic gland is where they come to maturity." Cal winked. "I sound smart when I say that huh? It's a bridge we will cross if we get to it. Anyhow, Jude, who is an expert will be able to tell if they're, well, ready to blow. Rest assured we're not gonna shoot them like a dog."

"That's good to hear. We'll be by, thank you."

Cal nodded and turned. He saw Glen shaking his head. "Dude, what?"

"Shoot them like a dog. Yeah, you don't sound cold."

Cal shrugged. "I have no idea what we'll do, that just came out."

"Are you okay?" Glen asked as they walked back to the car. "Are you worried about Mark."

"I am. I very worried. It's been a day and a half since I got him in touch with Dirk's sister."

"I get it, we don't know if they made a connection. If they did, that's a long haul. You said yourself the roads are bad."

"You're right."

Cal wasn't convinced, but he couldn't dwell on it, he had to focus on keeping his town and his mother safe.

They drove back to Ma and Joe's where Jude and Connie were inside.

"Oh, you're back, thank God," Connie said. "I was worried."

"We're fine," Cal replied and stepped in farther.

On the bar were more silver mini arrows, and Cal noticed them right away. "You have been busy. You think we're gonna get hit by a group or something."

"I think," Jude replied. "The longer they search for a host, the more they will hunt."

Glen spoke up. "Here's what I don't get. They're human right? They aren't zombies or rage infected, they have their thoughts."

"But they are distorted," said Jude. "I can't say for sure on anything because this has never gotten this far. Close when my great grandfather released it. But according to that journal and what the doctor from the UK said, the hunger and need to replicate drives the host to the point they can't control themselves."

Glen nodded. "They got some good information from that guy before he died. But what do we do if they do come in a large group. I mean we are right off a main exodus route."

Cal lifted an arrow. "We take them out. Trust me they want to die, they just don't know how."

Connie shook her head. "Cal, these things throw the acid vomit at you. Not to mention drop so many parasites, they infect everyone. They can't control it, it's as if an uninfected person causes an instant gag reflex."

"Wow," Glen commented. "Connie, that's super insightful. And right on. Each potential victim is a trigger."

"I'm not worried," said Cal. "You're only a trigger if you're not immune."

Glen chuckled. "Dude, this isn't a virus. There's no immunity to this thing."

"Invisibility then?" Cal questioned. "Whatever you call it. Jude?"

Jude nodded. "There are some the parasites do not want as hosts. They aren't triggers. They can fight the storage hosts."

"That's me." Cal smiled. "I'm immune or rather ... invisible."

Glen grunted. "I wish you would stop saying that and taking chances as if you are. One parasite rejected you. It doesn't mean you're an unwanted host. The only way that can happen is if by chance you're already a host or terminally ill."

Before anything further could be said, a clearing of a throat drew their attention.

Cal spun around and grinned. "Mark." He rushed over to him and embraced him. "Brother, thank God."

"Markie." Connie shrieked and ran to him. She hugged him as well, then looked at Alicia. "Oh, wait until your brother knows you're alright."

"He's here?" Alicia asked. "He and his family made it?"

Connie nodded then turned to Mark. "Cal and Glen went looking for Martie but no luck."

"We did," Mark stated. "She's in the car."

Looking perplexed, Connie tilted her head. "Why is she in the care. We should take her to see her family. They're at the Caldwell rental."

Mark shook his head. "She won't budge, she was exposed to the parasites."

Jude asked. "How long ago?"

"About two hours, maybe four."

Jude shook his head. "If she was infested and she's not dead, she can only be a storage host and she should still be safe to see her family."

Cal pointed. "We have that TSA scanner. We'll scan her tonight."

Alicia spoke up, "If you tell me where my brother is staying, I'll take her to see the kids and tell her she is safe."

"It's mile from here," Glen answered. "You can't miss it. Make a left at the crossroads, follow those two blocks and it's the only blue modular home on that street. Can't miss it."

Alicia nodded. "Thank you. I'll see you in a bit, Mark."

"Yes, and thank you again." Mark walked to the bar. "I need a drink." He paused when he noticed the arrows. What is this?"

Jude replied. "Silver. An immediate line of defense."

"Yu have a lot," Mark said. "Which is good because there are a lot out there. It's only a matter of time before they reach Needville."

"See," Cal said. "We'll be ready. Or rather, I'll be ready."

Glen huffed. "Can you stop please. You are not an invincible hero. You act like you can go out there all one-man band and take them out."

"I can," Cal replied. "It's not like a pack of wild dogs. They don't attack unless you trigger them. I don't."

Another huff and Glen shook his head. "You are not invisible or, how do you put it, immune, they'll get you. Mark." Glen faced Mark. "You're the expert. Can you tell your brother that he can get hit as easy as anyone. That he's not some invincible, invisible host."

"Actually," Mark spoke solemnly. "He is."

<><><><>

At first Connie nearly collapsed to the floor, then she cried for a moment before she poured a drink and regained her composure.

"Mark, sweetie," she said with quivering words. "You're expert. You're the smartest man I know. Tell me this is or could be the one percent that you're wrong."

Mark drew in his bottom lip and shook his head. "No, mom. I'm not wrong."

Connie whimpered. "Cal."

Cal winced. "Mom, stop. There's a ton of bigger fish to fry right now, so stop."

"Stop? Stop?" she asked. "You're my son. Look at Glen. This is devastating to him as well."

Glen leaned against the bar, his head hung low. He waved out his hand. "I just can't. Don't." He closed his eyes tightly.

"Oh my God." Cal threw his head back. "Mark, please tell them I'm alright."

Mark held up his hand. "When Cal told me about some minor symptoms, I guessed it right away, then we ran tests. He has a malignant growth on his left kidney. Biopsy confirmed it is a malignancy."

"When?" Connie asked. "When were you going to tell me."

"I was scheduled for surgery tomorrow," Cal said. "I planned on telling you beforehand. I didn't want you to worry. But then, you know the world fell apart. So, you see, that parasite rejected me because he doesn't want me. None of them do."

With a sigh, Glen looked up. "Why do you sound so happy about this?"

"Happy?" Cal asked. "Because the one thing that could kill me is the one thing that will allow me to save this town, to protect my family. I can do what none of you can," Cal said. "I can fight them, and I will win."

TWENTY-FOUR

A VIEW FROM OUTSIDE

Houston, TX

Who was Harding Taylor? He was a man. Any man. In fact, Harding Taylor represented every man, every person on the face of the earth as the unprecedented, extinction level event unfolded at lightning speed.

His thoughts, fears, worries, uncharacteristic behavior in the wake of it all was no different than anyone else's behavior.

It wasn't a fight or flight for survival. It was fight *and* flight.

From his point of view what was a blip on the news, a tragedy with celebrities, steam rolled into devastation. There were no answers and even if there were, there was no way to get them.

No phones. No internet and now, no electricity.

Fight and flight.

Harding decided on flight.

He'd fight if he had to, but flight was the current choice.

Everywhere was a reminder of what was happening. He tried to think of the helpful hints so called experts gave on the news before it went down. He bashed his brain thinking of that

269

recording from the emergency alert system that played over and over again. One he swore he could repeat verbatim. But the moment it stopped, Harding couldn't recall too much of what was told to him.

What to do if faced with an alpha, how to spot on.

He had heard from others that failed that the roads were increasingly impassible. Highways jammed with stalled or wrecked vehicles, traffic lights out and Alphas searching the road for meal selections like a buffet.

He had heard rumors two days earlier when there was a speck of internet that the city was getting people out on busses, trains and ships.

The bust station was insane, so he headed toward Amtrack.

In what looked like rush hour on maximum overdrive when he arrived. But it was his best shot. Actually, his only shot, he abandoned his car in traffic blocks beforehand. Turning into one of those people that jammed the roads.

He moved with the wave of people, trying to push through families to get to the station. It was easier for him, he was alone. No one to tote along, hold on to or account for.

It took him an hour but when he finally got close to the building, he saw at that at one point earlier, they had been scanning people. The body scanner archway still remained, but those who manned it, left their post.

It was people fighting to get on a train. Any train leaving the city.

The line extended far and wide as people pushed to get through.

He kept a look out for his friend James. He worked with him at the insurance company and James had put off leaving. Swearing that staying put was the best thing to do, even though James' pregnant sister begged him to leave. He was firm on not leaving. Something told Harding that James wasn't far behind in abandoning Houston.

The noise level was unbearable, people screaming, shouting and crying. He witnessed two fist fights, but Harding kept going, he just wanted to get on the train, more so just in the station.

Eventually the trains would stop running.

As he finally neared the doors, Harding saw it on the outside wall of the Houston Train Station. A off white building always clean was now spray painted with the red words, 'This is how it ends.'

As if something from a movie.

It got him to thinking about an old piece of prose.

A dismal poem made popular by TS Eliot included similar words, 'This is the way the world ends.' A fragmented piece of poetry, filled with scattered thoughts. It inferred that the world would go quietly and not with a bang. Many believed it to be written about a plague, when in fact, it tells of a world drying up, life becoming dust. That was what Harding interpreted it as meaning.

Because in no way would a world go out with a whimper.

Man was too resilient. They would kick and scratch for a chance to survive, as everyone was doing at that station.

Harding was a tall man; he had the advantage of seeing ahead if he stood on tip toes. He saw two police officers doing their best to help people in.

With a strange feeling in his gut that it was his last chance, he ditched his bag and slithered his way through the throngs of people. He lost count of how many people hit him, kicked and pulled at him. He didn't care. He was getting on that train.

He was close, maybe five feet. He could see the windows and how crowded it was. People stood int the aisles, crammed in.

The someone shouted out, "Oh my God, it's the last train."

A wave of screams rang out, it made his ears ring and everyone behind him rushed forward.

The moment of the push projected Harding forward and he lunged for the open doorway. He was on the opening step when someone pulled at him to make their own way. It was a woman. Harding didn't know that until he shoved her from him and watched her fall to the ground.

It was as if she wasn't even there, people stepped on her, trampling her, her body was a stepping-stone. The police officer near the door disappeared. Probably the same fate as the woman or maybe he made it inside.

The door closed and hands kept trying to open in.

Standing on that step, two others behind him, Harding watched the people grab on to the train. In such desperation, they held on as it started to move, each dropping off one by one.

When the train cleared the station, he let out a sigh of relief. He didn't know where he was going, but was certain the train would take them from the city. There was no way it was making another stop. It was filled to capacity.

He planned on staying right there near the door, it was too crowded to even go into the main cars. He had room to breathe. No one shared those steps with him, the closest was the man in the baseball cap at the top of the steps.

So many people were crying at first, it was an orchestra of sobs. Then it grew quiet sans a few sniffles and coughs.

Perhaps people were in shock.

In his little nook of the train entrance, Harding felt safe, out of the woods. That didn't last for long. Not fifteen minutes into the fast-moving train ride, he heard a scream.

A loud, loud shrill scream, which then caused an eruption of screaming.

Hurriedly, Harding looked behind him, the man in the baseball cap charged for the train car in some heroic move. Before long multitudes of screams filled the car, and Harding watching people racing to get to the train car behind them.

It was as if they didn't even see him, and that was a good thing.

Eyes tightly closed, Harding crouched down on that bottom step near the door. Damn right he was scared, he knew what was happening.

Something horrifying, deadly. It was what the news warned about. It had to be.

It was happening.

All while the train kept rolling.

Faster.

Faster.

The screams had a domino effect, they moved away like thunder, growing distant, weaker, until done.

He stayed there for the longest time, knees bent up, crammed against that door with his hands to his ears. Harding didn't know how long. He had no plans on moving until the train stopped.

It just…stopped.

Not hearing anything, Harding slowly stood and peered out the door window. They weren't at a train station, they were in the middle of nowhere.

Fearful, he turned around, at the top of the three steps were two bodies. They looked like they just dropped.

"Someone," a woman cried. "Oh God, is anyone else alive?"

After hesitating, Harding stepped up. And moved to the car. It was difficult. There was no stepping over bodies easily, he had to maneuver his foot so as not to step on someone one.

He saw the woman mid car, standing between the row of seats. She was older, maybe in her seventies. Her hands covered in blood. As she seemed to be staring down to someone or something. He didn't walk to her because it was impossible.

The dead lay everywhere. He didn't see anyone bloody or murdered. How did she get the blood on her hands.

The woman made eye contact with Harding. "My husband. The man just…he shot this stuff on him. There's nothing left."

She shook her head sobbing, "Why didn't he get me? Why am I not dead? He just walked by me. Why?"

"I…I don't know."

"Did he walk by you, too?"

"Who?" Harding asked.

"The man who started all—" The woman never finished her sentence, because she screamed. It was horrifying.

Why was she screaming. Harding realized she wasn't looking at him and he turned around.

He jolted at the sight of the man standing there on top of the bodies. His face pasty white, blood smeared around his mouth. He trembled some, coughing.

Two words.

The man spoke two words.

"I'm sorry."

His chest protruded, head went back, and his jaw dropped at least six inches.

There was no time to register what was happening or to even run. Before Harding knew it, the man ejected from his mouth a blasting red, blood substance. It landed smack center of Harding cores. It didn't hurt when it hit him, but after a moment it was the most excruciating, burning pain Harding ever felt. Insides sizzling, collapsing.

The pain didn't last long.

Harding died within thirty seconds.

His train ride to safety was over.

TWENTY-FIVE

DESPERATION

London, UK

Farina hadn't planned to sleep in her car when she was done with her final day of work. She already packed what she needed and planned, like she had done the previous night, to sleep in the reception break area of the lab.

She never planned on staying in London more than another day.

It was over. At least for what Farina could do. She had to worry about herself. For her husband's sake she needed to survive and get to him.

Every hour she stayed in London increased the chances that she wouldn't.

Nothing went as planned.

The only part of the plan that was still on the table was leaving at first light when the roads were lit by the light of day.

Once the power went out it was black.

The emergency lights in HTD lasted two hours and as they flickered their last bit of juice, Farina and Stephen, with the supplies they gathered, made their way to car and then to a parking lot four blocks away.

It was just as dark outside. An overcast night gave very little moonlight, there were no parking lot spotlights or streetlamps.

With very little conversation between them they shared cold stew from a tin and sipped whiskey they found stashed in the director's bottom drawer.

At first it was fine. Just quiet, then things turned.

Farina likened her and Stephen to that neighbor everyone had. The neighbor that would cook or grill outdoors and the aroma carried to everyone.

She reclined her driver's seat, resting her elbow on the edge of the car door and leaned toward the window. It was hot and she tried to catch a breeze for comfort. Farina had just become comfortable, her eyelids fluttering in that mediation state just before sleep when she was jolted awake.

A 'rustling in the seat' sound broke the silence, quickly followed by Stephen's, "Oh, shit. Shit. Shit. Shit."

Farina tried to process what was happening. She heard the tapping, and she shifted her eyes over to his hand as he frantically tried to close the window.

"Turn on the car. Turn it on now."

Eyes casting upward, Farina saw the man outside Stephen's window. His chest broad, arms back, mouth wide.

Hurriedly she turned over the engine. As soon as she did, Stephen's window went up. As soon as it secured in a closed position, not a split second later, the window was blasted with the red regurgitation.

Hand shaking, Farina pushed the button to put her own window up and was thrown into a state of panic when she saw another host, this one a woman, preparing to release by her window.

She wasn't alone. There were more. At least a dozen.

The window went up and Farina avoided being blasted in a nick of time.

"Go. Go," Stephen ordered. "Go."

She threw the gear shift in drive just as another host blasted the front windscreen, making it impossible to see. Farina didn't care. She slammed her foot on the accelerator immediately hearing and feeling the 'thump' of hitting someone.

It wasn't the only person she hit.

Thump. Bang.

Impact after impact. Bodies rolling against the roof as she plowed through.

Farina tensed up trying not to scream, feeling internally every person she hit.

She couldn't see. The instinct of turning on the wipers made everything worse. As if she ran into a mud puddle and tried to clear it. They smeared everything in a thick velvety manner. Farina pressed and held the button for windscreen fluid. The continuous flow of substance sprayed against the red on the windscreen eventually clearing it enough for her to see outlines of images.

She kept it going, wipers at fast speed until the windscreen was clear enough for her to see.

Stephen closed all the vents and turned on the interior light.

"Do you see any?" Farina asked.

"No. I'll keep looking."

"Where do we go?"

"I don't know," Stephen replied. "Just drive. Keep going maybe we'll find someplace remote."

"Should we head to Swayfield?" Farina asked.

"We can try, but it may be too dark. Just whatever we do, we need to save enough petrol to get to Swayfield."

Farina nodded her agreement. They were in a very metro and crowded area and it was far from safe. She was scared, fearing the parasites in the bloody substance would make it into the car. They couldn't put the windows down or turn on a fan. For one hour at least they had to drive around in the airtight vehicle.

The heat was intense and so was the stress. Any relaxation she received from that tiny bit of whiskey was gone.

Farina could barely breathe, barely think. Her heart raced so fast she thought it would burst from her chest. So close to leaving, so close to finding sanctuary in a remote village and they were locked in a box of horror. A concrete jungle with so many streets and buildings. It was hard to know where she was driving and if she was just going in circles.

The side windows were covered, seeing out of them was impossible, but at least Farina could now see out the windscreen. Not that she wanted to. Seeing ahead brought the frightening sight of what was out there. *They* wandered the streets. Men and women, but no children. Farina wondered about that. Why hadn't she seen any children. Were their delicate bodies too fragile to handle being storage hosts. Did they just succumb like Susan did? Those out on the streets at night, waking in the dark had to be storage hosts. Anyone else was either gone or dead. There weren't moving in thousands or even hundreds like some zombie horde in a movie. Dotting the sidewalk here in there, moving about at a slow pace, looking, searching. It was as if they were suddenly energized the moment the car drove by them.

Attention was caught, something stirred in them and they came for the car.

Farina knew they, like Tip the Drummer, were in control of their faculties. Until, as Tip told Farina, he was exposed to something that stirred the eruption of the parasites within.

In a desolate city, void of life, void of possible new hosts, those already infected were subconsciously frantic to find someone, something to release upon. They didn't know they were until they caught the scent.

All of them. All of the created storage hosts went from tragic victims to being nothing more than desperate hunters in the night.

TWENTY-SIX

LAST STAND

Ma and Joe's – Needville, PA

The fires of Houston lit up the eastern sky. Glen knew that's what it had to be, a dull glow that had been growing. It reminded him of the wildfires in California. In the distance but still threatening.

In the years he had been at Ma and Joe's, he had never seen that many people in the building. The structure fire code estimated it held three hundred. It was so packed for the meeting and free food, Glen was certain there were more. Only once had he seen close to that many people and that was when Ma and Joe's had the Bingo Mania giveaway.

He was glad he fired up the grill in the back in case the power went down. Glen wasn't sure how they still had it, most of the area had gone dark the day before. The grill provided an extra area for cooking all that food, the kitchen in Ma and Joe's just wasn't big enough.

Another reason Glen was happy about having power…the TSA Body scanner.

Every single person that walked in, walked through the scanner and did so happily.

No infestations, at least none that Mark or Jude saw. The only one that didn't go through was Martie. She was waiting until the thirteenth hour, a time she knew if she had been infected by a parasite, that it would show.

And that's where they were. Approaching that final hour. The time frame where she'd know the truth. Even if the power did go out, Glen was ready with the generator.

Mark assured her, even though Glen was certain Martie knew, that she would have warning signs. Which was one of the reasons she wouldn't eat. Glen tried to get her to try one of his famous burgers, but she said she was scared. She recalled that Brick had severe indigestion before he 'erupted'. A sign that his esophagus was already compromised.

The meeting didn't last long, just long enough for everyone to agree on a course of action and to get volunteers. It ended right before night fall. While a handful of people stayed at Ma and Joe's to enjoy a little normalcy of music and drinks, the rest left to hunker down and secure their animals as well. The radio would provide them contact with Cal who would patrol the streets.

Even Connie left. She took a bottle, of course, along with Alicia, but promised Cal she would lock up the house until Mark got there.

Terminal illness was a shield against parasite infestation. The parasites would avoid those who with illness, leaving them to wither and die in an hour. If there was no scent to catch, no host body to pursue, they wouldn't move.

After getting assurance from Jude and Mark, four towns-people volunteered to patrol the streets and keep people safe. Four people other than Cal who were sick with cancer or a severe anemia like Sickle Cell or Aplastic.

They just had to wait it out.

Watch carefully those who drove through town or even stopped. Those fleeing were still driving by, that was evident by the burnt wreckage outside the bar.

It wouldn't take long. A couple weeks of diligence and would starve out the parasite one way or another. No more hosts or no more people.

The storage hosts would expire eventually. Even if they continued to pass the parasite, they couldn't live longer than a couple weeks without food.

Storage hosts couldn't eat.

If they hit the eruption stage and didn't have a host to infect, they would relinquish anyhow from any and every body orifice.

The only way to stop the horrendous death and release of parasites from the body was to use silver to draw them to one point.

That was the topic of conversation with Martie and her family.

She spent time outside with them, keeping her distance. Glen was nearby and he hated hearing the desperate words of a woman who was scared she would leave her children.

"I don't want to projectile," Martie said.

"We will cross that bridge when we get to it," Dirk told her.

"We need to cross it now, Dirk." Martie glanced at her children then to Carrie. "This is a real possibility. I want you know I am not going to drag this out. If I have it, put me down. Do not let me get to that point." She held her hand up to Dirk stopping him from talking and she turned to his wife. "Carrie, I know you love my boys. So, I'm not gonna ask you to promise me something that I know you'll do. So, thank you. Just have that baby and give my…our sons a focus of love."

Carrie nodded, then cringed, her hand going to her stomach.

"Are you alright?" Martie asked. "Are you having pains?"

"I've been, yes. Mark is already aware."

Glen did his bartender thing, looking busy while listening to every word said. Did he hear right? Was Carrie in labor? He felt bad for her if she was. Mark was a great virologist or whatever he was, he just wasn't a baby doctor, did he even know what to do?

"Mom," Martie's oldest son spoke. "We love you. You're gonna be fine, okay. No parasite is in you. You're fine."

"Let's hope," Martie replied. "But if—"

"Martie," Dirk cut her off. "We'll cross that bridge when we get there. Alright?"

Glen watched the family interaction, like an audience, and he felt it in his gut when Jude and Cal walked up to Martie.

Cal placed his hand on her shoulder. "It's time."

<><><><>

Run.

James Conrad dropped his phone in frustration and when he lifted it the light illuminated the desecrated body of the old man.

He had pulled over to help the elderly man. In his rush to leave the city, he had made progress. Broke free of the chaos and he thought the spreaders.

Yet, the old man now lay on the road a victim of a parasite carrier, and someone stole James' car.

It wasn't a good situation.

James knew they recycled their parasitic load. Ejecting it in some sort of acid blood on to their victims. The substance turned insides into gel so the host could ingest and make more parasites.

He guessed.

James didn't know.

The news and updates had stopped, and he only had so much information. He had heard from his friend and coworker, Harding that whoever was a carrier passed it along and kept on going.

They also shed them and that was another reason James ran.

He made some distance from the body and did that 'horror film' mistake and turned to look behind him. When he did, he tripped over his feet and fell to the pavement. Not before he saw he was being pursued not by one but three people.

He was injured, knees burning, but that was nothing compared to what would happen to him if they caught up to him.

He scurried to his feet and without missing a beat, ran.

His goal was that bar on the side of the road, the one with the music playing and neon sign.

People were there.

Someone would help.

James kept thinking, Run, just run.

He did.

"You're going to be fine," Cal assured Martie as he stood behind her just before the archway that was set up a few feet inside by the front doors. "You got this."

Martie whispered. "I know it's in me."

"You don't know."

"I know. I have such a feeling."

"It's fear," Cal said. "Get it over with. Find out and be relieved. Because the not knowing is horrible, trust me."

Martie nodded nervously.

Cal looked over her shoulder. Mark and Jude stood together staring at the screen. Glen was there as well, a few steps behind them.

Her family waited. All standing there. Carrie held tight to her stomach, diligently fighting off what could only be labor pains. Putting on a front that she was alright. And those in the bar that didn't know Martie, tried to pretend they weren't paying attention. Cal knew they were.

Everyone wanted to know.

Mark instructed. "Step in. Arms out and take a breath."

Martie glanced at Cal and stepped into the archway doing as Mark instructed.

"Hold still," Mark said.

Cal shifted his eyes from Martie to Mark. He knew his brother better than anyone and would get the answer just by Mark's face, no matter how stoic his brother tried to project.

It was tough for a second to read Mark. The corner of his mouth raised some, then Mark looked at Jude. The second Mark did that, Cal knew.

Mark's head lowered for a second. "I'm sorry, Martie."

Several reactions swept over the bar. Martie gave none, bravely stepping backwards.

Carrie let out a whimper of a sob.

Martie's two sons rushed for her. she held up her hand. "Keep them back, Dirk."

Dirk grabbed on to the boys.

The youngest child cried out, "Mommy."

"It's our mom, let us hug our mom," her oldest said.

"Jed, no," Martie told him. "Stay with Dad. Stay away, what's inside of me I can't control."

Cal could see the pain on Martie's face, how badly she wanted to give her children one last hug, But she couldn't take that chance.

287

"Are you sure?" Cal asked Mark. 'Do you need to check again."

Jude replied. "We're sure. It's there."

Martie inhaled deeply, lifting her shoulders in a sign of courage and faced her sons. "Boys, if I could hold you right now, I would. But I can't take a chance they won't come from me. Know I love you both so very much. You have Carrie and your father. I will always be with you."

Both her sons cried out, "Mom!" painfully and Martie turned to face Cal.

"I may shed," she said softly.

"I know," Cal replied.

Her eyes cast down to the holster on his belt. "You have that knife. Is it silver?"

"It is."

"Can I have it?"

Cal reached for it.

"Cal!" Glen called out. "What are you doing?"

"What are the options here?" Cal asked.

"Not to give her the knife. Let's find another way," Glen said. "Mark? Come on. You're the big shot here. Jude, what can we do."

Jude sucked in his bottom lip. "I'm afraid not much."

Martie glanced back over her shoulder. It was hard, her family was crying. Cal knew how difficult a decision it was for her. He wasn't going to make it harder.

"Cal, please. The knife." Martie held out her hand.

Cal placed his hand on the blade.

"Help!" the man blasted through the bar. "Help! Lock the doors, Help!"

Cal spun around to the man that charged in the bar.

"James?" Carrie called out.

"Carrie?" James stepped forward. "Oh my God."

"Wait." Cal held up his hand. "You know each other."

James pointed. "That's my sister. But right now lock up."

"What's going on?" Cal asked.

"Those vomiting carriers," James said. "They're chasing me."

Jude rushed to the window.

"Shit," Cal cursed.

Splash.

Carrie groaned out.

Cal's eyes widened. "Did her water just break that loudly?" he looked at the huge puddle at her feet. "It did."

"Oh my God." Carrie buckled. "This is happening fast. I tried not to say anything."

Mark rushed to her. "How far apart."

"I have pressure."

"Shit." Cal repeated. "Jude?"

Jude looked back. "They're out there."

"Okay," Cal said calmly. "We can't get these people out. Jude there are two walk ins in the back. Get everyone back there. They're airtight. Everyone…" Cal shouted. "In the back."

Those in the bar ran to the back.

Glen pointed to Carrie. "What about her?"

"Get her in the units as well," Cal said rushed.

"She's having a baby, Cal," Glen stated.

"No shit."

"Oh my God, that has to be a code violation."

Cal grunted. "Go!"

Mark stepped to him. "Cal, what are you doing?"

"Taking them out. They won't hurt me. Go. Get her back there." Cal watched Mark hurriedly usher Martie's family to the back.

"Cal," Jude said. "Hit them with silver. If they had done it before a bullet won't kill them."

"I know. Get in the back"

"No," Jude said. "This is my fight too."

Martie looked at Cal. "I'll help you."

Jude handed Martie a mini crossbow. "One is loaded in." He handed her two small arrows. "You shouldn't need more."

"Can I use this on myself?"

Jude didn't answer.

The door to the bar kicked up with a bang and the large man stepped in. His face and shirt bloody, eyes holding a maddening look. He turned Jude's way and Cal could tell the host was immediately triggered by him.

Shoulder first, Cal did his best wrestling move and speared the host with everything he had. The force of Cal's body pushed the man out the door and onto the porch.

The man didn't go down. He stumbled back, regained his composure and looked beyond Cal, finding something or someone more enticing.

Who was he focusing on?

Jude.

He hadn't gone with the others and just being there sparked something in the bloody stranger.

The Host puffed out his chest, threw back his head and arms and dropped his jaw. Without hesitation, Cal whipped out the knife and in a swift backward swing, sliced the throat of the host.

As he teetered back, a tiny arrow hit him in his upper chest. Immediately it began to bulge as the parasites gathered to the silver. He dropped down.

Cal turned around. Martie held the crossbow

"Just making sure he doesn't blast those things everywhere out of his body," she said.

"You." Cal pointed at Jude. "Get inside, now!"

"No." Jude shook s head. "I told you, this is my fight."

"And your death."

"Guys," Martie called out. "Look."

Cal spun to see even more walking their way. To make it even more strange, Cars were stopping at random, with people stumbling out, focused on the bar. "They're driving now?" Cal asked.

"They're human, Cal," Jude replied. "They only stop following that human instinct when they see a potential host. Me. I'm bait. Use me."

Cal grunted. "Just keep a distance, away from the building, we don't need you to get one." He looked at Martie. "Ready? Hit them anywhere."

Martie nodded. "I'm going to need more of these arrows."

Jude handed her some.

"I'm ready," Martie said.

Before stepping off the porch of the bar, Cal lifted his radio. "If anyone from my appointed immune squad if listing, we can use your help at Ma and Joe's."

The signal was bad, and the words broke up on Glen's radio but he got the gist of it. Cal was placing a call for back up. If Cal was calling for help, something big was happening. Glen thought about going out to help, then changed his mind. He even briefly worried about Connie, then remembered she wasn't along.

Glen was squeamish as it was and being in a ten-by-ten sealed cold room with a woman on the floor about to give birth didn't help his wincing factor.

Sure, half of those in the bar went into the freezer while the other half crammed in the refrigerator, but Glen still felt bad for Carrie. He supposed the pain was bad, but it couldn't have been worse than having a room full of stranger in her personal space while her birthing ready nether region was exposed for all to see.

It was no wonder Mark was arguing with her.

"Carrie, you have to help me out here," Mark said, positioned by her feet. "You have to let this baby come."

"Uh, Mark," Glen said. "You're adding pressure she doesn't need. I'm sure ass a mother she knows best."

"Really, Glen?" Mark snapped. "What do you know about this?"

"I know yelling at her isn't helping," Glen said.

Carrie cried. "I can't do this."

Glen asked innocently. "Would it help if we all turned and faced a wall. I know I can't pee if someone is watching—"

"Glen!" Mark barked. "It's not the same thing. She is holding back."

"Then it is the same thing."

"No," Mark said frustrated. "She is holding back. She won't let the baby come and it has nothing to do with people in the room. And she needs to let go and give birth. The top of the baby's head is protruding from the—"

"Stop. No." Glen said. "I don't need to know."

"Mark," Carrie wept. "I don't want to do this. What if it has parasites."

"It doesn't. He or she doesn't. We're in an airtight room."

"Oh my God," Glen exclaimed. "Could we run out of oxygen. Or die from Carbon monoxide poisoning? Maybe that's why she—"

"Glen, I swear to God," Mark spoke through clenched jaws. "You are not helping., Go stand in a corner."

"This is why I always like Cal better." Glen shook his head and stood by the lettuce bin.

"Listen to me, Carrie," Mark spoke soothing. "None of us in this room will let anything happen to your baby. Your husband is here, brother, your kids. You got this. For Martie, do what she asked. Have this baby."

A part of Glen wanted to look, maybe see the miracle of life come arrive in a world so dark. Not that Carrie would mind, after all she was there for everyone to see. Just as Glen started to turn, he heard Carrie groan and grunt this really loud and awful sound. It was then he decided he'd rather watch the wall.

Swayfield, Grantham, UK

The car ran out of fuel, puttering out a short one hour walk from Farina's in law's place. They shouldn't have run out at all, but they were kept hitting detours trying to get out of London. Cars and trucks just abandoned on the road, blocking so many routes they could have taken.

Finally, they got free and clear. Only once did they get out of the car and that was two hours after the attack, sweaty and hot. Farina needed to make sure they were in the clear for parasites on the car.

Despite the fact that they checked and checked again, she still worried that one had made it into the vehicle unnoticed.

After hours of what felt like suffocation, they rode with the windows down until they couldn't ride anymore.

They pulled off to the side of the road, hopefully, she'd retrieve it at a later time. Having only one small flashlight, Farina and Stephen waited to the sky began to lighten before walking that final back, two lane road.

Farina didn't mind the walk as much as the items they carried.

She felt safe and free from any 'spreaders', they stopped seeing cars or wandering storage hosts not long after getting free of the city.

She began to think there was no way they were making it out there, and the 'run for the hills' mentality of those untouched was actually the best action to take.

Then she saw the body.

It would have scared her had its condition not filled her with hope.

It had grown light enough out that she didn't need the flashlight to get a good look at the body laying on the road.

A woman and she looked as if she were walking and dropped. She lay on her side, one arm reaching out. While Farina couldn't see any decomposition on the arm or side of the face, no distinctive bloating, there was the slight distressing smell of death and that told Farina the body had been there for around ten hours.

The corpse was untouched by animal life, which wasn't surprising given the circumstances of the events.

It was when Stephen used his foot to roll her over that Farina got her first glimpse of what it looked like when a storage host died still carrying a load of parasites.

The woman had not been killed. Her face had no signs of blood on her shirt or face. The dark color on the jaws wasn't present. A bruising they all carried from the widening of the mouth.

Her skin was white, eyes dark and sunken in. The woman's lips were cracked. The one thing that that made the distinction that she was a storage host was her neck. It was large and wide and the mass extended from chin to the U of the clavicle. It swelled like a water balloon and sounded like one as well when Stephen turned her over, swishing and moving when she rolled to her back.

"Jesus," Stephen gasped. "She looks like she has the bubonic plague gone mad."

Using the tip of her foot, Farina tapped slightly on the neck.

"Farina. No stop," Stephen cringed.

"You're right. I need to be careful." Stepping away from the body, Farina set down her bags. She grabbed a mask, gloves and goggles and placed them on.,

"What are you doing?" Stephen asked.

"She's been dead longer than an hour. She was a host."

"How do you know."

"This." Farina pointed to the neck. "Bet me that's parasites. She didn't have a host to project to and she died before she could. They never come out if there's no direction."

"But we've seen them projectile without hitting anyone."

"We have, but someone was always around to trigger the reflex."

"So, she choked to death."

Farina shook her head and opened the woman's mouth. "My guess. She died of severe dehydration." She glanced back at Stephen. "If they don't eat, they don't drink."

"Do we know for a fact they don't eat."

"I don't but assuming the esophagus is compromised, eating would be difficult. So would drinking."

"So, one of them could die in little as three days?"

Farina smiled. "Yes."

"We'll still don't know that she's a storage host. I mean, she could have the plague. Or infection."

"One way to find out." She reached for her back pocket and pulled out the small butter knife.

"Farina no."

"Stand back." Reaching around the woman's neck, Farina barely touched the tip of the knife to the skin farthest from her when the neck just popped. The tiny incision split wide open as the thick, red, gel substance rolled out and plopped on the ground.

The doctor in her found it fascinating. "Stephen, shine the light on it," she requested.

He did and gagged. "It looks like maggot covered afterbirth."

"It does. There has to be tens of thousands of them," Farina spoke in awe.

"No wonder this thing spread so far and wide so fast."

"No wonder."

"Can we go?" Stephen asked. "As disgusting as this is, there is nothing we can do with this information."

"Not right now. Maybe in the future."

Farina stood, taking off her goggles, mask and gloves. She grabbed hand sanitizer from her back placing it on her hands and arms before walking the road with Stephen.

As they hit the main portion of town, everything was dark.

It would have worried Farina had it not been so early and black out hit the country.

"Is that a light in the pub?" Stephen asked. "Looks like a lantern."

"Brett's parents own that pub." Farina picked up the pace, hurrying there. She paused by the exterior window and sure enough her mother-in-law was behind the bar, it looked as if she were wiping glasses.

With a gasp of relief that she was alright, Farina rushed inside. "Mum."

Her mother-in-law dropped a glass in shock. "Farina, doll, you made it." The older woman rushed to her. "Oh, we've been so worried. Wait until Brett and Dad see you."

"They're okay?" Farina asked.

"Yes. They are."

"Mum, this is my coworker, Stephen. Stephen this is Eunice."

"Pleasure," Stephen said.

"Mum, why are you here."

"Working. I always prepare the pub this early," Eunice replied.

"Mum, there's a global emergency."

"Yes, well, no one around here seems to be worried about it," she smiled. "Have to keep the spirits flowing. But have to manage it. Not sure when we'll have more. Dad said he'll make it." Eunice chuckled.

Farina shook her head in disbelief. Her mother-in-law didn't seem phased by anything. "Mu, there is a lock down order."

Eunice waved out her hand. "Like I said, no one here is worried. Besides, it's no where near us. We're safe."

"Actually," Stephen spoke up. "Down the road—"

"We left the car," said Farina cutting him off. "Ran out of petrol."

"Oh, we have some extra in the shed," Eunice replied. "Dad can take it down. Right now, let me walk with you to the house. I'll grab my keys from the back."

Once she had slipped to the back of the pub, Stephen turned to Farina. "You cut me off when I was going to mention the woman on the road."

"Yes. I did. She doesn't need to know. They've been living in their own world here. Happy. Let's not change that. I honestly feel we are safe here."

"Ready." Eunice came from the back. "I'll fix us a nice breakfast. You two must be starving."

"I am," Farina replied.

"Let's go."

Eunice led the way as they walked to the door. Farina looked at Stephen giving him a reassuring look. They made it. She truly believed her words that they were safe for the time being in the small village. Judging by the woman on the road, it wouldn't be long before they were safe for good.

Jude likened it to the craziest video game he ever played. He had a hard time thinking of a better word than trigger, but that was what he was.

Just his presence caused those on the verge of expulsion to wildly pull over and aim for him.

When one went down, another showed up.

Cal was a mad man with it, getting up and close to each host to take them out.

His entire life was spent trying to prevent what happened to the world. He feared it would one day happen but didn't imagine how bad it would get.

He worried about his family, wondering if the outbreak had reached them. There was no communication whatsoever, he was in the dark.

Because the storage hosts were rare, they weren't barraged by them.

Jude didn't blame them. They didn't know. They had thoughts and fears the same as anyone else. They didn't want to hurt or kill anyone. When it was time to release, they weren't in control.

Needville was safe.

It would be safe. Cal and the others who were immune to the parasite would work diligently to keep strangers out. That was the only way to keep the town safe. Secure the residents in their homes, let no one in, and wait it out until the storage hosts died.

At the moment there was only one person carrying a parasitic infestation.

Martie.

Jude felt horribly for her. She was losing her life and fought diligently with Cal as if trying to make a difference at the end of her life.

But Jude could see it on her face and in her coloring.

Martie's time was limited and coming to an end faster than she wanted.

He was the last one.

The man nearly wrecked his Volvo into a telephone pole just at the turn that went into the main street of Needville.

Cal wanted to check the town. He thought it was over. That the influx of highway storage hosts had come to an end. He realized at that moment he couldn't go into town. Not with Jude. Doing so was like being the pied piper.

When the man stepped from his car in a maddening way, Martie was the one that took him out.

She sailed one mini arrow at him, landing it center of his belly. It was an instant effect; one Cal hadn't seen because he and the others killed the hosts with silver. Sure, the kill caused the parasites to go to the wound, but not like this. The arrow did what it was intended to do. The simple object no bigger than a fat needle impaled the man. Within second a huge bubble formed around it. Like a giant pimple ready to burst. But it didn't. The man fell to the ground.

Dead.

Cal didn't know why that killed him; he assumed cardiac arrest. That had to be it. Only an autopsy would tell, and he was certain his brother would probably take on that task.

"Good job," Cal said to Martie.

Jude approached. "We should head back to Ma's. Get the others secure in their homes. Patrol the street."

Cal nodded. "Agreed. Ready, Martie?"

She didn't move. Her arm still extended the handheld cross-bow like a gun as she stared down to the body.

"Martie."

"You have to kill me, Cal," she whimpered.

"We need to wait. I know this frightens you," Cal replied. "But I'm sure there's time."

"There's not. Tell Jude to step away and kill me."

"What?" Cal asked.

"Shit," Jude whispered behind Cal.

"Please, Cal." Martie sobbed.

"Martie listen…"

Martie turned around. When she did, her body shook, and neck tensed up as she faced Jude. "Cal," she said struggling, "tell my kids…I love them."

With her last bit of strength, fighting with everything she had, Martie brought the mini cross bow to her gut. The simple 'click' released an arrow into her. Her head lowered as she looked down to the immediately growth in her abdomen, then she raised her eyes to Cal.

Cal rushed to her, grabbing on to Martie. He didn't fear a parasite, he had no reason to.

302

A look of relief swept over her face as her eyes met Cal's.

"I didn't hurt anyone. That's all I—" Martie stopped.

Cal felt the weight of her body as the life left her. Holding on to her, Cal lowered to the ground, keeping her in his arms. He felt she deserved more than dying like that in the middle of the road. At least he was able to give her one last moment of human contact before she left the world.

Even though victorious in the battle on the road, Cal had to face the hardest one.

Facing her children.

Glen paced and it annoyed the hell out of Mark.

Everyone else had settled, not saying a word. The newborn baby girl was swaddled in an apron in Carrie's arms.

"Can you stop?" Mark asked.

"I can't breathe," Glen replied. "We need to get out of here."

"Cal will come for us."

"Cal could be dead," Glen said.

"How? How?" Mark snapped. "These aren't vicious animals. They go on instinct and their instinct isn't to get Cal."

"What are we gonna do about that?" Glen asked.

"About what?"

"His, you know, problem."

Mark huffed out. Actually, he hadn't thought about it. Cal's illness, his condition, one easily treated in a modern world. But the world was no longer modern. Mark readied to tell Glen the infamous line of 'we'll cross that bridge', when the cooler door open.

Cal and Jude stood there.

Glen wheezed out as if the air that came in was lifesaving.

The baby cried.

Cal glanced down to the baby then to Mark. "Everyone okay?"

Mark stood. "We're fine. Baby and mother are fine. We heard you call for backup."

Cal nodded. "Yeah, the squad right now is going door to door making sure everyone is alright. I wanna check on mom."

"For sure. Cal…" Mark hesitated. "Martie? Where is she?"

Cal shook his head, then peered to her family. "I'm sorry." He paused when the sound of sadness and sobs came from her children. "Just know, she didn't suffer, she didn't turn. She took care of it herself." He stepped back. "Come on, let's get all you folks home."

Glen walked up to Cal and hugged. "Thank you for all you did."

"Sure. I think I'll have a drink though."

"I'll get it." Glen walked out, pausing outside the door to inhale. "Thank God I can breathe."

Everyone slowly poured out of the cooler. Except Mark. He stayed behind a few minutes.

Martie's death profoundly affected him.

Her sons were grieving their loss of their mother and it was all Mark's fault.

At least he felt that way.

"Brother?" Cal called him. "You coming?"

"I did this to her, Cal," Mark said. "I ordered the quarantine. I ordered them to find her. Had I not, she'd have been with her family."

"And possibly none of them would have made it," Cal said. "What?"

"Mark, they're here because of you. Had you not quarantined her, they never would have come to Needville."

"You don't know that."

"Uh, yeah, I do," Cal chucked. "This is cattle country. Who comes to Needville. Have a drink with me brother then let's go check on mom. Round one is over with tonight."

"Sure." Mark nodded sadly. "Cal?"

"Yeah." Cal stopped walking.

"When this is all said and done with, I am going to focus on you. Okay? You may be immune to the parasites but you—"

"Mark, stop. Okay." Cal gave a swat to Mark's arm. "I'm not worried about it. We have bigger fish to fry. We have a world to save."

Mark believed that. Cal wasn't worried. He never really cared about himself, just video games, their mother and doing his job.

Cal may have been all about saving people, but when it was all done, Mark would be all about saving his brother.

TWENTY-SEVEN

Three Months Later
Swayfield, Grantham, UK

The fall weather had finally set in and it was a nice change of pace for Farina when she did her morning chores.

The cooler air, being able to wear that sweater Eunice made for her. Farina loved the simplicity. Her marriage while always a good one, was even better in Swayfield.

It was as if she never knew the parasite outbreak. Other than the body on the road, nothing or no one came to the village.

She was far removed, and the chaos and death was a memory she tried to bury.

Farina didn't know for sure if it was over globally. It didn't matter. In Swayfield it was, and live was good.

She was the town doctor but before Farina could go to her little office next to the pub, she collected the eggs from the coup.

"I brought you tea," Brett stood on the other side of the fence. He held a steaming mug. "Yours grew cold."

"Thank you." Farina carried the basket. "Look at this huge egg." She lifted it as she walked to him. "I think it may be a double yolk. I have never seen one this big."

"Let's save it for ourselves, shall we?" Brett handed her the mug, then he cast his views to the sky. "Do you hear that?"

At first, she didn't, not until Brett called it to her attention. The distant sound of fluttering that grew louder and louder.

A helicopter.

It became so loud it was deafening especially as it hovered above them. The wind from the chopper blade blew Farina's hair, whipping up dust around the coup and sending her chickens in a frenzy.

That lasted only a moment and then the helicopter left.

"That was odd," Farina said.

"Odd?" Brett asked. "That's your reaction? We haven't seen anything in the sky in months. Something is going on. A rescue."

"Rescue?" Farina laughed at that. "Who needs rescued."

"Farina, this is just not what I expected. They're looking for someone. Things must be up and running again."

"I don't care."

"You don't want to go back?"

"No."

Farina handed her basket of eggs to Brett, exchanging it for the tea. They had made it nearly to the house when a man in uniform jogged his way to them.

"Excuse me," he called out. "Are you Doctor Ainsworth."

Farina stopped. "I am."

"I'm Captain Newman from His Majesty's Royal Air Force. Doctor Kingsman said you would be here."

"He's alive?" Farina asked in shock.

"Yes. He sent us looking for you, his team."

"Stephen is here as well, please tell him we're fine," Farina replied.

"Ma'am he needs you in London. Or rather wants you there."

Brett asked. "Why? Is the outbreak still going on?"

"No, sir," Newman answered. "Just trying to get things back together. We have forty-five percent of the population still remaining. But things are in disarray and all medical professionals are needed."

"So, in short, London is a mess," Farina said.

"Yes." Newman nodded.

"Am I required to go?" Farina asked.

"Requested not required."

"Captain, my husband will help you locate Stephen, but I have patients to see this morning. Please give Doctor Kingsman my best."

"Farina," Brett said. "This is your work in London."

"No, Brett, my work there is not what it was. It won't be for a while," Farina replied. "Here is my work." With her mug in hand, she nodded an acknowledgement to Newman and went into the house.

There really was no question or debate on what she would do. Farina knew what she left behind that day she drove from London. She couldn't imagine a beautiful gleaming city, in her mind it was destroyed. A downfall by chaos and death.

She wasn't ready to face the aftermath, one day. Not yet. Perhaps it was a selfish decision on Farina's part not to go back.

She was content and happy in Swayfield and her life there, even more happy that she knew that the outbreak was indeed over.

Needville, TX

Cal never wore a belt in his life. Maybe in the fifth grade, but by middle school they just weren't cool. He wore one now and he tightened it another notch. More weight had dropped from him. It pissed him off. He didn't feel too badly. He had his days, sick to his stomach, pain that was intense. He was proactive about it.

Pain pills washed down with a beer in the afternoon always kicked him into drive.

It wasn't the smartest thing to do, but it helped.

The parasite outbreak kicked his ass.

He and Jude were road warriors for over six weeks. Going out, searching for Storage hosts. He was certain he didn't get them all, but they made a dent.

It the months since it all began, it finally calmed down.

Half of Houston burned to the ground, creating a cloud that darkened the skies for weeks.

Needville survived.

The power still hadn't come back on, and Cal supposed it wouldn't unless they did something themselves.

No phones. No internet.

He had no idea what was going on with the rest of the world and frankly, Cal didn't care. He cared about his town, his family, and worried about his brother. He hadn't heard from Mark in weeks.

Mark left Needville on a search to find what he needed for Cal.

A quest that really shouldn't have taken him more than a few days.

Connie feared the worst, Cal told his mother Mark was fine. Though he didn't one hundred percent believe that.

Two o'clock Cal stopped at Ma and Joe's, down his drink with his pills.

"One more left after this." Glen slid him the beer. "Chuck said his brew will be ready next week."

"I have an old bottle of vodka at the house," Cal replied. "I'll be fine."

"I'm sorry man."

"Don't be." Cal turned to look at the door when he heard it open. He would be lying if he were to say he wasn't hoping it was Mark. Every time Cal heard a door opened, he hoped it was his brother.

It was Jude.

"You need to take a break," said Jude.

"I'm fine. I look worse than I feel."

"Really?" Jude asked.

"No." Cal shook his head, sipping his beer. "I have good days. I have bad. This is a bad day."

"Don't tell your mother," Glen said.

"Oh, I won't." Cal looked at Jude. "Taking off again?"

"Yep. Tracy is all ready."

Cal laughed. "You're the only man I know that has named a horse Tracy.,"

Jude shrugged. "I like the name. Think I'll head west, See what's there. Find you some more poison."

"I appreciate that." Cal lifted his beer. "You know this isn't over, right?"

"Yep."

"What? The parasite shit?" Glen asked shocked. "It's over."

Jude shook his head. "No. It's out there. It's in an animal, probably a wolf, waiting. It won't spread like it did before. Not as many people. But let's not kid ourselves, it's out there."

Cal raised his beer. "I'm safe."

"That's not funny." Mark's voice carried into the bar.

Cal nearly dropped his beer in shock., He turned, saw his brother, set down the beer and raced to him.

"Hey." Mark hugged him. "I'm sorry. I ended up having to walk the last hundred miles. But I'm here."

"You need to go see Mom," Cal stated. "We'll head over together."

"Stop." Glen held up his hand. "I'm glad you made it back. Did you get what Cal needs."

"I did. We're gonna start treating him right away," Mark replied.

Glen heaved out a breath. "Thank God."

"What?" Cal joked. "No more shield from the parasites?"

"I'd rather have my brother," said Mark.

"I got chills," Glen said. "That was sweet."

311

Cal finished his beer and set the bottle on the bar. "We're headed to our moms. Jude. Don't leave until we get back." He snapped his finger. "Glen, save me that last beer."

"You got it." Glen gave a thumbs up.

"Let's go." Cal put his hand on Mark's back and walked with him from the bar.

"Where's Jude going?" Mark asked.

"He does this road trips, checks for signs of parasites and life. His always said his fight is not over."

Mark stopped on the porch. "Neither is yours."

"I know."

"I promise you, with everything I am, I am gonna fight this with you and for you. You'll beat this."

"Brother, this is nothing compared to what we fought already," Cal said, tossing his arm around Mark's shoulder and giving him a hug as they walked.

What his family and friends didn't realize was that Cal was good with whatever happened to him. He felt victorious. The human race faced something incomprehensible and won.

Not completely. But they were alive, that was a win.

Things would never be the same, life would be simpler. Cal also knew that even though, out there somewhere, the parasite was still thriving, still a threat, for the most part, it was over.

His town and his family were safe. At least for the time being the fight against them was done.

Things were calm.

For as ever long or short as his life would be, Cal could live with that.

Jacqueline Druga is a native of Pittsburgh, PA. Her works include genres of all types but she favors post-apocalypse and apocalypse writing.

For updates on new releases you can find the author on:
Facebook: @jacquelinedruga
Twitter: @gojake
www.jacquelinedruga.com

Made in the USA
Middletown, DE
12 December 2022

18257997R00179